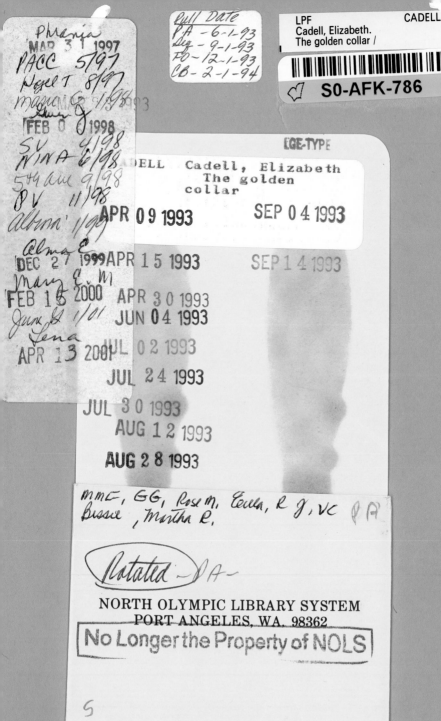

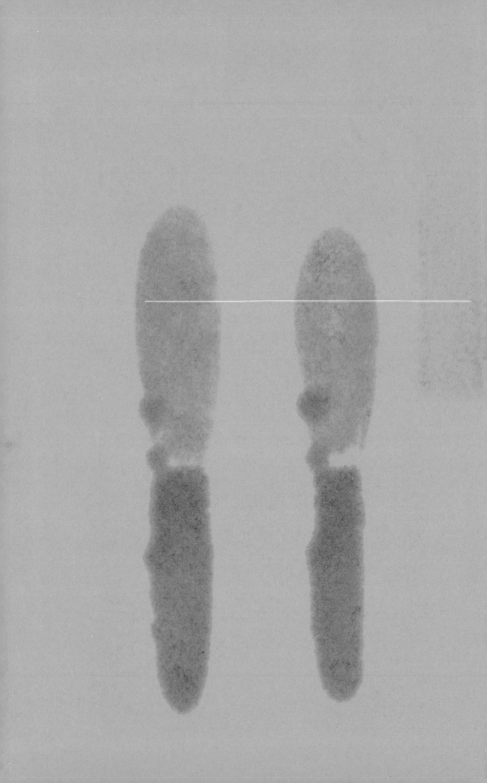

THE GOLDEN COLLAR

By Elizabeth Cadell
in Thorndike Large Print

THE CUCKOO IN SPRING

The Golden Collar

ELIZABETH CADELL

THORNDIKE PRESS • THORNDIKE, MAINE

Library of Congress Cataloging in Publication Data:

Cadell, Elizabeth.
    The golden collar.

    Reprint. Originally published New York: Morrow,
c1969, c1968.
    1.Large type books.   I. Title.
[PR6005.A22506   1985]   823'.912   84-24131
ISBN 0-89621-599-7

Large Print edition available through arrangement with
Brandt & Brandt Literary Agents, Inc.

Cover design by Laslo Nosek

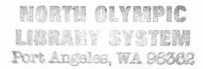

THE GOLDEN COLLAR

CHAPTER 1

There was only one car standing in the courtyard when Henry Eliot arrived. As he drove through the wide, arched entrance, he identified old Mr. Pugh's Rover, its bodywork scarred and dented, its driving seat covered with the pink, crumpled cushions needed to bring Mr. Pugh's legs within reach of the pedals. Mr. Pugh himself was on his way to the front door. He turned to respond to Henry's greeting.

" 'Morning, Henry. Magnificent day, eh?"

"Lovely. Any idea what this meeting's about?"

"Not a notion, not a notion." Mr. Pugh glanced up at the cloudless sky and spoke yearningly. "My word, I'd give something to be working in my bit of garden. On days like this I write out a rough draft of my resignation."

"Isn't anybody else coming?"

"Sir Bertram told me he'd got one of the lawyers over from Portugal. He said he'd sent the car up to London to bring him down here for the meeting."

"Any trouble?"

"That we shall soon see. I've heard of none, but when Bertram rang me up at breakfast time and asked me to be here by eleven, he sounded rather 'er um.' "

Rather "er um," Henry knew, was as near as Mr. Pugh would ever get to biting the hand that fed him.

"Can't see why I'm wanted," he commented.

Mr. Pugh glanced at his watch in the nervous, fussy manner that misled newcomers to the firm into thinking him too old for his job.

"Ten to eleven. We'd better go in, hadn't we?"

Henry had a mental picture of Sir Bertram standing at the head of the table in the large, firelit library, waiting for the chimes of the clock to end before drawing out his chair and declaring the meeting open. But that would not be for another ten minutes, and there was no point in being too early; it didn't do to truckle under to bosses, even if, or especially if, they were doubling as future fathers-in-law.

"You go in; I'll be along in a minute," he told Mr. Pugh.

He walked round the side of the house and up the steps to a wide, flagged terrace, his eyes on one of the windows of the floor above. But lovely as was the sight he expected to see, there were other attractions on the way that slowed and finally halted his progress. Motionless, he let his eyes roam over the lines of the lovely old building.

Like everything else owned by Sir Bertram Stonor, it could stand scrutiny by experts; the house itself, its contents, its staff and its unobtrusive luxury were all of a perfection which Henry had once believed Sir Bertram took for granted, but which he now knew to be the sources of intense, almost inordinate pride.

He turned and looked at the garden spread below him, glowing in the late May sunshine. There had been a little rain that morning, and drops still glittered on leaves and petals and gave a sheen to the expanse of smooth lawn. The carefully-tended flower beds were bright with colour. Farther off, the trimness of lawn and flower bed merged into woodland; below the trees he could see clumps of daffodils, their pale segments curving from the delicate golden chalices. Beyond them was a carpet of white narcissi threaded with purple violets. To the left was the path that led to the shrubbery and to the famous rhododendrons which Mr. Pugh regarded with such wistful envy.

Henry drew a deep breath. This was how springtime England could look — and usually didn't. How much, he wondered, had his recent decisions been influenced by this setting? This was Sir Bertram's house, but it was also his office; though he had premises in London to accommodate his staff, the greater part of his business — and it was world-wide — was conducted from this Sussex mansion. Here he held all meetings; here his employees came when summoned; against this background Sir Bertram judged new recruits, applying tests which were not all connected with their professional skill. Those who failed were promptly dismissed, or appointed permanently to the provisional staff.

Henry had got in without difficulty — with what he now felt to have been far too much ease. A struggling architect, he had in January submitted to the Stonor Development Corporation designs for one of their much-advertised projects in Brazil, and the first step in his advancement had been an invitation to lunch at this house. At lunch he had met Marly Stonor, Sir Bertram's only daughter, and his future had been settled on two fronts, the personal and the professional. How many men, he wondered, how many young men would have been able to turn down offers so seductive, put to him in such surroundings? Now he was on the Stonor staff for good, and he was to marry Marly Stonor in July, and it was only on mornings like this, which recalled the warmer climes in which he had planned to pass his life, that he wondered if on that January day he had been bemused — or bribed.

He came out of his reverie and remembered that he had been summoned to a meeting. He turned to retrace his footsteps and halted as a voice floated down to him.

"You'll be late."

He looked up. She looked, he thought, as lovely as the morning. Her hair was blowing loosely about her face; her shoulders, and as far as he could judge, other parts of her too, were bare.

"You'll catch cold," he warned in his turn. "Why aren't you down?"

She gave a great yawn.

11

"Half-past three," she reminded him.

"You got an hour's sleep more than I did — and look at me."

She was looking. It was a possessive look — and a satisfied one. Like her father, Marly Stonor was discriminating; like him, having chosen, she was tenacious and did not give up until she had got all, or nearly all she wanted. In Henry she had found what she desired in a husband; he was tall and good-looking, he was the right age — thirty to her twenty-six — and he had a quiet, easy, relaxed manner which soothed when it did not irritate her. His lack of money was no drawback, since she had so much. His rooted dislike of social gatherings was annoying, but it was something she felt competent to handle.

"Coming back to town with me?" he asked. "We could have lunch and —"

"You're lunching here."

"Who said so?"

"Father said so. A friendly end to a probably unfriendly meeting."

"What's it all about? All I got was a phone call telling me to be here. I wouldn't have said it was much trouble to tell me why. Has anything gone wrong?"

"Nothing that Father can't put right." She

12

spoke with a confidence founded on experience. "He's angry, though. If you stand there much longer, you'll be late and that'll make him madder. He's got one of the Portuguese lawyers here. If you have to go out there, I'm going too."

"What the devil could I do in Portugal?"

"Speak the language, for one thing. Go on in, before Father sends for you. See you at lunch."

She withdrew and closed the window, and Henry remained staring up at it for some moments, the sun warm on his back, a cold feeling in his heart. Three, two months ago, the withdrawal of that lovely body, that flawless face would have left him with a sense of helpless longing. Today, though the feeling of helplessness persisted, all longing was gone.

He turned away, entered the house and made his way by the shortest route to the library, bypassing the servant who was waiting to give him ceremonious conduct. He knew that he was the only man in the Stonor organization who had ever ventured to disregard the formalities, but he had seen nothing in his contract to prevent him from finding his own way about the house, and had done so even before his engagement to

Marly Stonor. He had considered himself as well able as Sir Bertram to define the boundaries between guest, employee and future son-in-law.

As he walked down the last wide, softly-carpeted corridor to the library door, he reflected that it was this house — fully-staffed, beautifully-run, that marked more than anything else Sir Bertram's ascendancy over his competitors. There were other millionaire heads of other powerful corporations, but they could not rival Sir Bertram's skill on the domestic level; few commanded so superlative a staff, none could match his rub-of-the-lamp technique in conjuring chefs and butlers from the air.

Henry opened the library door and entered. The first chime sounded and there, as he expected, was Sir Bertram with one hand on the back of his chair, observing the eleven-second silence and gazing across at the portrait of his grandfather, the first baronet, who also stood with his hand on the back of a chair and who looked as heavy-jowled, as keen and as confident. On a small table below the portrait was a silver-framed photograph of the late Lady Stonor, not much missed by her husband, but a severe loss to her couturier.

Aside from Sir Bertram, Mr. Pugh and Henry, only one other person was present, a short, dark, well-groomed man of middle age, with large, grave eyes and a calm, grave manner.

"Eleven o'clock." Sir Bertram was opening the meeting. "Good morning, gentlemen. Mr. Pugh has already met Senhor Moreira out in Portugal. Senhor Moreira, this is Mr. Eliot, my daughter's fiancé and one of my architects. Henry, this is Senhor Moreira, who is the head of the firm of lawyers looking after my interests in Portugal. He arrived last night. I asked you to come to this meeting because you have a personal concern in the matter we are about to discuss. Shall we sit?"

Henry sat down, battling against feelings which Mr. Pugh would have called disloyal. He was becoming used to Sir Bertram's highhanded methods; this was not the first time he had been summoned without being told why, and it would not be the last. All he objected to was the public and, in his view, tardy reference to his personal concern. There was only one matter connected with Portugal in which he could possibly be involved — a piece of land in the province of the Algarve which Sir Bertram had discovered on a recent visit to the country, and which he was buying as a wedding present for his daughter. Mr. Pugh had begun the negotiations for its purchase; later, Marly had told Henry casually that there had been a hitch in the proceedings and that the matter had been placed in the hands of lawyers in Lisbon. No mention had ever been made by Sir Bertram to Henry concerning the purchase, and Henry had asked no questions. Marly's interest in the matter had been negligible; when the land was hers, she would go and look at it, but for the moment there were more pressing problems — her trousseau, for example.

But now Sir Bertram had chosen to link Henry with the project and Henry saw that matters were not going well. Sir Bertram wore a heavy frown, and the Portuguese lawyer looked as though he had been subjected to some severe preliminary examination. Henry waited expectantly.

Sir Bertram looked across at Senhor Moreira and spoke in his most overbearing manner.

"I think we had better begin at the beginning, Senhor. As I told you earlier this morning, your letter came as a great shock. I had understood that since you took this matter over from Mr. Pugh, things were proceeding smoothly. I should like to be informed of exactly what has gone wrong."

Senhor Moreira took his time in replying, and Henry looked at him with dawning respect; when Sir Bertram rapped out a request for information, most people hesitated to say something. But the Portuguese was preparing his words, his well-shaped hands moving without haste, opening the file of papers he had brought with him.

"To answer you, Sir Bertram," he said at last in careful but correct English, "I might appear to be making excuses for my firm. This is far from being the case. We have, from the beginning, acted under great difficulties; we have done everything that could be done. At the risk of displeasing you, I would like to remind you that you did not approach us until the lawyers you had sent out from England" — he turned and gave Mr. Pugh a slight, apologetic bow — "had become entangled in —"

"All I wanted," Sir Bertram broke in angrily, "was to buy a piece of land. Not a vast tract, not an entire region; simply a strip of land. I saw the land when I was out in Portugal in February. I came back here and instructed my lawyers to buy it. After what seemed to me an inordinate series of delays, they announced that the land was not for sale. As the owner had begun by stating clearly that it was, I decided to transfer the negotiations to your firm in Lisbon. After more delay, you wrote to me to say that you could do no more than confirm what Mr. Pugh had told me — and now, on your arrival in England to discuss the matter with me personally, I learn to my astonishment that you reached this conclusion without having made any approach whatsoever to the owner of the land. I find this quite incomprehensible. If you have an explanation, I should like to hear it."

In films, Henry mused, the big boss always spoke like that, and then the hero scraped back his chair, tossed the papers into the big boss's face and made an impressive exit. He had yet to see anybody leave Sir Bertram's presence in this manner, but this Portuguese lawyer was doing pretty well in his quiet way; he was simply sitting there waiting for Sir Bertram to run out of breath. Only then did he speak, his voice as calm and as quiet as before.

"Let me review the matter, Sir Bertram," he suggested. "You found a most desirable piece of land in the Algarve, one of the few coastal strips still undeveloped between Faro and Sagres. You were not unreasonably elated. You sent your excellent lawyers" — once more he sketched a bow in Mr. Pugh's direction — "out to Portugal to arrange the purchase. They ran at once into difficulties because the alleged owner was hard to find. He was located at last, agreed readily to sell the land, and then —"

"Vanished," came in Mr. Pugh's mild tones.

"Naturally," Sir Bertram said heatedly. "He'd lied about —"

"No." Senhor Moreira spoke very quietly, but there was something in his tone which checked Sir Bertram. This Portuguese, Henry realized with boundless admiration, was the only man in his experience who had ever brought off this feat without finding himself out of a job. But Senhor Moreira was proceeding with his survey.

"Nobody lied, Sir Bertram. There were no lies. The man believed the land to be his to sell. But it was not his. It belonged, it belongs to the owner of the adjoining property, a very large, very old Quinta called the Quinta do Infante. Members of the Silva family have lived there for many generations. The Quinta is enclosed; it is entirely encircled by a high wall. The land of which we are speaking is outside the wall, between the Quinta do Infante and the sea but it belongs indisputably to the owner of the Quinta, Senhora Silva."

"Then why on earth —"

"Twenty-eight years ago," Senhor Moreira continued, ignoring the interruption, "Senhora Silva gave permission to an old servant, a pensioner on her estate, to build a cottage near the beach, and to keep a fishing boat there. He was a widower; he sent for a married daughter to look after him, and she came with her husband. Later, the couple had a son whose name is Manuel Janqueira. The baby, with its parents, stayed on at the cottage after the death of the old man; they did not in fact leave until the Algarve was, so to speak, discovered; hotels and villas began to spring up, and two years ago Manuel Junqueira and his parents left the cottage and went to Albufeira to work for the high wages offered by the tourists. The parents died there. Manuel Junqueira, twenty years old, was located by Mr. Pugh and agreed to sell both cottage and land. I do not know whether, after seeing Mr. Pugh, he found that he did not in fact own land — but that was not why he vanished. He vanished simply because he was called up to do his military service — in his case, naval service. While Mr. Pugh waited for him in Albufeira, Manuel Junqueira was on the high seas.

"In Portugal, twenty-eight years ago, when the cottage was built, there was no system of land registration. There were no title deeds; in many cases, properties of this kind passed from one owner to another by nothing more binding than word-of-mouth. I do not know whether Manuel Junqueira, born and brought up in the cottage, ever troubled himself to inquire who owned the land. He may have been aware that it once belonged to Senhora Silva, but he may have assumed that it had passed to his parents by what are known as squatters' rights; in another two years, this would have been the case, for after thirty years, land so given becomes by law the property of the person to whom it was given."

"What I can't understand," Sir Bertram said impatiently, "is why no approach has ever been made to this Senhora Silva. You knew this Junqueira didn't own it; you knew she did. So why you couldn't —"

"I will explain. I am personally acquainted with Senhora Silva. My firm has for many years represented her family, and I know a great deal about them. I know enough of Senhora Silva to be aware that she has refused absolutely to sell any part of her estate. But in the past two years she has been so pestered by people wishing to buy, strangers who forced their way in and behaved as if she was only wishing to be offered more money, that she has closed her gates. She now refuses to see anybody who wishes to discuss the sale of land."

"And so?" Sir Bertram demanded.

"And so I felt that the only hope for you was by an indirect approach. She knows nothing yet of your wish to buy and that means that Manuel Junqueira is unaware that there is any legal hitch; if he knew, he would have written to Senhora Silva and he would have learned that the land was not for sale. She would have compensated him, because she is a generous patron but the matter would have been at an end. So we —"

"What's the matter with a straightforward business approach?" Sir Bertram asked irritably. "You've heard of bargaining, haven't you?"

"I think I said — did I not? — that in this case, money is not a great consideration. I thought it foolish to risk going myself to Senhora Silva. I went instead to a gentleman called Senhor Crespo. He is a distant cousin of mine; he has lived all his life in the neighbouring village of Caravela, he knows all the Silva family intimately, and is a close friend of the present owner. I begged him to see Senhora Silva, explain matters to her and ask her to meet me for a friendly discussion of the situation. He did so and Senhora Silva agreed to see me. My cousin wrote to me in Lisbon and I was on the point of going down to the Algarve, when you telephoned from London and asked, I may say insisted, on my coming to England."

"If you could see the pile of papers, letters, explanations and general mess I've been made to wade through since this thing started, you'd have insisted too," Sir Bertram told him sharply. "This is the first clear exposition I've been given since February. Now I know where I am. Now I can see my way. The best thing would be for me to go out and speak to this Senhora Silva, and I shall tell her plainly that . . ."

He paused. Senhor Moreira had said nothing; he was not even looking at Sir Bertram; he was idly turning down the corners of the papers before him, his expression mild and somewhat abstracted. Yet there was in the air a strong suggestion that he did not think

Sir Bertram's proposal worth considering.

"On the other hand," Sir Bertram proceeded smoothly, "it might be better not to go myself. I can hold myself, as it were, in reserve. I shall send out Mr. Eliot."

"Yes." Senhor Moreira looked up and spoke unhesitatingly. "Yes, that is a very good idea. Mr. Eliot is in all ways suitable. He is to marry your daughter, and I understand that this land is to be a wedding present to her. He will be able to act for you."

"That's all, then." Sir Bertram pushed back his chair. "But before we adjourn, I should like to say that in my view, too much has been made of the difficulties. I see nothing whatsoever to prevent a direct approach to the owner. She owns property in a province which is still attracting buyers, and this is simply her way of sending up its value. I can't see the smallest reason for a cap-in-hand approach, but you and Senhor Moreira, Henry, must arrange the details between you. Just get me that land. I don't care how. Just get it."

Henry, with some surprise, recognized in the tone a hardness usually reserved for Sir Bertram's most important projects. Following the others to the door, he pondered on the reason for this — and suddenly he understood why Senhor Moreira had been summoned, why the meeting had been called, and why he was being sent to Portugal. The position was no longer what it had been when Sir Bertram returned in February. This was no longer a purchase and a present — it had become a major deal. And it had become a major deal because Marly had aroused the envy of her friends by telling them that her father's wedding present to her was to be a sea-fringed strip of the Algarve. Everybody knew what Sir Bertram had promised; it was unthinkable that everybody should learn that he could not carry out his promise. It was no longer a mere family matter; the eyes of outsiders were on him. He had made a lavish gesture, and Henry knew that he would go to great lengths before admitting that it had been an empty one.

Sir Bertram led them to the garden room, where drinks had been put out.

"Henry, you'll go out at once," he said. "Marly will go with you. I need hardly impress on you the need for absolute discretion once you get down to the Algarve."

"That," Senhor Moreira said, "is essential. Nobody should know of this."

"A large part of the Algarve," Henry pointed out, "is populated by Marly's friends. They all know Sir Bertram's buying land out there."

Mr. Pugh, pouring himself a weak whisky and soda, glanced speculatively at Henry. He had liked him from the moment he entered the firm, but in the early days, the liking had been tempered by the suspicion that this young man knew on which side his bread was buttered. Lately, he had become anxious lest Henry did not know what was good for him.

"If Marly goes out too," he offered, "it'll look nice and natural."

"That was the idea," Sir Bertram said coldly. "And even if Marly's friends do know I'm buying land, not one of them has any idea where it is. It's completely secluded and it's almost impossible to find, because anybody approaching it from the land side imagines it to be part of the walled property."

"Which in fact it is," said Senhor Moreira. "But I agree with you. Only when seen from the sea does it appear as it is — a separate piece of land with a beach of its own. I do not think Miss Stonor's friends will find it. When I return tomorrow to Lisbon, I will get in touch with my cousin, Senhor Crespo, and tell him that Mr. Eliot and Miss Stonor are arriving."

"You can explain, if you have to," Sir Bertram said to Henry, "that you and Marly are taking a trip out there to inspect the land. Not a word to anyone about difficulties, until we've ironed them out."

"I think it honest to say," Senhor Moreira put in quietly, "that I do not have much hope that Senhora Silva will sell." He raised his glass. "But I shall drink to Mr. Eliot's success."

Henry was not drinking; he was waiting for Marly and contemplating going upstairs to see if she could be induced to hurry. Then he saw Mr. Pugh put down his empty glass and wander into the garden, and decided to follow him. He caught up to him as the old man turned in the direction of the rhododendrons.

"Is this the first time Sir Bertram has found himself up against a non-seller?" he asked, adjusting his steps to the other man's leisurely progress.

"Eh? Oh, no. Dear me, no. But I will say that he seems to be taking this matter seriously — too seriously, perhaps. If it falls through, he'll take it hard."

27

"That sounds as though you agree with Senhor Moreira."

"Oh, I do, Henry. I do. Yes, I do. You must remember that I started all this — my first experience of trying to do business with Latins, and I hope my last. I looked rather a wooden leg at the meeting just now, but I assure you I was following all the details, and I feel that even now Sir Bertram hasn't grasped all the difficulties. I wish you every success, but . . ." He stopped abruptly and pointed a reverent finger. "Look, Henry. Just look."

"Yes. Double daffodils. Has he ever —"

"Ah! But look again! Queen Anne's daffodils. Not the Stuart Anne — no, no, no."

"No," agreed Henry. "Do you think Sir Bertram —"

"I don't think anyone's ever really got to the bottom of it, you know, but in my opinion, the Eichstatt theory's as sound as any."

"Eichstatt?"

"In Bavaria. The Prince Bishop of Eichstatt employed a chap called Besler, B—e—s—l—e—r. He died, Besler I mean, somewhere round 1620, but I'm not strong on dates, not at all sound. I saw his book once, Henry; my word, magnificent engravings.

Mag—ni—fi—cent. Besler's *Hortus Eystetten-sis*, that was."

"Really? Well look, about Sir Bertram and —"

"Now, Eichstatt's not far from Austria, and you remember that Louis XIII of France married Princess Anne of Austria? Well, *that's* undoubtedly the Anne of the daffodils. The marriage took place in 1615, so the date could be right, don't you see?"

Henry nodded absently. He was wondering how it was that girls wore next to nothing but required a whole morning to put it on. Why couldn't a girl hurry down on a lovely morning like this to enjoy it? Some people might also wonder why she wasn't hurrying down to enjoy the company of her fiancé. A month or so ago, Henry knew, she would have but he was aware that the heat no longer scorched for either of them.

"This Senhora Silva," he asked Mr. Pugh, who had now left the daffodils, "didn't I hear she had English connections?"

"Eh?"

"This woman who owns —"

"Ah yes, I follow you. No. No English connections now. Her sister was married, a long time ago, to an Englishman. He died, and his widow went back to Portugal."

"Any children?"

"Senhora Silva? No. She's a widow too. She was born a Silva and she married a cousin of the same name. I had no idea that she owned this piece of land, but as you now know, it adjoins her Quinta, and in the course of my inquiries I got to know a lot about her. No, she had no children. The sister had one child — a daughter."

"Sister dead?"

"Yes. The daughter lives with the aunt, and . . . Henry, just *look!*"

They had reached the rhododendrons, and Mr. Pugh was lost to everything but their beauty. Henry, glancing back at the house, saw no sign of Marly. Servants were placing long chairs on the terrace; Sir Bertram and Senhor Moreira were walking outside to enjoy the sunshine. Sir Bertram seemed to be making a speech — probably the one on Portugal that Henry had heard so many times; he could join them and listen to Part 2: *Observations on the Natives,* or he could stay here and brush up his rhododendrons.

"*Thomsonii,* Henry, beautiful, don't you agree? I've seen them darker than this, but I like the rose pink best."

"Beautiful," Henry agreed. "Did you hear Senhor Moreira saying that —"

"*Glaucophyllum*. I can show you an even better one in my garden, more purple than pink. What was that you were saying?"

"Was the Quinta do Infante the husband's property?"

"Oh, no. No, no. It was owned by the two sisters. Senhora Silva is the surviving one."

"Then the niece must own part of it."

"No, she doesn't. When her mother married and went to England, she sold her share to her elder sister. I got quite interested in their history while I was out there. I didn't of course know that they owned the land Sir Bertram was after, but I knew their property was close to it, and I made a few inquiries about them. The family records go back, I understand, to Henry the Navigator. Were you ever in Portugal?"

"I did a brief tour of the North a few years ago. Didn't have time to see the South."

"It's a lovely country. Mark you, if I had to live there, it wouldn't be the Algarve I'd choose."

"Why not? Lost its character since the boom?"

"Parts of it have, yes. Not all. But progress has come, and the first thing progress does is standardize. You'll see more plastics than pottery out there, more's the pity. I don't suppose I shall ever be out there again, but I'm glad I saw it in its Biblical stage."

"The more progressive, the less picturesque?"

"Exactly. If you . . . come and look at this, Henry. *Magnolia campbellii*. Found in Sikkim. D'you know, I've actually seen it out in March — a mass of delicate but quite sizable pink flowers. Beautiful, beautiful."

This time, Henry's agreement was less abstracted; his eyes were on Marly's approaching figure. She was coming across the grass; at her feet gambolled her two pugs, one black, one brown. She was wearing a suit of pale green; her hair, which she did in a variety of ways, was today drawn back from her forehead and confined by what looked to Henry a band of gold mesh. Though he thought women's current fashions more hideous than anything since hobble skirts, he had never seen Marly in anything that offended his feeling for line.

He left Mr. Pugh and the rhododendrons and went to meet her. She put her arms round him, drew his head down to hers and kept her lips on his until she ran out of breath.

"There!" she said, releasing him. "A nice morning greeting for you."

Her voice was slow, almost a drawl; her manner matched it. He had never seen her hurry. She loathed games; when he tried to make her run, she moved like an unsteady calf. She swam moderately well, with well-coached, studied strokes; she danced beautifully. She ate and drank what she pleased and nothing made any difference to the elegance of her figure.

He had seen her first at the upper window from which she had leaned that morning, and he had thought her merely a pretty girl; only when she came downstairs could he see the lovely line of neck and shoulder, of thigh and long, slender legs. In the first few moments his feeling had been one of purely professional pleasure — and then she had turned her glance on him and he had ceased to think purely and had begun to assess the competition.

He was still assessing it. To be in love had meant, in her sense, that they were lovers. They were to be married in two months, but there had never been — he had ceased to hope that there would ever be — any falling away of the hordes of men who surrounded her. He was not surprised. She was beautiful, she was gay, she was good company. She was also rich, though this factor was not so important in a set which Henry, without envy, termed gold-plated. The surprise, he knew only too well, had been all on the other side; they had not expected him to last. Even now they had doubts — and more and more frequently, he had doubts himself. For he had shed most of his illusions; he was not the first, he would not be the last. She lived fully and freely, and for all her unhurried manner, she lived fast. He was not a weak man, but his instinct had warned him to make concessions. For a time, he had hoped to hold her and he had succeeded in her sense, but not in his own. So far, he had matched her pace, but he was beginning to flag; if he fell behind, she would not wait for him. And he no longer wanted her to.

Her arms were round him again; over her shoulder, on the terrace, he could see Sir Bertram looking indulgent and Senhor Moreira looking the other way.

"What kept you upstairs all this time?" he asked her.

"I was ringing up the Colstons. You're ordered out to Portugal, aren't you?"

"Yes. So are you."

"That's what I thought. So I rang them

up and spoke to Cousin Tim, and we're going to stay with them."

"You. Not me."

She made no protest. Her use of the plural had been, he knew, a polite pretense; the Colstons were no more anxious to entertain him than he was to be entertained by them.

"What did you tell them?" he asked. "The whole thing's marked Top Secret."

"I just said that we were coming out to look at the land, that's all. And they said Fine, come here, which I knew they would. You'd stay there too, if you didn't have silly ideas about Edgar."

"Edgar's got silly ideas about me; he thinks I don't mind watching him playing those we-grew-up-together games with you."

"We *did* grow up together."

"He didn't grow up at all. Come on inside; I haven't had a drink."

They waited for Mr. Pugh, who informed them that he, too, had Pink Drift in his garden.

"My wife's very fond of it," he said as they walked to the house. "It's a hybrid that's come on a lot recently. You know it, of course? It's a cross between *scintallans* and *calostrotum*."

Marly's cool blue eyes were on him, their

expression a mixture of tolerance, amusement and contempt. Henry left them as they joined Sir Bertram, and took Senhor Moreira's empty glass.

"Same again?" he asked.

"Thank you." Senhor Moreira followed him and stood waiting as Henry poured it out. "And so, Mr. Eliot, you are going to Portugal to see Senhora Silva. I have already wished you success."

"But you think I'll fall on my nose?"

"If you wish to express it in that way . . . yes. I do. Your only hope is my cousin; you must rely absolutely on him."

"I will. All the same, I'm surprised to find myself agreeing with Sir Betram — couldn't this gate-closing be a build-up?"

"You mean that Senhora Silva is pretending to be reluctant? If you think that, you will be going to Portugal for nothing. You must clear your mind of such illusions."

"You clear them for me," Henry invited.

"I will try. I will begin by reminding you that a few years ago, the Algarve was unknown."

"In the sense you mean, yes."

"Overnight, what is called a tourist explosion takes place. Speculators appear. Poor fishermen, poor peasants find themselves rich, because the cry is for land — land, land and more land. I assure you — for in Lisbon we have had to deal with countless clients who have bought land in the Algarve — I assure you that people buy without thought, without knowledge, recklessly. There are houses being built where there is no water, or on land which in the rainy season will be a swamp. Villas are built in a hurry, sold and resold. Everybody who has a meter of land is ready to become rich. So Senhora Silva, who has a great deal of land, has been . . . please tell me the word."

"Besieged?"

"Thank you. Besieged. This expresses it absolutely. My cousin told me that strangers, complete strangers, have demanded to see her, and spoken insultingly to her of large payments of money. She —"

"Couldn't we say she's too sensitive? Most people offered large sums of money would open their gates instead of closing them."

"This I know. But if you were a widow living quietly in your home, not wishing to go up in this explosion, would you wish to be —"

"Besieged? Probably not. I'd appoint an agent, yourself, or your cousin, to sift the offers before calling me in."

"How can I convince you, persuade you, that there are still people in Portugal who do not wish to slice pieces from their property?"

There was a weariness in his tone that made Henry flush. For a few seconds he saw himself as he thought Senhor Moreira must see him, a young man digging himself into rich soil, making the most of his luck, marrying the boss's daughter.

"Look, I'm sorry," he said. "I'm only trying to learn. At this distance, if you want me to be honest, Senhora Silva appears to be just what Sir Bertram called her, an owner trying to send up the value of her land. If we're both wrong, then tell me why."

"Because neither of you knows anything about the kind of person you are judging. Make no mistake, Mr. Eliot, within her boundaries, Senhora Silva is a queen. She is not wealthy in the way that Sir Bertram understands wealth, but she is not poor, and she has things that you used to have here in England, but do not have any more: loyal retainers, dependents, whole families living on her bounty, families whose every member she knows and cares for. Her life is simple, her house, compared with this, is shabby, but in her own domain she is what I called her — a queen. This you will have to remem-

38

ber when you — if you approach her."

"I'll remember. I'll doff my hat and bow my head. But if she isn't rich, has she any special reason for refusing to profit by the general scramble for something she appears to have too much of — namely, land?"

"That is not so easily answered. A person's reasons are his own, private, unknown to others. Senhora Silva does not have to give reasons."

"I suppose not. Is there any chance of an oblique approach by way of the niece?"

"Useless. The niece has no property and no authority."

"One other thing: If Senhora Silva herself gave an old man permission to build on this piece of land, why, when he died, didn't she take it back again? The land, I mean."

"I am surprised that you ask this, because I understand that you have lived in Brazil, and there — I know this because I myself lived there for many years — there you would have seen similar instances of generosity of patrons to their dependents. Not only was he given permission to build; his cottage was paid for by Senhora Silva. She was not likely to hurry down when he died, to turn out his daughter and her husband and small son. What is more, when her own niece recently found a use for the empty cottage, Senhora Silva paid a monthly rent to Manuel Janqueira. Incidentally, why are we not speaking Portuguese? Sir Bertram told me that you speak it fluently."

"With, as you hear," Henry said, breaking into Portuguese, "a strong Brazilian accent. Why did Senhora Silva's sister sell her share of the property when she married?"

"Because she expected to spend the rest of her life in England. But her husband died young, and she returned to Portugal, to her sister. Since we are speaking Portuguese, I can tell you that my cousin, Enrico Crespo, is not only a friend of Senhora Silva; he is also her suitor, if you can understand the pace of —"

"I understand very well. My mother had a Brazilian suitor who called on her every third Sunday and asked if she had reconsidered."

Senhor Moreira laughed.

"Were you born in Brazil?" he asked.

"No. I was taken there as a two-year-old. My father died when I was thirteen, but my mother wouldn't come back to England. She would have liked to have kept me out there, but I had a strong-minded uncle in England who brought me back and put me through school and the university. My mother went to live in Madeira — she died there two years ago."

"What part of Brazil were you in?"

"Santos. I've been back once; I've got good friends there. In fact, I was considering joining a firm of architects out there when I met Sir Bertram and got the offer of this job. Any more advice before I meet Senhora Silva?"

"I do not think so." Senhor Moreira's eyes were on Marly, who was coming to join them. "I think you will do very well without advice." In English, he said, "You are going to Portugal with your fiancé, Miss ʔʔonor?"

"Yes. Shouldn't I be the one to tackle Senhora Silva?"

Senhor Moreira had no time to reply; Sir Bertram had signalled. Marly led them to the dining room. They took their places, and Mr. Pugh nodded towards the centerpiece, an ormolu vase filled with palest pink roses and sprays of lilies of the valley.

"Your work, of course," he said drily to Marly.

She ignored the remark; he knew quite well that she did nothing in the house except live in it. She picked up her fork and began to eat the salad in the small wooden bowl beside her plate — crisp green leaves, glistening and aromatic.

"Well, Marly." Her father addressed her across the table. "I suppose Henry has been talking to you about the trip to Portugal?"

"He didn't have to tell me I was going — I guessed. I rang up Cousin Tim and told him we were coming."

"I hope you didn't tell him why."

"I said we were going out to look at the land. Aren't we?"

"Yes, but —"

"I want to be back fairly soon. I don't want to miss everything."

"Such as what?" Henry asked.

"Oh" — she waved her fork — "the Derby, Ascot, Wimbledon."

"And your wedding," Mr. Pugh put in courageously.

Once again, she ignored him. Senhor Moreira spoke in his pleasant voice.

"If you get this land, Miss Stonor, what will you do? Build a villa on it?"

"If Henry and I ever come to an agreement about what it's to be like. He wants it small, for us. I want it large, so that we can invite all our friends. What's the point of going out there for holidays if you can't be gay? Henry drew me the most perfect house

42

with guest chalets and a pool, and said This is what we're *not* going to have."

" 'He only does it to annoy. Because he knows it teases,' " Sir Bertram quoted in the loud, heavy tone he used when he wished to be jocular. "That's so, isn't it, Henry?"

"That's so," Henry agreed. He certainly did it to annoy, and it certainly teased, but so far, he had not been able to decide how much sense of ownership he would feel about the land after his marriage to Marly. At the moment, he felt none whatsoever. He was going out in obedience to orders, and whether Senhora Silva said Yes or No mattered little to him personally. Professionally it would matter a great deal; Sir Bertram wanted the land badly, and Henry knew that failure to get it would rest squarely on his own shoulders.

"Henry isn't going to stay with Tim and Wanda," he heard Marly saying to her father.

"Good. Then they won't be able to pump him," he answered.

"Then where?" Senhor Moreira asked.

"Choose me a nice hotel," Henry asked him.

Senhor Moreira bowed, and turned to look at Marly, who was sitting at his other side.

"I'm going to talk to Senhora Silva," she told him confidently. "That can't do any harm, can it?"

She had spoken lightly, but the dark eyes regarding her remained unresponsive. When Senhor Moreira spoke, his voice was sober.

"Harm? I hope not," he said slowly.

CHAPTER 2

Three days after the meeting with Senhor Moreira, Henry was with Marly Stonor at London airport, awaiting the flight to Lisbon.

The plane was punctual. When they boarded, Marly took her seat, adjusted her safety belt and settled down to read; she hated flying and had long ago decided that this was the best way of passing the time on the journey. Henry, finding her unresponsive to his attempts at conversation, gave up at last and ordered a drink, and when the steward went to get it, found to his annoyance that an elderly passenger seated across the aisle, who had been glancing at him with interest, had now decided to be friendly.

"Long time gettin' us off, weren't they?" he began. "And they never tell you what the 'old-up is, that's what gets me. They put you off by calling it a technical 'itch. 'Eh, Miss" — he stopped a stewardess as she went past, and blinked his mild blue eyes in awed recognition of her grace and beauty — "sorry to trouble you, Miss, but could I 'ave a plain soda? Yes, just soda water, that's right. No, nothin' in it; I 'aven't got a 'ead for anything stronger. Lovely girls, these," he remarked to Henry as she went to attend to the other. "Well-trained, too. I've been told they could deliver a baby if a mother was, so to speak, took short. You staying long in Lisbon?"

"No."

On his other side, Henry felt Marly stirring impatiently; his disinclination or his inability to discourage friendly overtures from strangers was one of the things about him that annoyed her most. All he had to do, she had pointed out countless times, was to pretend that he was stone-deaf, or if he preferred, say "Quite" to every remark until the message went home.

"I'm goin' on to the Algarve — that's the bit down at the bottom," the man confided. "Know it at all?"

"Quite."

"Tried Estoril, but the Algarve's warmer.

My wife got keen on a 'ouse we saw when we was there some time back, and I'm going out to take another squint at it. My name's Easter, by the way, Walt Easter. Not Christmas, I always say, and not Whitsun, just Easter. Good way of remembering."

"Quite."

"She couldn't come with me this trip — the wife, I mean — but she'll follow me out if I fix up anything. Always miss 'er when she doesn't come along."

The blue eyes seemed to grow misty. They were faded, but still round and candid and guileless; they gave the last touch of retired-old-salt to the chubby, pink face and fuzz of white whiskers.

"You going out there on business?" he asked Henry.

"No. That is . . . no."

"Wish I was in business again. Didn't want to retire, but you know 'ow it is? You 'ave to get out and make way for the young 'uns. Four sons, all in the old firm — not bad, eh?"

"Quite."

"I go in now and then to see what they're doing, but they don't tell me much. Not that I ask. Joyce — that's the wife — said they were to be left alone to do things their own

47

way. No pushing them around was what she meant. So I leave 'em alone, and now they're running the business. Shoes. I started out in a little back street in Camberwell — if you was Professor 'iggins, you'd 'ave spotted I came from Camberwell, wouldn't you? — and then I branched out when I married, 'cos the wife brought a bit o' money with 'er, not much, but a 'elp, and we opened in the West End and never looked back. It was Joyce gave me the pluck; I'd 'ave done it in the end, but not then, but she said, 'Oh, go *on*, Walt' — so I did. Got a pitcher of 'er with me — 'ere she is. Bit faded — the snap, I mean — but you can see 'er if you look close. Looks thinner there; she's put on weight since that was taken."

Henry looked at the likeness with as much politeness as he could summon. Mrs. Easter's eyes were as candid as her husband's, and had a mildly patient look, as though she had become accustomed to being exhibited to total strangers. He returned the talisman to its owner and then leaned back and closed his eyes.

"Goin' to 'ave a bit of a nap? Good idea." Mr. Easter's voice floated across the aisle. "Might try the same."

He tried, and to Henry's relief, succeeded.

He turned to Marly, who raised her eyes from her book long enough to inform him with some asperity that just so long as he encouraged bores, bores would continue to accost him.

"It's the way you look," she complained.

"How the hell can I help how I look?"

"If you didn't seem so . . . so *approachable* . . ."

"You mean I encourage them?"

"I mean you don't *dis*courage them. Why can't you practice snubbing people?"

"Get back to your book. How's that for a start?"

She never liked his attempts at humour; he was prepared to admit they were feeble, and was not surprised to see her turn away and resume her reading. She did not close the book until the plane was coming in to land.

Senhor Moreira was waiting for them. Ceremoniously he introduced his wife, his partner and a nephew with an imposing title who had just joined the firm. Senhora Moreira was neither young nor handsome, but after one swift glance at her clothes, Marly awarded her a place among the top ten of her private fashion list. The party drove to lunch at a restaurant. On the way, as there would be no time for sight-seeing after lunch, Senhor Moreira pointed out buildings of special interest. Henry took in as much as he could of the sunny city; Marly, seated beside Senhora Moreira, was busy writing down the names of *modistas*.

Lunch over, they came out to find the hired car which Henry had chosen in preference to flying down to Faro.

"It has been a pleasure to see you, even for so short a time," Senhor Moreira assured them. "Good luck," he added to Henry. "I have written to my cousin Enrico to say that you are coming."

They took their leave and began their journey south. The weather was perfect, the sky a mild, unclouded blue. The air was warm, the sun caressed Marly's bare arms. The countryside was lion-coloured, the sea a deep blue that bore no resemblance whatever to the steel-gray, tossed waters of the English Channel over which they had flown.

Henry drove. Marly, as usual, did the navigating, steering a true course between hotels and restaurants, guided by stars; her favourite scenery was the sign suspended outside internationally famous hostelries. As they neared the province of the Algarve, she noted briefly the low, white houses with their distinctive, lacy chimneys which a casual glance at a guide book had led her to expect. One foreign country, she claimed, was pretty much like any other foreign country; all you had to do was remember a few dates and avoid mixing your periods. She believed ninety per cent of travellers to be pretentious bores stretching a smattering of art or architecture as far as it would go. If they were honest, she said, they would admit that ruins, whatever they had been a few thousand years ago, were now nothing but a collection of cracked pillars.

Henry had ceased to try and interest her in the things that interested him. He had once dreamed of marrying a woman with tastes not unlike his own. The only tastes he and Marly shared were for French films, Italian glass and Chinese food.

His eyes were on the road, a part of his mind was on his driving, the rest was free to wonder what had happened to the sanity, the clear-headedness he had once possessed. Hair like spun silk, a face pale and provocative, a body soft and yielding . . . these he had gained in exchange.

The swiftness of her surrender, far from filling him with a victor's confidence, had left him with a shaking sense of insecurity. Seeking reassurance, he had asked her to marry him. She had laughed, but she had agreed — and even before the engagement ring was on her finger, he had learned that marriage would not stop her from doing anything she wanted to do, and that in trying to bind her, he had done no more than put a noose round himself. He was trapped. He was caught without hope for release, for if there was any way in which a man like himself could extricate himself from a situation like this, he did not know it. She had not pursued him. There had been no pressure — except that of his own desires. Only she could free him, and he had no hope that she would. Marriage was on her program — with him or with somebody else. He filled the bill because he supplied the one thing lacking in her life — novelty. He had been, he still was, to her, a new kind of man. His views, his principles could still amuse, even though they irritated her. She had thought him easy to read, to know, to manage, and was learning that he was not. The program would be carried out. They would marry, and he would get what he had once desired so ardently and now desired not at all.

He heard her speaking.

"Can we get to Albufeira in time for dinner?"

"Probably. But won't the Colstons be expecting us?"

"No definite time. We'll have coffee there."

They drove on through country which, though it could not rival the grandeur of the scenery he remembered from his brief tour of the north, seemed to Henry to have a miniature appeal of its own, with small, white villages and small, white, flat-topped houses and small, fertile farms and he knew that down here, there was shelter from the strong summer winds that bedevilled the western stretches of coastline.

They reached Albufeira at dusk and drove down steep, narrow streets to the restaurant chosen by Marly, and Henry, looking at the tall, modern apartment houses, the smart, bright little shops, wondered, as he had so often wondered before, why the sunseekers, in taking over new playgrounds, seemed to go out of their way to destroy the original charm and character of the region.

They took their places at a table on a terrace that seemed to overhang the sea; in the buzz of chatter round them, Henry could hear no Portuguese. The service was good, the food superb; if this was Portugal, Marly said, she was prepared to award it the Stonor Star.

"Only it isn't," Henry said.

"Isn't what?"

"Portugal."

"Oh, don't start that," she said irritably.

"All right, I won't. Start what?"

"That dreary drone about despoiling the land and polluting the peasants. What do you expect people to do when they come to live out here? Settle down in a fisherman's hut and can sardines?"

"No. All I'd like to see is a bit of originality, that's all. We haven't passed one villa here that you haven't seen in Sitges or Torremolinos or Nassau or Bermuda or any other dozen places I could name. I wish I understood the rich. All these people are rolling; if they weren't, they couldn't stay here. So why do they go on putting up these featureless, uniform, custom-built villas-with-pools?"

"Instead of putting up what, for instance?"

"Houses that blend with the landscape. Houses more suited to hot climates. Houses that have cool, shadowy places to sit in. Shutters placed outside the glass, not inside.

Corridors, to give you moving air. Patios, for privacy. More shade, more —"

"What if you happen to like a custom-built villa-with-pool?"

"Then you've come to the right spot."

"What do you imagine people want when they're on holiday?"

"I don't imagine, I know. A package deal. Air travel, bedroom-with-bath, a well-stocked bar and a filtered pool — and they don't care whether they're in Portugal or Pernambuco."

"Quite right. Now choose the wine."

She seldom argued, unless it was to get her own way. She regarded their differences of opinion, more and more frequent of late, as a sign that he entertained some odd ideas which she would make him shed in time. Ordering and sampling the wine he had chosen, he felt a wave of depression sweeping over him, and decided to attribute it to the heavy lunch he had eaten and the miles he had driven. But he knew that these moods preceded all the parties to which he accompanied Marly, parties at which he knew he would meet what he thought of as the Colston type. They would soon be at the villa, and he would begin the usual struggle to endure the noise, the barbed pleasantries,

55

the off-beat jokes and the latest scandals. He disliked dancing, but he would have to shuffle round a space no bigger than a carpet, peering down at a mask of make-up and an over-exposed bosom. He detested dance music, but it would blare all night and people would scream in order to make themselves heard above the din. And Marly would bloom like a flower, while he would retreat by degrees to a far corner and stay there looking, if he could believe her, like a bishop in a brothel.

She herself was as out of place, as bored, as resentful at the concerts to which he took her; she yawned when he played her his favourite records. He liked horses and rode well; she could not understand how anybody could clamber on to the back of any animal, or endure holding carrots before a slobbering set of teeth. He liked reading; she seldom opened a book. These, and other differences, he had once tried to disregard; now he knew that they formed an unbridgeable gap between them, a hopeless barrier to their eventual happiness.

The Colstons' villa was about two miles east of Albufeira, built a little inland; they drove up to find it brilliantly lit. When

Henry parked the car and walked round to the other side of the house, he saw a terrace on which was assembled a large and noisy gathering of the kind he had expected. In the kidney-shaped pool, people were still swimming; dinner was a cold buffet laid out on long tables inside the house, to be eaten when and where the guests chose.

There was a momentary silence as Henry and Marly appeared, and then Colonel Colston, a tall, still-handsome man of about sixty, detached himself and came forward with outstretched arms.

"Marly! Marly, my dear!" He kissed her on both cheeks and held her at arms' length to study her. "Here you are at last! You're late. Hello, Henry."

Henry shook the proffered hand and felt no resentment at the marked decrease in cordiality. He bowed to the small, plump, rather fluttery Mrs. Colston, who had followed her husband and was holding Marly's hands and regarding her affectionately.

"It's lovely to see you, Marly! Come and meet everybody. Edgar's here, you know."

Henry had already seen Edgar, who was threading his way between the tables on the terrace, brandy globe in hand, coming without haste but already calling to Marly over intervening heads.

"Darling! Why so late? We expected you to arrive hours ago!"

He ignored Henry, who watched the three — father, mother, son — as they drew Marly away to be introduced to the other guests, a number of whom she already knew. He remained on the terrace, poured himself a cup of coffee from a tray on a side table, and surveyed the party without pleasure. He felt that the well-worn comparison to tropical fish might well be used again to describe this gathering — colourful, darting, purposeless — but the fish didn't make this deafening noise.

He had met the Colstons several times since his engagement to Marly, for they paid frequent visits to England. Their chief source of income came from their flair for getting to the right places just before the right time, anticipating tourist booms with an accuracy which Marly called uncanny but which Henry thought merely canny. On arrival, they bought land, built a house and settled in — permanently, they said. This fiction was maintained until someone showed a disposition to buy, at which point the Colonel's fictional doctor gave him fictional advice to move at once to a drier or milder or cooler or wetter climate. They had moved, with immense profit, from Bermuda and the Bahamas to Spain and Sardinia. Theirs was a good partnership; the Colonel liked to build houses and his wife liked to furnish them; both had a sense of style as well as a semi-professional charm that kept the minds of buyers from dwelling on tiresome details like drainage or construction or water supply until the sale had been completed and the Colonel and his wife were out of range.

The guests at this villa looked to Henry like the guests at any other holiday villa of this type; he recognized two actresses, a television announcer and a pale-faced playwright. There were no painters, unless you counted Edgar, whose work hung on the walls of the drawing room. Henry had not yet succeeded in deciding how far jealousy blinded him to their merit, if any.

Mrs. Colston was coming towards him. Born Winifred, she was now Wanda, which suited her better. She referred to herself as petite, and might once have been justified, but her pocket-Venus look had become dumpiness. She had an affected manner and, like her husband, a remarkable talent for picking up and storing useful items of gossip.

"Henry, we've been neglecting you," she

said. "Good gracious, you haven't even got a drink!"

"I've had some coffee, thanks."

Marly was the center of an all-male group; Edgar's arm was round her waist; more of the cousin stuff, Henry told himself, and schooled himself to tolerance. The Colonel was revolving with an elderly partner in the center of the drawing room, which had been cleared for dancing. At a signal from his wife, he grafted his partner on to a hapless young man who was trying to make his way to Marly, and then came and took Henry's arm and led him to the end of the terrace.

"Want to have a chat with you before you go off," he said. "No, no, no; don't go screwing your head round to see what Marly's doing. She's having a good time, as usual. You'll have to get used to it, my dear fellah, just as I had to when I married Wanda. Mark you, I was a good bit older than she was, but that only made it worse; soon as we got to a party, she was whisked away and I had a job finding her again. Popular little thing she was, pretty as a picture and wonderful company, as you can still see. Now how about a drink?"

The Colonel, Henry reflected, managed to make a better pretense at cordiality than his wife, but he knew that they both resented bitterly his engagement to Marly. There had been a lifelong friendship between her and Edgar, and his parents had probably felt they had good grounds for hoping that the two would marry. Henry knew he could not expect Colonel and Mrs. Colston to love him, but sometimes he felt that he preferred Edgar's open and unmistakable loathing to this false, grating pretense at politeness.

"Pity you're not the social type," the Colonel observed. "You'll have to learn to join if you're going to marry Marly. Can't understand a young chap like you wanting to skip out on a good party. You've got to be social. You've got to learn to get along with people."

Not people in crowds like this, Henry thought. Elbowing, pushing, jamming and jostling — how could they endure it? Thank God he hadn't got the kind of job that forced him into it; he wasn't touting anything and he wasn't one of those poor devils who had to keep in the public eye.

"Tell you what I wanted to ask you," the Colonel said, with the air of one who has sufficiently prepared the ground. "Has Sir Bertram run into any kind of snag regarding this land of his?"

61

"Snag?"

"That's what I said, snag. Anything gone wrong with the negotiations? Now don't try this man-with-a-load-of-secrets act with me, Henry, my boy; I'm Sir Bertram's cousin and I'm also in his confidence. I suspected there might be something wrong when Marly telephoned out of the blue and said you were being sent out here. If there was anything wrong, he needn't have sent you. Why couldn't he have got in touch with me? After all, I've been here for some time and I could have scouted round and reported back. Marly says you're out here to see some old fellow who knows something or someone to do with the Quinta do Infante. What's the Quinta do Infante got to do with it?"

"Sir Bertram sent me out to look at the land. That's the reason Marly came with me. It's for her, and she's never seen it."

"Well, I may as well tell you that Marly told me that the land doesn't belong to the fellow who owns the cottage on it. It belongs to . . . wait a minute and I'll recall the name . . . yes, Senhora Silva. If you're hoping to get in touch with her, you'll be out here a long time. I tried to see her about letting me have a piece of her several-thou-sand-acre spread, and didn't get past the gate. Who's this old fellow Marly says has a special pull?"

Henry saw Marly coming to join them. Her hand was in Edgar's, her face had the rather still look it wore when she was most enjoying herself. Edgar was looking as he always looked to Henry — insufferable. He had a long face, long hair and long-lashed eyes and liked people to point out his resemblance to Byron, which to Henry's fury they frequently did.

"Have you finished with Henry?" Marly asked the Colonel.

"You can have him," the Colonel said stiffly. "He's trying to tell me that you're both out here for the swimming. You might inform him that I've a far greater right to put matters straight than he has."

"He's under strict orders to be discreet," Marly explained. "Don't try to pump him."

"Discreet. That's the word I've been looking for," put in Edgar. "Discreet. I knew he had some quality, some elusive quality I couldn't pin down. Discretion. It's very frustrating to have to be discreet; you can't tell old friends that Senhora Silva can only be approached through a guy named Crespo. If you *do* get into the Quinta do Infante, Henry, you mustn't be too disappointed. It doesn't measure up to its interesting old walls."

"You've been inside it?" Marly asked in surprise.

"No, darling. Nobody gets inside. But I'm told it's a vast white elephant of a place with peeling plaster and wormy floorboards and a parcel of retainers hanging about doing God knows what — praying, I daresay. And they say that if you do manage to make your way in and mention property, or money, you get thrown out for using dirty words. I only hope Senhor Crespo can fix up an entrée for you. If you get an interview, you must tell us about it, they say she's quite, quite unhinged, like that woman in the mouldering house in Dickens. Speaking of old women — Colonel, have you brought up the subject of Pearling?"

"Good Lord, no, quite forgot," his father answered. "Look here, Henry. I've had a letter, one of those damned letters people are always sending, asking me to look up this or that entire stranger, or show somebody round, or put somebody up. There's this woman called Lady Pearling staying at the hotel Marly tells me you're going to. I've been asked to show her this house, but I don't want to."

"Why not?" Marly asked. "She's rich

enough to buy a dozen like it. I've met her."

"Well, I haven't and I don't want to," the Colonel said. "I've been making a few inquiries. They say she looks at houses pretending to buy, but when it comes to signing, she signs off. She's sure to see you with Marly, Henry; if she wants you to bring her out here, don't."

"You'll be sorry," Edgar said. "She's a two-time millionaire."

"What's two-time?" the Colonel asked irritably.

"Her husband left her the Pearling fortune, but when she married him, she was the ABC heiress. You know — Allen's Baby Cars," Edgar explained.

"Those perambulators?" the Colonel asked.

"If you can call them mere perambulators, yes."

"I see. Well, I don't care how many fortunes she's got," the Colonel said. "Just keep her away from here, Henry."

Henry promised to do his best, and decided that he had had enough of the Colstons. Marly did not see him to his car; she remained on the terrace, standing between the two men and turning back towards the drawing room before he had gone out of

65

sight. Which was as well, he thought grimly as he drove away. In his present mood, he would have accused her of talking too freely about the reasons for their journey and she would have lost her temper and then somehow Edgar would have been dragged in and they would have had the kind of quarrel that left him bitter and resentful. It was better to go away like this and leave her in the setting in which she fitted so well — too well.

The hotel was large and luxurious. He was shown up to a room on the second floor, at the southwestern corner of the building. He tipped the dark, bright-eyed little page, opened a glass door and stepped on to a spacious balcony which he saw was built diagonally and which he shared with the occupant of the room next door; the only division was a chest-high stone partition surmounted by an iron railing. As he stood looking out, a light came on in the adjoining room and a portly form emerged, and Henry was surprised and displeased to recognize Mr. Easter's pink face and white whiskers. He was wearing gray and white striped pajamas.

"Coo! 'ow's that for co — in — cidence!" he exclaimed with undisguised wonder and joy. "Thought you was stopping in Lisbon. Glad you decided to come and 'ave a look at this place." He raised himself on tiptoe and leaned forward in an attempt to peer into Henry's room, then he lowered his voice to a whisper. "Owe you an apology, 'smatter of fact," he said. "Thought you was alone on the plane. Saw you was sitting next to a pretty girl, but didn't get the connection, like. Then I saw you go off together. Could 'ave kicked myself. But I knew 'er; seen 'er picture in the papers. She's Sir Bertram Stonor's daughter, isn't she?"

"Yes."

"Thought I recognized 'er. Not married to 'er by any chance?"

"Not yet. We're engaged."

"There! An' I kept you talking, and I bet she thought I was a fat old nuisance. Well, well, well, I wish I was young an' engaged again. If I was, it'd be to the same girl, an' that's a compliment after forty-nine years married. Got some land 'ere, 'asn't 'e, Sir B?"

"No. Yes," Henry corrected himself, and saw a frown of bewilderment on Mr. Easter's face.

"You in 'is firm, by any chance?"

"Yes."

"Stonor Development?"

"Yes."

"Last time I was out 'ere, I met one of those lawyer chaps who work for 'im. 'e 'ere too?"

"No."

"I see," said Mr. Easter, though it was obvious that he didn't. "No 'itch, I suppose?"

Henry, at this point, realized that he should fall back on Marly's final injunction, which was to say: Mind your own bloody business. But he had in fairness to himself to admit that Mr. Easter's frank approach made nonsense of more subtle methods of questioning. This childishly simple I-ask-you-tell technique was extremely difficult to parry; if they sent people like Mr. Easter to China, he would come back with all the information anybody needed.

"You're thinking I'm a ruddy Nosey Parker," Mr. Easter said. "An' that's what Joyce says too, but I'll risk embarrassing you, and tell you that if I don't like someone, and even Joyce admits I'm good at sizing people up, then I give 'em a wide berth. It's on'y when I see an upstanding young chap like you, who might be my eldest, Leslie — though 'e's fairer, and per'aps not so wide across the shoulders — as I say, it's on'y when I like what I see that I stick my neck out. You're about twenty-nine, right?"

"Thirty," Henry said into the expectant pause.

"That's what I thought. Our Les is twenty-nine. Yes, when I see a chap like you, who's got what you might say a friendly look, I risk putting out a 'and. We're all getting nice and classless, they say — which I think is a bit of a mistake, myself — but there's still a lot of people walking round looking down their noses at the Walt Easters. I wasn't meaning to nose into your business, but last time I was in these parts, Sir B. 'ad got 'old of a nice piece of land — the best bit 'ereabouts — and the deal looked nicely sewn up. After a new bit, is 'e?"

"No."

"That's what I meant. I just wondered if somebody 'ad slipped up. This bit I'm speaking about was a bit out near that Quinta do Infante, as they call it."

"Quite."

"There was this lawyer arranging the sale, and 'e'd located the owner, who'd got a little 'ouse built on the land. That the same?"

"Quite."

There was a pause. Mr. Easter opened his

mouth and closed it again. His eyes rested unwinkingly on Henry's face.

"I think I'll have a shower," Henry said.

"I'll go to bed," Mr. Easter said. But he spoke absently, and when Henry turned to close the door leading to the balcony, he could see the white fuzz of hair, and Mr. Easter's large, freckled hand still clasping the dividing railing.

The next morning, a single glance through his uncurtained window brought him out of bed and on to the balcony. He stood for a time, his feet bare on the sun-warmed stone floor, and forgot everything but his delight in the peaceful scene spread below him. He saw fertile fields, the amber and rust-red roofs of a village, pinewoods and, beyond, the sea, blue and shimmering in the sunshine. Then his glance came back to the area round the hotel and the impression of peace vanished. Large coaches stood on the drive, cars with foreign license-plates drove up and expensive luggage was lifted out. Porters and pages in smart uniforms smiled at newcomers and bowed to departing guests. The old world, Henry mused — and the new.

He rang for coffee and asked if there were any messages for him. Learning that there were none, he got out a map and spread it on the bed and after some difficulty found the village named Caravela in which Senhor Crespo lived. It was some miles away, in the direction of Faro, at the end of a thin, straggling line that the map seemed reluctant to call a road. He sat for a time in thought, and then decided to drive over and find the Crespo residence.

He did not hurry. The business which had taken Senhor Moreira speedily to London, which had brought Marly and himself so promptly to Portugal, seemed on this warm, still morning to be less than urgent. There was no point in rushing; he had no desire to disturb the prevailing peace.

When he went downstairs and made some inquiries at the reception desk, he was told that anybody he met along the road would be able to tell him where Senhor Crespo lived; he was very well known. He was a very pious gentleman and very learned and his mother was also very pious, in fact saintly, and it was a pity she did not go about as much as she used to, to visit her friends. Telephone? Yes, there was a telephone.

Telephoning, Henry learned that Senhor Crespo was at Mass with his mother. An English gentleman? Perhaps he could telephone later? Perhaps Senhor Crespo would return soon, perhaps not; sometimes, after Mass, he took a walk. . . .

Henry put down the receiver and walked out to the car. On the wide glass-enclosed terrace he saw several old ladies, and remembered Lady Pearling and wondered if she was one of them. He thought they looked lonely, but they also looked warm and comfortable and prosperous, which made his first impulse of compassion give way to the feeling that they ought to be at home, wherever home was, making themselves useful in looking after their grandchildren, if any.

Brooding on old ladies, he missed a road sign to the right and had to reverse. Entering the side road, he found himself on a surface which deteriorated steadily and at last became so bad that he was thankful he was not driving his own car. On both sides of the dirt road he saw workers, for the most part women, toiling on the land; he drove past trees laden with fruit, ready or ripening: olives, almonds, figs, cherry, lemon and orange. All this, he mused, and fish too; the Moors must have hated leaving.

He rounded a curve, the road dipped, and as it rose again he saw on his left a high wall, clearly the boundary of an immense property. From the knowledge of the district gleaned from his meeting with Senhor Moreira at Lisbon, he was aware that there was only one house of this size in the vicinity, the Quinta do Infante. This was its western wall.

For a moment, he had an impulse to drive round the perimeter of the property but first things came first, and at the head of this morning's list was Senhor Crespo.

The road became all but impassable. He took a dirt road that led to the right, and as he did so, understood for the first time why the land-hunters had not found this particular piece of land, for the wall of the Quinta went on, seemingly endless, losing itself in a pinewood that stretched to the sea. Nobody, without penetrating the wood, could guess that before long, the wall turned at right angles, and that beyond it lay a screened, secluded strip of seashore.

He drove reluctantly on, overcoming the temptation to explore. Before him he saw a small white village; as he reached it, he saw that miniature though it was, it contained a square, a church, a communal washing tank and dark, Moorish shops set in streets just wide enough to allow passage to a laden donkey. There was a *chafariz*, a stone fountain; flanking it was a wall decorated with blue and white *azulejos* depicting a blue and white St. Sebastian pierced by blue and white arrows.

He stopped the car, got out and stood looking round for a residence worthy of a pious and learned gentleman and his pious mother. Only one was possible, a large, square, two-storied dwelling set in a spacious garden, its front turned away from the glare of the sea. On the gate hung a bell; Henry walked up and rang it, and the clang brought the inhabitants of every other house to their doors, but evoked no response from this one.

He rang again. It was a double note, harmonious despite its tinniness, and he thought he might be able to compose an accompanying chant. There was plenty of time, and nobody would interrupt him; as far as he could see, the villagers were going on with whatever they had been doing before his arrival.

At the fourth clang, a woman appeared from the steep path leading down to the beach; with her came an old fisherman, wrinkled and weather-beaten, on his head the traditional long-tailed woollen cap. Henry addressed them.

"Does Senhor Crespo live in this house?"

The question was not answered for some

time. The woman, on hearing Henry speak, had turned to call to her friends at the washing tank, inviting them to come and listen to the gentleman who had come from Brazil. They came, the suds drying on their hands, and stood round, smiling and expectant.

"Senhor Crespo," Henry repeated. "I'm looking for him."

"Ah." The fisherman grunted. "This is his house. But the servants are not here."

Without warning, the woman gave tongue; there rose a prolonged shriek or wail of the kind Henry had heard issuing from the mouths of the fish-vendors in Lisbon.

"Deo — linda!"

"Guilhermina!"

"A — de — lia!"

From afar, voices replied. They were coming, the crowd told Henry. Deolinda had gone to fetch the bread. Guilhermina had gone with the gardeners to fetch firewood for the kitchen stove. Adelia was down on the beach, buying fish. The other servant, Fernando, had accompanied Senhor and Senhora Crespo, who after Mass had gone for a little *passeo*, a little walk. They would be back soon, unless they lingered by the way, as sometimes they used to do before the Senhora had her illness, when the weather was good, as it was today, not too hot and not too cold.

The tale was interrupted by the arrival of the three who had been summoned. Elbowing their way to the front, they heard Henry's greeting with surprise and delight and they took up the threads of the narrative. It was strange, very strange that an *estranjeiro*, a foreigner, should come on this very morning, for it was a special occasion. It was the first time that the Senhora had been out of the house since her recovery. She had come back from the very mouth of death only because the whole village had prayed to Our Lady of Fatima, and Senhora Silva herself, a lady living in a great Quinta not far away, came to sit by her bedside and pray also. That so frail a lady of such great age should recover from so serious an illness was a miracle.

A miracle, the audience agreed.

Henry felt the years falling away. He had grown up among people like these, who took their time to get to the point, if they ever got as far as understanding that there was a point. The sun was beating down on his back and he could smell the pines and he could hear the lap-lap of the sea below the promontory on which all the newly-washed clothes flapped and danced. The wind was strong, but warm. Senhor Crespo was still in his mind, but no longer in the forefront of his mind; he was out walking, he would return, and it was no use asking when. This was not a land in which you could ask when and be told when; that kind of thing was all very well for people who wore watches and were forever looking at them — but here . . . Calma, amigo. Calma. Relax, friend.

Relaxing, Henry refused the servants' invitation to enter the house. He stayed where he was, and answered questions about himself and forgot Senhor Crespo altogether until one of the servants touched him on the arm and pointed.

"Look, Senhor. They are returning."

Far away, Henry saw a long procession. It was approaching slowly, so slowly that but for the reassurances he had just received, he would have taken it to be a funeral. He made out, as it came nearer, a wheeled chair. Seated in it, propped up on cushions, was a tiny, black-shawled figure so fragile, so wisp-like, that Henry's reverence for Our Lady of Fatima took a sharp upward curve; to snatch this human crumb, this morsel out of the jaws of death was indeed a miracle. Pushing the chair, flanking and following it, were retainers, friends or hangers-on. Leading the procession, leaning on a stick, was an elderly, thin, upright figure, Senhor Crespo, Henry decided. He had an almost unlined face, a neat, pointed beard and immense dignity; Henry thought he could have passed for one of the more benevolent Borgias.

The procession halted. Senhor Crespo welcomed Henry to Portugal, thanked him for coming, wished him a happy visit and then with ceremony led him up to his mother. Henry, bowing, laid his lips on the little proffered claw and released it gently. A voice like a thin silver piping floated up and asked him why he spoke with a Brazilian accent, and informed him that she, too, had once lived for a year at Santos, with her husband.

It was an auspicious beginning. When the chair was wheeled towards the house, Senhor Crespo walked on one side of it, Henry on the other. Falling into step, Henry glanced at his watch; it was forty minutes since he had arrived at the village.

It was another fifteen before the old lady had been lifted tenderly out of the chair and carried into the house. Then Senhor Crespo, having seen her safely to her apartment, returned to Henry and made his apologies for having kept him waiting so long.

But in Henry's mind, the matter had lost the last vestiges of urgency. He followed his host round the side of the house to a vine-shaded terrace. They sat at a small, round, marble-topped table and Senhor Crespo called for wine and a bottle was brought and poured out and drunk while the old man in his gentle, cultured voice explained something of the anxiety they had recently been through, and their thankfulness at his mother's recovery. As he was speaking, a servant, his manner fatherly and devoid of any tinge of obsequiousness, stopped and removed his master's dusty boots, replacing them with a pair of soft calf slippers; a fresh handkerchief was brought and sprinkled with lavender water and handed to Senhor Crespo so that he could cool his heated forehead. Henry received no handkerchief and no lavender water, but his shoes were gently dusted and a soft brush removed the marks of travel from his jacket. Then the servant went away, to return with more wine.

"You left my cousin Urbano well?" Senhor Crespo asked, when the glasses had been refilled.

"Yes. We had a very pleasant lunch in Lisbon."

"It was a pity he could not come here, as he had hoped — and as we had hoped. He was summoned to London. His wife is charming, don't you agree?"

"Very charming indeed."

"She was a da Souza, and very good-looking. Not now, we must admit, but when she was young. And so graceful. My mother has always been very fond of her. Before the accident, they used to like to meet and go on little tours — my cousin Urbano always owned large cars which my mother found more comfortable than my smaller ones. It is a pity to think that she will never again enjoy those drives."

"Wouldn't they do her good after her illness?" Henry ventured to suggest. "I mean, change of air, change of scene and . . . and so on?"

Senhor Crespo, who had been sipping his wine, put down the glass and stared at Henry in amazement.

"But Senhor," he asked in a hushed tone, "did you not hear about . . . but yes, Urbano must have told you, and perhaps you did not understand. It was not my mother's illness that prevents her, that prevented her from taking these tours. It was the accident."

"Accident?" In spite of himself, Henry heard a note of awe in his tone. "What accident?"

"My cousin did not tell you?"

"No.

"That is extraordinary. That is really extraordinary."

"Was he involved in the accident?"

"Involved, no. When it happened, he was in Lisbon but of all our relations, he was the most upset. He wrote to tell us of his horror for what had happened."

"What was . . . I mean, what *did* happen?"

"I will tell you." Senhor Crespo gave Henry more wine as though he were giving him strength to hear the recital. "I will tell you. It was in March. My mother wished to go and visit friends of hers who had come for a few weeks to stay at their house in Portimão. I drove her in my car. Since the time when she gave up her carriage, she would not buy a car of her own, because she felt that her coachman was too old to learn to drive it, and she could not trust herself to a chauffeur. I myself, Urbano, and one or two friends — these were the only people she would ever allow to drive her. And always, we had to drive with the utmost care, her nerves would not stand anything else."

He paused, took a sip of wine and sighed.

"Even to recall it fills me with dread," he said. "It happened at the place where the road from this village joins the road to Faro. We reached the junction. I stopped the car, I looked to left, to right. I sounded my horn many times. Then and only then did I venture to move forward and make the turn. And as I did so . . . Boom!"

Henry saved the bottle just in time. Senhor Crespo drew a pen and notebook from his pocket and proceeded to sketch the position of the cars involved in the crash.

"I was *here*. I was on the correct side of the road, driving at the pace of a snail. Along came this brute, this pig, this taxi. It made to pass, but without leaving sufficient room. There was an impact. From the opposite direction came a cart which barely avoided being overturned, but fortunately the man kept his head and pulled up the donkey in time."

"Your mother was injured?"

"My dear Senhor, she was prostrate. She was unconscious. I opened her door. I touched her, I called to her. I asked the brute of a taxi driver for water, but he was occupied in seeing if there was any damage to his car — *his* car, Senhor. Not *my* car, which he had run into. I told him that my mother was senseless, perhaps dying, and what did he do?"

"Go for help?"

"You may think so," Senhor Crespo said bitterly. "All human people must think so but he did nothing of the kind. He abused me. He shouted. He made wild accusations: I was driving in the middle of the road, I came out of a side road without warning . . . without warning! I had given him no room to pass. And the cart driver, he too began to accuse me. When the matter came before the police, they spoke against me and I did not get one centavo's worth of compensation."

Henry uttered some sounds of sympathy. This was not the business upon which he had come; he knew that it was time to recall his host and put an end to reminiscence. But before recalling his host, it was necessary to recall the business upon which he had come, and on this his memory appeared to be hazy.

"Was the car badly smashed?" he asked.

"Badly? My dear Senhor, there was a gash, a deep gash, no less than a meter in length, running from the door handle to the radiator. The other car, which the man had been so careful to examine, had no mark. No mark whatsoever. The injury was all to me and to my poor mother, who from that day to this has never entered a car. I sold mine and I did not buy another. I could not bear another shock of that nature, and it would of course kill my mother. It was undoubtedly the collision, the doctor tells me, that brought on her illness."

He leaned over to refill Henry's glass, and Henry snatched it out of reach.

"No. Thank you, no," he said.

"But your glass is almost empty."

"No more, thank you." Henry made an effort to clear his mind. Car . . . collision . . . Senhora Crespo. No, not Crespo. Senhora . . . yes, that was it. "Senhora Silva," he brought out with infinite relief.

"Ah, Senhora Silva," echoed Senhor Crespo, and shook his head sadly. "That, too, was a shock."

Henry waited. He would have given much to be able to give way to the pleasant languor that was stealing over him. But he had to stay awake. He was feeling very warm — too warm. Senhor Crespo was sipping his wine. Though he sipped so delicately, he had emptied more glasses than Henry had done, and

Henry realized in panic that he had not only to keep himself awake, but keep Senhor Crespo awake too.

"Senhor Moreira told me," he said, "that Senhora Silva knew nothing about the proposed sale of the land."

"Nothing. Nothing. And I, her oldest friend, had to tell her. She was greatly shocked."

The little fountain in the courtyard sent out jets as delicate as spiders' webs; they fell into the basin with a cool trickle of sound. The wind rose and fell. A wasp came to hover round the wine. From the house there was no sound whatever; no doubt its mistress was asleep and all the servants were whispering . . . and Senhor Crespo's eyes were closing . . .

"What," asked Henry in a loud voice, "was she shocked about?" He felt remorseful at seeing the old man start, but went on steadily. "Was it because the land had been offered for sale?"

"Exactly." Senhor Crespo straightened himself in his chair. "She had allowed an old servant to build a house, she had even paid for it, and what was the result of this generosity? Manuel Junqueira was offering the land for sale, when he was not even the owner. And what does this mean? That once again she has to endure the importunities of strangers who wish to persuade her to sell her land."

"All I —"

"Do not blame her, Senhor, if she seems to you unreasonable. I have been here, I have seen for myself how she has been pestered. Not by one, not by a dozen, but by scores. When she said she did not want to sell, she was treated like a market woman; people tried to cajole her. If you will believe this, some brandished checks in her face and told her to fill them in for whatever sum she wished. It was extremely . . . it was extremely . . ."

"Sordid?"

"Thank you. Sordid. And then she closed her gates, and after a time it seemed that the rush, the frenzy was over. She could be at peace. And then I, her oldest friend and greatest admirer, I had to go to her and tell her that once again, she was being begged for land. Yes, at first it was a shock but I reassured her. I said that this time, the petition was from friends."

"What did she say?"

"She asked me what I knew about you. I said that Urbano Moreira had written to me that I could have every confidence in you. You would, he told me, make a sympathetic approach."

"Did she say when?"

"She did not give a day and a time; she said only that she would receive you. It was not possible, until I had spoken with you, to arrange the meeting. But now I have seen you, and we can speak of dates. Perhaps next week or the week after that, whatever suits you both."

"I was instructed," Henry told him, "to treat the matter as urgent. I don't want to inconvenience Senhora Silva in any way, but I would be grateful if she could . . ."

He paused. Senhor Crespo was shaking his head sadly.

"We must leave it to her, Senhor Eliot, we must leave it to her."

"Do you think she'll sell?"

"Sell? Oh, I do not think so, Senhor. I do not for one moment think so. But she will see you. So much we have accomplished; she will see you."

"But the only reason for seeing me is to discuss the sale."

"Perhaps I should not have ventured to give you my opinion. I am only an intermediary. I did what my cousin asked, beyond that it is no affair of mine. It is between you and Senhora Silva, and it is not for me to conjecture what she will say to you."

There was silence. Through the bushes Henry could see Deolinda going up to the house, a large basket of washing balanced on her head. A cat walked delicately along the low wall, glanced suspiciously at Henry and scrambled out of sight. Somewhere beyond the wall an oxen cart creaked. Slowly, Senhor Crespo's eyes closed, his head nodded, his snores were as subdued as all the other sounds in the sun-steeped garden.

Henry rose and crept away. Something had been accomplished — Senhor Crespo had said so. Exactly what progress had been made would perhaps become clearer in the relatively less somnolent surroundings of the hotel. The intermediary had done his work and was sleeping after his labours. Next week, or the week after . . . it all depended on the extent of the shock suffered by the Senhora at the thought of having more open checks brandished in her face.

As Henry drove away, the village was left behind and the high wall of the Quinta do Infante was coming into view. But this time, Henry did not skirt it and drive on. Somewhere, he knew, there must be a road that led to the piece of land for which he had come to negotiate. Senhor Moreira had not been certain where it was, and Senhor Crespo had fallen asleep before he could ask him, but there was undoubtedly an entry to the land from the village of Caravela.

He found it at last, but he hesitated before taking it; it was scarcely more than a bridle path, weaving among the pine trees, which seemed to grow more thickly towards the sea. But it was worth a try. Sir Bertram might never own the land, but he was here as his emissary and it would be as well to know what he was buying.

He drove with the greatest caution. He knew that he was trespassing, but there was no sign of the cottage which had been built near the water's edge, and he doubted whether he would ever reach it, for the car was lurching alarmingly and the path becoming all but invisible.

Then he saw a clearing ahead of him and drove from the dusk of the trees into a sunlight that almost blinded him. He stopped the car, got out and saw before him a sight that held him spellbound.

Behind him was the wood. Beyond the clearing, the ground sloped gently down to an almost perfect semi-circle of beach, its sand so smooth, so golden, so untouched that it was hard to believe the foot of man had ever disturbed it. The sea licked gently, lovingly at the bay's edge; the wind that had agitated the garments on the Caravela clotheslines could not penetrate this sheltered cove. A blaze of gorse marked the line of the trees round the clearing, wild flowers carpeted it. Nothing could be heard but the lapping of the water. And closing round him, Henry felt a peace that had a quality of infinite remoteness, making him forget where he had come from or why he was here.

When he remembered, when his senses cleared, he understood for the first time what Sir Bertram was in danger of losing, and understood that the loss would also be Marly's . . . and his own.

Standing staring at the scene before him, his mind sketched swiftly the kind of house that Marly would build here. He saw the trees felled to clear the site, the beach a line of straw umbrellas, the sea with a floating bar; he heard the shrieks and cries of holiday-makers, the impatient hooting of cars. Marly's friends . . . here.

He turned towards the car, and hesitated — and then he got in and drove on. There was more to see. He could thread a way through the trees, and the surface was unlikely to be worse than that along which he had come.

He went yard by yard. Soon he reached a well-defined footpath. Farther on he saw wheel tracks; they came from his left, and he guessed that in the Quinta wall there would be a gateway giving access to the wood. He went straight on — and at last, following the curve of the beach, he saw another small clearing, and on it, a little white house, without doubt the one built twenty-eight years ago by the grandfather of Manuel Junqueira.

There were signs of occupancy, but he did not pause. He was moving so slowly that as he drove under a line of wash hanging almost motionless on a clothesline, he had time to study the garments — all very small, all identical — a row of patched shirts so shrunken that the arms were the same length as the bodies.

The road had up to now been sandy and covered with pine needles; it changed abruptly, and he found the car bumping over piles of stones and sand that seemed to have been heaped into mounds. The car springs would not stand much more. Henry decided to go back.

And then he wished that he had not come so far, for he saw that what he had driven up to was a humble kind of crèche. Outside the little house was a long, trestle table; seated at it were two rows of small, dark-haired children, some mere babies. Two old women were carrying out bowls of stew or soup and breaking up hunks of bread and filling brown mugs with milk. Low, child-size trundle beds were lined up under the trees. There was no sound save that of the clink of crockery; a savoury smell filled the air.

One of the women looked up and saw Henry and gave a startled cry. The children raised their heads and stared. There was a moment's dead silence — and then, without warning, loud shrieks rose and blasted the peace of the grove. Henry saw children scrambling off the benches and coming with a rush towards the car — coming, he saw, with howls and imprecations. To his bewilderment and dismay, they gathered round, clawing at the car, kicking it, hammering on it with small, furious fists.

The noise reached pandemonium. Henry started to get out of the car, was met by a shower of sand from the attackers and decided to sit where he was until the women could restore order.

From the doorway of the house a girl appeared. For a moment she stood in amazement, taking in the scene; then she came down the steps, made her way round the table, reached the children and shouted a brief order. The noise died down to sobbing, and the girl addressed Henry and, to his amazement, spoke in English.

"Will you kindly tell me what you're doing here?" she inquired.

"Trespassing," Henry said. "I'm sorry. Would you mind calling off the wild Indians?"

She had been frowning; now he saw her lips set in an angry line.

"Why should I?" she demanded. "They've a good right to be angry. You've wrecked their work."

"I've what?"

"You heard what I said. You've driven right over their work, the work they took a whole morning to do. Get out and look — if you're not too frightened."

He got out and looked. The children swarmed round him, howling and pointing. All were barefoot. All wore the kind of shrunken shirt he had seen on the clothesline; some also wore shorts, but the younger

93

ones wore nothing but a shirt, and Henry was wondering why when a thin stream emerged from a little boy and told him.

He followed the pointing fingers. At first he could see nothing but the road along which he had come, with its rocks and its mounds of sand.

"I don't understand . . ." the words were lost in the surrounding noise, and he raised his voice. "I'm sorry, but I really don't see what . . . would you kindly control this mob, so that I can hear you?"

She restrained the children and spoke in a voice cold with rage.

"It was a competition. They spent all the morning making designs of their own. They worked with sand and stones, and some of them did quite recognizable figures, which were going to be judged later, when they'd had their after-lunch rest. Then you came along and drove over everything and ruined it."

"I'm sorry," Henry said again, and moved — too late to evade a well-aimed kick on the shins delivered by a small boy whose strength seemed out of proportion to his size. He looked at the girl to see if she intended making any protest, and saw her looking pleased. Her reproach to the offender was no more than token.

"*Zeto, nao.*"

"I can speak Portuguese, too," Henry said furiously. "If you won't tell him to use his feet for standing on, then I will. If he'd had boots on, he'd have taken my skin off. Look!"

He drew up a trouser leg to examine the mark on his shin; seeing it, the children crowded round Zeto to congratulate him.

"It serves you right. Why shouldn't he kick you?" the girl asked Henry. "You had absolutely no right to come here. This is private property. It belongs to —"

"— the Quinta do Infante, which belongs to a lady called Senhora Silva. I've said I'm sorry."

"Saying sorry doesn't involve much effort. Those children worked —"

"— the entire morning. You said so before."

"To trespass on the borders of a property is bad enough. To drive right through the wood, past the beach, right up to this house —"

"I simply wanted —"

"Please don't make excuses. And please go away. The children haven't finished eating."

"I was only going to say —"

"— what you said before. You're sorry. We're sorry too — sorry you came. Good-bye."

"Good-bye. But before I go, I'd like to say that your attitude has —"

"If you don't go, I won't be responsible for your injuries. The children can't be held off for much longer."

She gave a signal to the two women; between them they herded the children back to the table, leaving Henry to extricate his car and get away as best he might. He made his way, hot with humiliation, back to the dirt road which would lead him to the main road, driving angrily, his mind playing back the scene and giving himself a more dignified role.

The girl . . . they had spoken of a niece. But if this was the niece, and if she wanted to do good works, why run her crèche in a fisherman's house in the woods instead of in one of the outbuildings of the immense Quinta? And if she was indeed the niece, he thought bitterly, his mission had begun well. A splendid start — and a fitting end to a totally unproductive morning.

He looked at his watch. He was expected to lunch at the villa and he was already late;

he would have to drive straight there instead of going to the hotel to have a shower and change into a fresh shirt. And at the Colstons there would be the same crowd of loud-voiced strangers, and the Colonel would be waiting to ask him more questions.

When he reached the house, he parked his car with a dozen others and walked on to discover that lunch, like dinner last night, was the buffet kind, with more than thirty guests milling round the long tables set out with food and drink. He looked for Marly; she was as usual the center of a knot of men, but for once there was no sign of Edgar.

The Colonel called to him jovially.

"Come along, Henry, come along — you don't deserve a drink, but I'll give you one. You can join Marly later. We waited lunch for you, and then decided you'd got lost."

He was leading Henry to a table, throwing out brief, casual introductions. No surnames; this is Dulcie and here's Edwina, you remember her, and Diana and Marietta, you know them of course, how d'you do, yes, heavenly weather, no, haven't been in the Algarve before, yes, know one or two people here, excuse me . . . ."

They paused at the table and the Colonel

gave cold beer to Henry and helped himself to a plate of lobster salad.

"Find that fellow you went looking for?" he inquired between munches. "Marly said you'd gone to see this fellow called Crespo."

"Yes, I went to his house."

"Anything to come of it?"

"No."

"Didn't think it would. Tell you what, Henry — I've been talking to Wanda, and she and I came to the same conclusion; far better if you got in touch with Marly's father and advised him to give up the whole idea. If you like, you can mention, just mention casually, that I shan't be staying in Portugal much longer — the doctor's advised me to move. Lovely here in summer, but too wet for me in winter. I'm thinking of trying Corsica. I was there some time back, and Wanda and I both liked it. You and Marly could buy this villa as a little place for your holidays, and —"

"I'm afraid Sir Bertram is very keen to get this land, if he can."

"Ah, well." The Colonel took Henry's empty glass and set it down with a bang. "Just as well, as it happens. I've practically promised this house to a fellow who saw it a few months ago; he's back again to clinch the deal. Matter of fact, I think he's staying at your hotel."

Henry thought of Mr. Easter, but this seemed an unlikely setting for him. It was not a Walt and Joyce atmosphere.

"Help yourself to anything you want," the Colonel said, moving away. He bumped into an elderly woman and apologized. "Clumsy of me. Let me present Marly's fiancé, Henry Eliot. Henry, this is Mrs. Restington. American, charming, newly-arrived, staying at your hotel. Excuse me, will you?"

"I've seen you around," Mrs. Restington said, fixing small, shrewd gray eyes on Henry. "When's the wedding going to be?"

"July."

"And where?"

"In London."

"Well, if I thought I'd be there in July, I'd ask you to ask me. I just love weddings. But I'm only going to London for a little while, on business; after that, I'm coming back here and I'm going to stay here."

"Settle here?"

"That's right — settle here. Settle down here — if I like it. If I don't like it, I'll go and settle down some place else."

"Are you looking for a house?"

"Yes, I am. That's why I'm here today;

someone told me about the Colonel and I phoned and he said to come right out. All my friends say I shouldn't be buying a house at my age, but if there's one thing I can't stand for long, it's hotels. I like to have my own kitchen and I like to sleep in my own bed. This house would do fine, but the Colonel says there's someone else who's going to buy it." She broke off and addressed Marly, who had joined them. "I've just been telling your nice young man that I want to come to your wedding, if I'm around. I suppose you've come to take him away from me?"

Marly smiled, nodded, linked her arm through Henry's and led him down to the pool, now almost deserted. He sat on a wicker chair and she took off her sandals and sat on the pool's edge, dangling her bare legs in the water.

"What sort of morning?" she asked.

"Complete waste."

"I thought so, when you arrived. You looked moody but then you always do, at parties, so I couldn't be sure. No contact with Senhora Silva?"

"No. The pace out here is —"

"— slow, dead slow and stop. Well, I'm not going to stop. I like it out here. I want a house out here. When can I get to see that land?"

"I drove up to it."

"What's it like?"

"It's a beautiful piece in a beautiful setting."

"Well, what did you expect? Why else would Father go to all this trouble? Now perhaps you'll be more anxious to think about the house we'll build on it."

"I've been thinking . . ."

"Well? What about?"

"Money. The kind of money it would take to run a house" — his eyes went to the villa — "a house like this, out here."

"Why worry? We'd only be here for part of the summer. Don't get difficult again, we've been over all this. I've got enough money to do it, so we do it. If we pretend we're going to live at your financial level without help from me, then we're both fools."

"There's nothing foolish in assessing what we'll be able to afford. What's become of Edgar?"

"He's in Albufeira, arranging for an exhibition of some of his pictures. I didn't go with him because I thought you might show up with some news about Senhora Silva. If

I'd known you were going to see the land, I'd have gone with you." She took her legs out of the water and swivelled round to study him. "What's wrong with you? The morning couldn't have gone as badly as all that."

He was silent for a time.

"Senhor Moreira," he said slowly at last, "said that Senhora Silva had a niece."

"So what?"

"I think I might have run into her. I did a detour to look at that land, and came across a sort of crèche."

"Crèche?"

"Some children, very young, having a meal outside that cottage that was built on the land. They lived there or spent all day there. This niece, if she's the niece, was in charge."

"What does she look like?"

He recalled the oval, angry face . . . and other details which he had seen and noted without being aware of it. He could have given a vivid answer to the question, but something — not caution, but a desire to keep Marly's destructive instincts at bay — made his reply brief.

"Smallish. Darkish," he said.

"Young?"

"About twenty-two, I'd say."

"Pretty?"

More, far more than pretty. He felt as though he held a picture which he was screening from Marly's gaze — a sketch, as yet incomplete . . .

"Well, is she pretty?"

"You can't really tell when a girl's shouting at you," he replied. "I was trespassing and she didn't like it."

"Didn't you tell her who you were? Didn't you ask —"

"We skipped the courtesies. We had a shouting match and she threw me out. I'd run the car over some designs the kids had been building with sand and stones, and they all came at me, yelling. So there were no friendly exchanges. If she's really the niece of Senhora Silva, I've made a poor start."

Marly frowned. She sat pondering for some time, and then looked up and spoke decisively.

"Look, I've got an idea. We'll go together, tomorrow, and see her, and you'll find you're wrong. Why would the niece want to work all day at a crèche?"

"She is the niece." Henry spoke with conviction. "She spoke English, and now I remember old Mr. Pugh saying something about her mother having married an Englishman. Yes, she's the niece."

"Then we'll certainly go and see her — to erase the bad impression you made. Once she tells her aunt what happened, you'll have less chance than ever of an interview. We'll go there and present a better image."

"And how do we do that?"

"Easy. We tell her that you came back here and told me what you'd done, and you were terribly upset and couldn't sleep for worrying about the poor children, and so you and I decided to go along to the crèche and take something for them — toys, sweets — by way of apology."

"And when we've handed over the toys and the sweets, we say: Could you now take us along to your aunt and persuade her to sell us her land?"

"*We* don't say it, we let *her* say it."

"From what I saw of her this morning, she's more likely —"

"Oh, Henry, don't be a *bore!*" She lingered despairingly on the word. "You had a wonderful chance at getting at Senhora Silva without wasting time with useless go-betweens, and you mucked it up. And when I try to retrieve matters, you do nothing whatsoever but make objections. Just *think* for a moment: Father's been held up for weeks, in fact for months, and so far, all that's happened in a forward direction has been a lot of chit-chat by a bunch of lawyers, first in England and then in Portugal. And then you're sent out here and the only liaison you've got is this half-baked old man in some village or other, who claims to be a friend who can get you into the Quinta. You heard what Cousin Tim said — getting behind those walls is almost impossible — and now, when you've actually made contact with Senhora Silva's niece, you do nothing to follow it up. It shouldn't be difficult to make an impression on a girl who's reduced to sitting in a pinewood looking after a bunch of children. We'll go there tomorrow morning and use some high-pressure charm, and after that we'll go ahead and tackle the aunt."

There was a pause. Henry had risen and was staring at his reflection in the pool's green, gently-moving surface. Here he stood, firm on his two feet, listening to Marly making plans and down there, the water showed him as a bobbing, grotesquely-dancing figure. A puppet. . . .

Something seemed to have happened to him. Some spring within him seemed loose, adrift. He took his eyes from his restless reflection, only to find them drawn irresistibly back. Successful architect, a Stonor man. Accepted lover, beauty and riches within his grasp . . . or a fool caught in a net of his own making.

The water made sucking, sneering noises. The figure continued to caper, flung this way and that, dark and shapeless on the pool's brilliant surface.

"Well?" he heard Marly ask impatiently, after a time. "Do we take them toys?"

He spoke absently, without turning.

"What they want more than toys," he said, "is diapers."

"Is *what?*"

"Diapers. Nappies."

"What in the world are you talking about?"

He faced her.

"Even you must have heard of diapers," he said. "They weren't wearing any."

"How in the world would you know they —"

"How would anybody know? By looking."

She got up in a slow, fluid movement and pushed her feet angrily into her sandals.

"Sometimes," she said furiously, "you really go out of your way to drive me crazy. Are you coming tomorrow, or aren't you? I don't want to sound offensive, but I would like to remind you that you're being paid to get through to Senhora Silva, and this plan seems to me better than anything that's yet been suggested. Are you coming tomorrow, or aren't you? If you won't go, I'll go by myself. Or with Cousin Tim, or Wanda, or Edgar."

Her eyes were cold and angry. As Henry looked, they seemed to turn brown. Her hair no longer looked blonde and straight and fine; it was dark and stringy. Her lips —

"Well, *say* something!" Marly shouted.

"Yes," Henry said. "Yes, I'll go with you."

CHAPTER 3

By half-past nine the next morning, Henry was ready to leave for the Colstons' villa. He knew it was rather early to expect to find Marly up and dressed, but if by any chance she was ready, they could get away without being held up by the Colstons, all of whom he knew to be late risers.

He was passing the terrace of the hotel, on his way to the car, when an imperious voice called his name. He turned to see a gaunt-looking, white-haired woman beckoning to him from her chair beside one of the glass-topped tables. Reluctantly, he obeyed the summons, feeling reasonably certain as he approached that this would be the Lady Pearling of whom the Colonel had spoken.

She told him at once that she was, pushed out a chair and ordered him to sit down. She was wearing a long-out-of-fashion suit made of shantung silk — he remembered seeing his mother in one just like it — and a small, round, locally-purchased straw hat. Her shoes were as sturdy as barges. If he had been asked to guess what she was, he would have said a retired governess or headmistress or Girl Guides Commissioner and he would have added that she was anything but rich. Anybody who looked less like a millionairess, he thought, it would be difficult to meet.

"I knew your name," she told Henry, "because an American woman staying here, a Mrs. Restington, said she'd met you at a villa belonging to some people called the Colstons. Sit down, young man, sit *down*. I can't go on squinting up at you."

"I'm afraid I haven't really time to sit down," Henry told her. "I'm on my way to an appointment."

"With that Colonel Colston, I daresay. It's too early to go visiting."

"Not a visit. An —"

"Yes, yes, yes, you've said so," Lady Pearling snapped irritably. "When did a personable young man like yourself ever want to waste his time with an old woman like me? Sit *down*."

Henry sat. He did not share Marly's feeling that all women over the age of sixty should be shipped to a remote island with an accompanying supply of prelates, psychologists, psychiatrists and playing cards, but he thought he would not mind waving good-bye to this one. He disliked her loud, peremptory voice and, even more, her bullying manner.

"If you're going to see the Colstons," she said, "you can give them a message from me. That's why I called to you just now. Incidentally, do you spell your name with one T or two?"

"One."

"You never had an aunt named Ruby Eliot, by any chance?"

"No."

"Lucky for you. Dreadful woman. Now about these Colstons. I'd like you to tell them from me that I've been expecting them to look me up. Some friends of mine wrote to them without, I may say, a word to me before doing so. So far, they've given no sign, which is just as well, because before being looked up, I like to find out something about the people who are proposing to do the looking up. How much are the Colstons asking for their house?"

"I'm afraid . . ."

"Wake up, wake up, young man. I'll take your fine feelings as read; all I want to know is the price. Don't pretend you're not aware that this Colonel Colston goes from place to place making large sums of money by selling his houses just as his unfortunate wife has settled into them."

"On the contrary —"

"Ah. That means she's in the business too. Business it is, however prettily they try to cover it up. Not that I think the worse of them for carrying on a business; I've been in business, or if you like, trade, all my life and I wish I'd never given it up. Well, if you don't know the price of the house, find it out, will you? You might have to corner the Colonel — I hear they've got a constant stream of visitors going in and out of the place. One of them's the daughter of that fishy fellow who goes in for big property deals — forget his name — Stonor, that's it. Sit *down*, young man, I haven't finished."

"I'm engaged to Miss Stonor," Henry said from his full height.

"Nonsense. You look far too sensible to have got yourself tied up with a fast piece like that."

"I'd be very much obliged if —"

"— if I wouldn't say so. If you're engaged

to her, you should make it your business to know as much about her as possible. It needn't worry you. Young women nowadays have no morals whatever, and young men don't seem to mind. On the contrary. If you're really engaged to this girl, I shall give Mrs. Restington a piece of my mind. When I was speaking to her about you, she should have told me. Unless she didn't know."

"She certainly knew. She —"

"Then, like me, she found it hard to believe and hoped it wasn't true. These things often blow over. Tell me, have the Colstons ever mentioned my name?"

"No. Yes," Henry amended unwillingly. "I think Mrs. Colston said that she might be able to help you, as you're new out here."

"Ha!" Lady Pearling gave a loud, contemptuous snort. "I've been a new arrival in more places than she's ever likely to have seen, even with her roving husband. What I'm trying to find out is whether she and he can be useful to me, or only useful to themselves. And the answer, obviously, is that they're out to make what they can. I can see that you know it, but you won't talk because you're offended. If I can't say what I think at my age, which is seventy plus, when will I be able to? If you're waiting for me to say

I'm sorry I threw a little light on Miss Stonor's character, you'll wait a long time. All I'll say in excuse is that nobody, looking at a decent-looking man like yourself, would dream that he'd go anywhere near that loose-living set, let alone consider marrying one of them. Now, if you're going to see the Colstons, you can tell them I've been looking at houses, and I'm going round in a taxi today to inspect some more. In a day or so, I might go along and take a look at theirs. On the other hand, I might not."

"I'll tell them. Now I —"

"Wait a minute. What are you doing out here? Holiday?"

"In a way."

"What's your profession?"

"I'm an architect."

"Don't tell me you're tied up with the father as well as with the daughter. Are you?"

"I work for Sir Bertram Stonor," Henry said coldly, and marvelled that she had lived to reach seventy plus.

"Hook, line and sinker," Lady Pearling intoned. "You look too muscular to be an architect. The architects I've dealt with have always been a weedy lot. You don't play bridge, by any chance?"

"Seldom, and badly. I must go now, I'm afraid."

"Don't let me keep you. There's a four-some in this hotel, but one of them keeps getting up and going off in a huff when I tell her what she did wrong. I'm tired of it. You'll have to make a fourth. And as you go, tell that page boy I don't want any newspapers, English or any other. If I wanted to know what was happening in England, I should go and live there, which I haven't done for the past fifteen years. Good-bye."

Henry made his escape, pausing only to purchase, somewhat ostentatiously, a news-paper for himself. He got into the car and drove very fast, less anxious to reach the villa than to leave behind him the echoes of Lady Pearling's voice.

It was strange, on walking round to the front of the house, to see that the water of the pool unmoving, the surrounding chairs dry and unoccupied. Stranger still to see the Colonel already up and dressed, seated on a chair in the shade, the remains of his break-fast on a table beside him.

"Good morning. Marly expecting you so early?" he called as he caught sight of Henry.

"I told her I wouldn't be late."

"I suppose you're both going off to see

the Silva woman's niece?"

"Yes." Henry knew that the Colonel was waiting for details, but he did not supply them. He heard his contemptuous laugh.

"Still hugging those professional secrets, eh? My dear fellow, do remember that Marly's father and I were confiding in one another before you were born. Is he likely to let his daughter come out here and stay in my house without a word as to why she came?"

"I don't know." Henry tried to speak reasonably. "All I can do is carry out the orders I was given, which were to say nothing to anybody."

"I see. Well, you just go on saying nothing to anybody. Marly will continue to treat me as a member of her family, which I am. That's so, isn't it?" he asked her, as she came out of the house. "I'm telling your boyfriend that he's missed the point and misread your father's instructions. But he's decided to hug his secrets."

She smiled. She was wearing a beautiful linen suit, cool and green; in her hand were two gift-wrapped packages.

"What are *you* doing up at this hour?" she asked the Colonel.

He yawned wearily.

"Had to be up to keep an appointment — this chap I told you about is coming over to see about buying the house. Why he couldn't have come at noon instead of dawn, I can't tell you. However, business is business. Incidentally," he asked Henry, "have you seen anything of Lady Pearling?"

"She spoke to me this morning."

"Did she mention houses?"

"She said she had been looking at some, and might come out and see this one in a day or two."

"Well, you can tell her she's too late," the Colonel said with satisfaction. "You needn't sound too polite when you explain that this chap's buying it. I'm told she's as rude as she's rich." He paused as a maid approached to tell him he was wanted on the telephone. "See you at lunch," he said, as he went indoors.

Henry turned to talk to the car, but Marly pulled him round to face her, and took his hands and clasped them round her waist.

"You haven't said good morning," she reminded him.

"I know. Couldn't we wait until we were less . . . well, conspicuous?"

"Nobody's peering out of any of the windows, and if they were, what's a kiss?"

This one was less than ardent. Try as he would, Henry could not free himself from the conviction that Edgar was regarding them maliciously. He saw Marly draw back to smooth her skirt.

"Uncrushable," she said. "This is a new suit. Like it?"

"Yes. But isn't it too good?"

She frowned.

"How can a suit be too good?"

"What I meant was that you're just visiting this crèche, not declaring it open."

Her good humour had vanished.

"Are you trying to tell me what I ought to wear?" she demanded.

"No. But those shoes —"

"Too good?"

"You've got to walk through a wood, or at least part of a wood. I don't want to trespass again. Those shoes look as though they won't do the distance."

"Well, they can. But if you'd rather —"

She stopped. The Colonel had come out of the house and had called Henry's name in a hoarse, angry tone. He was advancing with long, purposeful strides. The smiling, genial figure which had gone indoors had reappeared with all affability gone and a face dark with rage.

"Hey, wait a minute, you!" he shouted.

Henry glanced over his shoulder to see who was being addressed; there was nobody behind him and he came to the astounding conclusion that it was himself.

"What the hell," the Colonel shouted, coming to a halt beside him, "do you think you're up to?"

Henry was speechless. Throughout his knowledge of the Colstons, he had seldom seen anything but the Colonel's bluff, slap-on-the-shoulder, help-yourself-to-a-drink manner. He had never taken it for more than a façade, and since his arrival in Portugal and his refusal to talk freely about the business on which he had come, the façade had cracked badly — but he had never imagined himself facing the Colonel as he was now, ugly with rage, spluttering with hate, stripped of every pretence of cordiality.

"What on earth —" Marly began . . .

"He'll tell you, ask him," the Colonel broke in savagely. "I would have thought that the first thing your father needed in the men who worked for him was the ability to keep their mouths shut when it was really necessary — a bit of elementary discretion, the glimmerings of know-how about when to speak and when to shut up.

I would have —"

"Would you explain what this is all about?" Henry asked.

"Yes, I'll explain." The Colonel saw an alarmed maid appear and disappear, and made an attempt to lower his voice. "I'll tell you. You informed that fellow, the buyer I had lined up for this house, who was on the point of signing, who was in fact coming here this morning to fix the whole thing up — you told him that the negotiations for the sale of Senhora Silva's land had broken down. That's what you did."

"I did nothing of the kind."

"Don't lie to me," the Colonel yelled furiously. "I might have known you'd do something like this. Ever since you set foot in this country, you've been strutting round telling me that you're the only one in Sir Bertram's confidence. Who the hell do you think you are? You tried to fob me off by pretending that you and Marly had come out here on a simple jaunt — d'you take me for a fool? And after all the pretence of being discreet — discreet, by God! — you blurt the whole thing out to the first passing stranger who tries to pump you."

"I've already told you —"

"And I've already told you that you're

lying. What you've done is go and blab the whole thing to that Easter fellow. If you had to spill information, why in hell did you choose Easter, of all people? Don't you know who he is? Didn't Marly's father tell you, when he was confiding in you, that Easter was the fellow who first went after that bit of land? Didn't he tell you that?"

"No."

"Well, I'm telling you. And let me tell you something else. I informed you clearly yesterday, in this garden, that Easter had made up his mind to buy this house. Knowing that, you let him know that there was a hitch over the Silva sale and naturally, he's got his nose to the ground and he's going after it again."

"I told Mr. Easter nothing whatsoever."

"You expect me to believe that he went to bed and dreamed it all? Marly herself told me, when she heard me mention Easter's name, that you'd got into conversation with him on the plane coming over here. And he told me himself that he was in the room next door to yours at the hotel, chatting chummily over the balcony. D'you expect me to believe that you never so much as mentioned the Silva land?"

"I only expect you to believe that I said

nothing to him to —"

"— make him smell a rat. Well, I think you're lying. I can —"

"Come on, Marly." Henry took her arm to turn her towards the car. "We've heard enough of this."

To his fury, she resisted.

"Wait a minute, Henry," she said. "You can't just walk away like that. You've got to clear this up."

"Clear this up? Clear this up?" The Colonel's tone was bitter. "That fellow was coming over here this morning to sign all the papers, and he rang up to say the deal was off. And when I asked him why, he told me that he'd heard that Sir Bertram Stonor had struck a snag and that the land was still on the market. Who could tell him that except someone who knew it? And who knew it but this precious fiancé of yours? It was in one of those get-togethers over the balcony that Easter got his facts, and I shall make a point of telling your father that if my affairs were in the hands of a man who couldn't help blurting them out to the first comer, I'd soon see to it he was on his way out and —"

"Heard enough, Marly?"

"Oh, don't take that attitude, Henry," she

121

said angrily. "If you're accused of something, all you have to do is prove —"

She stopped. Henry had walked away and was going with long strides towards the car. She hesitated, decided to follow and caught up to him as he reached it. He opened the door for her, she got in and they drove for some time in silence. After one or two glances at his face, she shrugged, settled back in her seat and sighed.

"Nice beginning to the day," she commented.

"Thanks for the splendid way in which you —"

"Now look, Henry," Her voice was hard. "I've told you before that the time to say things isn't afterwards, but on the spot. I know what you're going to do now, you're going to start abusing Cousin Tim and telling me exactly what you think of him. Why say it to me? Why didn't you say it to him? You always do the same thing — retreat. You never fight a battle on the field. Afterwards is too late. What's the *point* of not saying it at the time?"

His face was white and set.

"The point," he said, forcing himself to speak calmly, "is simply that one person yelling abuse is enough. It isn't a pleasant spectacle, but it's a damn sight more unpleasant when two people do it. I'm willing to stand up to anybody in a straightforward, reasonable argument. What I can't stomach is watching someone who without the slightest justification, without grounds, without proof of any kind, tells me, not once but three times, that I'm a liar. There's only one answer to people like the Colonel, and that's to leave them to shout it out alone. I could punch him in the face, but being about thirty years younger than he is, I'm disqualified."

"You're crazy. If you shout back, then you both get it out of your systems and the thing's over."

"You think so? Then let's go back and do it again. Your cousin Tim calls me a liar and I call him a dirty old man given to fawning over rich old women, a cheat who fills his house with so-called friends specifically chosen because they've got the money to buy his unsound houses; lamentable old poseur and a man who in general I wouldn't trust once he'd wandered out of my line of vision. You think that would have been better?"

"At least it would have shown you weren't afraid of him."

He brought the car to a stop and turned to face her.

"You really, seriously think that? That I'm afraid of him?"

"Well . . . in a way, yes. Look at the way you let my father talk to you sometimes. Why don't you —"

"— talk back and talk myself out of a job? If he did it too often, I would — but he doesn't. In the meantime, as you pointed out recently, I'm being paid to listen to him. And now that he's come up, did you hear what the Colonel said about Easter having been the first to go after that bit of land?"

"Yes. I should have warned you."

"Warned me against what?"

"Against that man Easter. My father told me that a man named Easter had saved him the trouble of searching for a piece of land. He didn't move fast enough, and Father got it — or thought he'd got it. When I heard the name on the plane coming out, I thought it might be the same. I would have said something but how could I imagine you'd get chummy over a balcony, and talk too much?"

"I didn't get chummy and I didn't talk too much. I haven't talked too much to anybody, but I think you have. I don't for a moment believe that your father meant you to talk so freely to the Colstons."

She laughed contemptuously.

"Henry, sometimes you sound mentally retarded! The Colstons are *relations*. Uncle Tim and my father are *cousins*. I've heard my father, all my life, discussing his business deals with Cousin Tim whenever they've met. It's one thing to talk to Cousin Tim; it's quite another to go and give it all away to that Easter man. You must see that, even though you're pretending not to."

He stared at her, began to speak, gave it up and started the car. He drove on in silence, so shaken that he wondered why his hands were not trembling as they held the wheel. The unhesitating stand she had taken, not for but against him; her knowledge of, her easy acceptance of the fact that her father had in some way out-maneuvered Mr. Easter, her hints that he was not qualified to take his place among experienced businessmen — each of these could be dealt with — but added together, they showed him more clearly than anything had yet done the terrifying gulf that yawned between himself and the woman he had wanted to make his wife. He had forced himself to accept their differences in background, in taste, in temperament; he had not considered moral values because he had not wanted to set himself up as a judge. But now he knew that in these, too, there was an unbridgeable chasm between them. Like her father, like the Colonel, she would always get her own way, fairly if it was possible, but if not, then by other methods. That was their way . . . and it was not his way.

He was to marry her and she would never change; so much he had learned. They would marry, and he would remain forever outside her circle, regarded as he was regarded now, good-looking, dull, intelligent but dreamy, a drag at a party and useless when it came to screwing down a bargain. They would marry, and the flame which had sprung up on their first meeting, which was now flickering, would die — and what use she would have for him thereafter, he did not know, but he could guess.

He brought his mind, with an effort, to Mr. Easter, who had at least proved Marly's theory that it was silly to talk to strangers. It was not reassuring to feel that without realizing it, he might have allowed Mr. Easter to guess the truth about the Silva property. He had, as far as he was aware, given nothing away but it struck him for the first time that the old man was perhaps not as guileless as he appeared; in between the family items and the frank, friendly questions, there may have been sandwiched a probe too swift to arouse suspicion.

The thought added the final touch to his mood of despair. His discretion, much less his veracity, had not been in question since he was a schoolboy. He would have called himself as discreet as circumstances required him to be, but the fact remained that he had talked to Mr. Easter, the land had been briefly mentioned and the Colonel had lost a sale.

He stopped the car at the edge of the pinewood and heard Marly's sulky voice.

"Look at that road! How far do I have to walk?"

"Not far. Give me those parcels."

"No."

He did not press her. He knew that she was posing as a warm-hearted girl visiting a crèche, bringing presents for the children. He too was bringing presents, but his were inedible, utilitarian and without the fancy wrapping.

"If you want to know," she informed him, "I'm not as keen on this idea as I was yesterday."

"Then why not call it off?"

"Because I want to see that land,

that's why."

"Well, come on and see it."

He had said nothing to prepare her for its beauty. When they reached the clearing, she stopped abruptly and stood gazing in silence at the curve of bay, and he stood saying nothing, waiting for her to speak.

It was a long time before she said anything. Then, with her eyes still on the view, she drew a long breath.

"I told you," she said.

"What did you tell me?"

"That it must have been something special, something extra-special like this — or why would my father have gone to such lengths to get it? Who else has a beach, a view like this?"

The sulky expression had left her face; in its place Henry recognized her father's look of acquisitiveness. Clearly revealed was the hard, business-like core that lay beneath her beauty. She had shed the attitude of passive expectancy which until now she had shown towards the purchase; she was alert, greedy, eager to bring the project to a successful conclusion. No longer was she content to wait for her father to drop into her lap yet another lavish present; now that she had seen what he was offering, she was filled with fear at the possibility that he would not be able to obtain it for her.

She raised a hand and pointed.

"We'll put the house there."

"If you get the land."

"Why shouldn't I get the land? Why shouldn't she sell? You can see she's never used it."

"The house is along that path. The house is being used, even if this land isn't."

They walked on slowly. When the little house came in sight, she spoke without hesitation.

"Guest cottage. Absolutely heavenly guest cottage. I'll build on a — what on earth are those?"

They had come to the clothesline with its row of short shirts, and she was gazing at them in amazement.

"Washing. Shirts, shrunken," Henry explained.

"How many children, for Heaven's sake?"

"I didn't count."

They could see the table laid with bowls and mugs. One of the old women Henry had seen the day before was bending over a tank filled with suds, washing still more shirts and spreading them on a sunny patch to bleach. In front of the house stood a cart, its donkey unharnessed and tied to a tree. There was no sign of any children.

From the house came an old man, his arms laden with empty cartons which he put into the cart; he saw the visitors, snatched off his hat, bowed and re-entered the house. And then from its other side there rose suddenly the sound of slow, rhythmic clapping, and children's voices raised in song. After the first few bars, Henry had to fight a strong inclination to put his fingers into his ears. It was all very well to talk sentimentally about childish carolling; to every ten toddlers who could sing, there were twenty who droned, or wailed, or chanted. These children were doing all three. The song was a sad one, with holy overtones; the voices dragged on mournfully, following or not following the tremulous accompaniment provided by an accordion.

The old woman had made no move to approach, but the old man must have announced the arrival of visitors, for in the doorway appeared the girl Henry had met the day before. She stood still for a moment, and he studied her with a detachment which had not been possible on their last encounter.

She was rather small — so much he remembered — but he had failed to note other things: her large, dark, expressive eyes, her smooth skin, tanned to gold, her dark, thick, wavy hair which looked as though it would resist any effort to turn it from its natural lines. Her nose was small; her mouth was slightly open as she stared across at the newcomers, then it closed and he saw that her lips were curving and well-shaped and firm.

"Good morning." They saw her greeting, but could not hear it above the caterwauling. As she came down the steps, the noise ended and an adult voice could be heard teaching the choir the words of the next verse.

Marly stepped forward. Henry saw her, fair and graceful and smiling, her manner a shade diffident, to match her words.

"We've come to apologize. My name is Marly Stonor, and this is my fiancé, Henry Eliot. He did an absolutely unforgivable thing yesterday, and we've come to say he's sorry. We've brought," she held out the packages in their bright green paper, "some sweets and things for the children."

There was no opportunity for audible thanks, the singing had begun again. They stood watching the girl hand the presents to the old man, who shuffled into the house with them.

When the verse ended, Marly went on with her speech, but to Henry's uneasiness, a touch of patronage had crept into her tone; it was now her fluent, easy, I-know-my-way-around manner.

"I hope you'll forgive Henry. Thank goodness I can say this to you in English. Henry said you spoke it quite well."

"I mustn't claim too much credit," the girl said gravely. "You see, I *am* English."

"Oh, really? I didn't —"

Marly stopped, since once again there was no point in going on. Verse three had begun. Once again they had to stand and wait, Henry feeling more foolish than he had ever felt in his life, Marly rapidly shedding the cloak of cordiality she had worn on her arrival.

The singing stopped, and in the silence they heard a swish of skirts. From behind them appeared a priest, in appearance a combination of the only two ecclesiastical figures well known to Henry, Savonarola and Friar Tuck; he had the latter's portly body and the former's impressive nose. He bowed as he passed Marly, murmured a greeting in Portuguese to Henry and was delighted to hear it answered in the same language. He paused.

"Ah, Senhor, you have lived in Brazil! I can hear this." He went forward and took the girl's hands in his. "Good morning, Teresa. I went to see your aunt, but she was not in, and so I came —"

He stopped. The accordion had broken into a gayer air, round the corner of the house came streaming the children, two by two, hand in hand, their bare feet stamping in time to the music. The older children, the fully-dressed group, were in the lead; next came the mini-shirts and then the accordion player, who was the other old woman Henry had seen the day before, serving at table. Last of all came the choir mistress and Henry's eyes fell on her, he forgot the children, the music, the priest, forgot even the reason for his presence here.

There was nothing to tell him who she was, unless it was the priest's unfinished speech. He had been to the house, and she was not there — because she was here. It could be no other. Her authority was proclaimed in every line of her figure and acknowledged by everyone present except himself and Marly. This was she. This was the chatelaine — no, not the chatelaine, the Dona. The Dona of the Quinta do Infante.

This was Senhora Silva.

Henry studied her with absorbed interest. She was about fifty-five, of medium height, her figure stout but rigidly encased in a black, perfectly-fitting dress. She had high cheek bones, large but rather lusterless black eyes. There was very little gray in her hair, it looked coal-black, drawn tightly off her face and arranged in a neat knot on the back of her neck. Her expression was so calm, so bland as to be almost cow-like, but Henry recalled Senhor Moreira's words and found himself in complete agreement with them, she had the air of a queen.

The accordion played the same bars over and over again. The children formed themselves into a circle, gave a few final stamps, and then there was silence, and Marly's long sigh of relief could be clearly heard, bringing the woman's eyes round to her.

"Ah, you did not enjoy the music?"

She spoke in English. Her voice was clear and direct, like her gaze — and like it, completely expressionless.

Marly's reply was offhand.

"I'm not musical, I'm afraid." She turned to Henry. "Look, we've got to go. We can come back when there aren't so many people around."

Henry could only stare at her, speechless. He had identified Senhora Silva so swiftly and with such certainty that he could scarcely believe Marly to be still ignorant of her identity. But for all his fiancée's intelligence, he knew that she could sometimes be slow to grasp a situation, and the insolence of her manner in answering Senhora Silva proved that she could have no idea whom she was addressing. While he was wondering how he could tell her, Senhora Silva relieved him of the necessity.

"You came to see my niece?"

The calm question brought realization to Marly and caused her, for the first time in Henry's knowledge, to lose her poise. Even when at last she spoke, it was in a stammer.

"You . . . you're not . . . are you Senhora Silva?"

"Yes. I am Teresa's aunt." She turned to Henry. "And you are Mr. Eliot, isn't it?"

"Yes, Senhora. May I present my fiancée, Miss Stonor? We came to —"

"Ah, yesterday you put your car over the children's work. Today, they wished to do it all over again, but it was the day I come to lead them in singing and dancing. It is good for them. Stonor?" She looked at Marly. "Then you are the daughter, perhaps, of this unfortunate gentleman who was mistaken over the ownership of my land?"

"Yes." Marly had recovered. "I've just seen it. It's beautiful."

"The view is good, yes. I do not often see it, only since my niece insisted on having a crèche here. Now when I come, I drive through the woods. Before, not."

Her tone had no rise or fall, the sentences went on, level and flat and expressionless.

"Now that we've met," Marly said, "I should like to tell you that my father is prepared —"

"Please, one moment." Senhora Silva raised a shapely hand. "Teresa, my fan."

Quietly, Teresa repeated the order to one of the old women, who called to the old man, who fetched the fan from the donkey cart. It was a circle of plaited straw attached to a long bamboo handle. Senhora Silva took it and began to wave it slowly to and fro before her face.

"The heat is trying for me," she explained, and turned to the priest, who had been standing quietly by. "This is our priest, Father Vieira. Father, you must speak English; you can if you wish."

"A dozen words only," Father Vieira protested. "And this gentleman speaks Portuguese — he speaks it well."

"Because he has lived in Brazil. This Senhor Crespo told me." Senhora Silva turned to Henry. "When I meet English people, I speak to them always in their own language. With my niece also, I speak English, for that is her language. For me, it is no effort, Portuguese or English, it is the same. Father, you heard Miss Stonor say that she is the daughter of this poor gentleman who thought this land was for sale? It is scandalous that this should have been going on and nobody telling me anything."

She said that it was scandalous in the tone in which she had informed them that she drove through the woods. Nobody ventured to break in on what she was saying. Henry did not know whether to put this down to the hypnotic effect of the monotone, or to her bearing of absolute authority.

She was moving towards the cart, to which the donkey had been harnessed. She handed her fan to Father Vieira and beckoned to the children.

"Come, you shall say good-bye to me."

They came eagerly, one by one, they raised their faces and she stooped for their kiss. Straightening after the last child had been embraced, she spoke to her niece.

"Teresa, tonight you must not be late, visitors are coming. Good-bye, Miss Stonor. Good-bye, Mr. Eliot."

She was about to climb into the cart. Marly stepped forward and spoke abruptly.

"We haven't talked about the land," she said.

Senhora Silva turned and looked at her. The arched eyebrows were raised, but nothing else had changed; Henry thought that this must be what was called blank astonishment.

"But yes, we spoke of it," she replied. "It is a pity your father did not ask Portuguese lawyers at once. This made a great delay."

"Then why make more?" Marly strove, unsuccessfully, to make her tone conciliatory. "The thing's been held up for months. We'd like to see you and discuss it. Not here. At your house, if it could be arranged."

"But certainly, this already has been arranged. Senhor Crespo, who is a very old friend of mine, came to me and told me that Mr. Eliot wished to see me, and I told him that I would be happy to receive Mr. Eliot at some time. No doubt he will communicate this, but you know, his mother is always going to die, and when this happens, he loses his head and everything that is inside it. She is very old, very delicate, poor thing. Twice in the last year we have thought she was going to be taken from us — isn't it, Father? — and each time, Our Lady of Fatima gave her back to us. Teresa, what is that you are holding?"

Teresa had sent one of the old women to bring out the presents; she explained that the visitors had brought them for the children. Henry was glad to see them. He had been for some time under scrutiny, and he felt that the boy Zeto and his friends were waiting only for Senhora Silva's departure before engaging in a renewal of hostilities.

"This is very kind," Senhora Silva said. "Teresa, you must make the distribution. And now I shall go. Father, are you coming with me?"

"Thank you."

"Then Alfredo will walk. Come."

Alfredo was at the donkey's head. Henry stepped forward and assisted Senhora Silva to step into the cart. She gathered up the reins, drew her skirt aside to allow the priest to take his place beside her, and bowed to Marly.

"Good-bye, Miss Stonor. Please give my compliments to your father when you go to

England again. I am sorry that he has had so much trouble, all for nothing."

The cart moved away, weaving in and out of the trees. The children stood waving half-heartedly, their eyes on the packages that Teresa was unwrapping.

"The lady you see here," she said to them in Portuguese when the cart had gone out of sight, "brought you these sweets. You must thank her."

There was a loud and hearty response, then eager hands were held out. Teresa handed the second packet to Henry; together, they distributed the sweets. Then Marly spoke with angry impatience.

"Look, do come along, Henry. Good-bye, Miss . . ."

"Kingsley. Good-bye. Thank you for the presents. Children, say good-bye."

Marly had turned away but she was too late to escape the friendly rush of children as they swarmed towards her, eager in the way of all Portuguese children to give or to receive a kiss. A dozen hands, sticky, grimy, reached out and clutched her skirt, leaving their imprint. She jerked away in fury.

"Get them off me, will you?" she ordered Teresa in a voice cold with rage. "Look what they've done to my skirt! Call them off!"

Henry went up to her, lifted the children gently one by one and put them out of her way. Then, with a nod to Teresa, he followed Marly.

They did not speak until they reached the car. He knew that she was regretting her outburst and getting herself under control, he also knew that when she was calm enough to review the visit, her reconstruction would contain certain inaccuracies designed to gloss over her part in the affair. He would let them go without contradiction, for a girl was entitled to indulge in a little face-saving.

But it would be difficult, today, to hold his peace, or to preserve peace between them. He was angry as she was, and he was filled with shame and humiliation. The visit had been a disaster, and he had been a fool to fall in with the plan. She had no business with Senhora Silva's niece. She had no business, as yet, with Senhora Silva. He remembered her words to Senhor Moreira after the meeting in the library: Would a visit to the Senhora do any harm? The reply had not been reassuring because Senhor Moreira knew only too well that an over-confident, arrogant, near-insolent approach would be disastrous. As it had been.

"Poisonous woman," Marly said as she

got into the car. "How did you know who she was?"

"I guessed."

"I can't see how, unless you're claiming it was instinct."

"It was her manner."

"Anybody can put on airs. I thought the girl was poisonous, too. When I think what could be done with that land, and when I think what they're using it for, a bunch of half-naked children yelling to an accordion, I want to scream. I tried to get you away. I can't imagine how you could endure it for so long."

"Is your skirt spoiled?"

"Of course it's spoiled. Chocolate streaks and patches of dirt. I wish I hadn't agreed to go with you."

Here it came. This was the point at which, she said, he should shout back. He decided, with an effort, to pursue once again his theory that it was better to quarrel one at a time. He was not afraid of her, and today he had been ashamed of her, but if he said a word now, she would work off her resentment against Senhora Silva on him for the rest of the day.

"Well, what's your next move going to be?" she asked. "Sitting and waiting?"

"If I don't hear from Senhor Crespo tomorrow, I'll go over and see him. But look, Marly . . ."

"Well? Look at what?"

"Don't pin too many hopes on getting that land. You heard what Senhora Silva said."

"That my father had his trouble for nothing. She's never met my father, so she doesn't know that when he goes to trouble, it isn't often for nothing. So far, nobody's said a word about money. Everybody's been hanging round, hat in hand, waiting to put the case to her through emissaries. Why do you think she hurried off in that donkey cart just now? To make it appear that she wasn't keen on selling, that's all. Did you see the girl's dress? Did you notice her shoes? Does a woman who doesn't need money go rambling around her own woods in a donkey cart? To me, the whole setup looked fourth-rate, which bears out everything you hear about the inside of her Quinta, falling apart, from all accounts. You can't tell me my father's kind of money, once anybody's crude enough to mention it to her, isn't going to talk. You wait and see: Once you get down to basic facts such as how much, and double-your-offer, she'll stop fanning herself and reach for the contract."

She waited for Henry's comment, but when it came, it was a mere monosyllable.

"No."

She turned in her seat to study his expression.

"You mean you're still taken in by all that build-up?"

"I mean no. She won't reach for the contract, because she won't sell."

"She won't sell," he repeated an hour later, to Mr. Easter.

He had taken Marly to the villa and left her there. She had refused to go to lunch with him until he went in and spoke a few conciliatory words to the Colonel and he had refused to enter the house until the Colonel had spoken a few conciliatory words to him. Their parting had been the climax of a disastrous morning, and they had parted with mutual relief.

He had left her and driven to the hotel. He parked his car, and then went on a grim search for Mr. Easter.

He was not in or near the pool. The bridge room was occupied by a foursome which broke up as he glanced in. He moved hastily out of the path of a woman stamping out in a towering temper, and fled at the sight of

Lady Pearling getting up to go in search of a replacement.

He had not tried the bar; soda water, he felt, was something you drank in a less spirits-smelling atmosphere. But it was in the bar that he located Mr. Easter at last, seated alone in a dim, deserted corner. He strode across and stood over him.

"What," he asked without preamble, "did I ever do to you?"

Mr. Easter, on the brink of a friendly greeting, gazed up with a look of inquiry. When he saw Henry's expression, he rose slowly to his feet.

"Anything wrong?" he asked.

"I merely asked you if I'd ever done you any harm. I'll make it clearer. Were you on the point of buying Colonel Colston's house?"

"Ah." With a grunt, Mr. Easter sat down again, motioned Henry to a seat opposite, and hailed the bartender. "Boy, waiter, steward, mozo, garçon, what's-your-name . . . oh, yes, you told me, Francisco. Francisco, bring me a nice cold soda water. Now, Henry — your name is Henry, isn't it?"

"It's what my friends call me."

"Don't say it like that," Mr. Easter begged reproachfully. "And don't be nasty before I've talked to you, Henry. Like Joyce always says: If you don't go too fast, you don't fall on your nose and 'urt it. What'll you drink?"

"Nothing. Beer. Were you on the point of —"

"Since it's coming up, Henry, yes. Yes, I was thinking of buying the Colonel's little property."

"In fact, that was the house you came out to take another look at?"

"That's the one, Henry."

"And you were going to clinch the deal this morning?"

"Well, I —"

"You were, weren't you?"

"All right, then. Yes, I was. But now look, I —"

"And then you telephoned to say you wouldn't, after all, be buying. So the Colonel was a little, just a little put out. So he told me I'd told you Senhora Silva's land was still on the market. Which I didn't."

Mr. Easter's face had grown pale. He gazed distractedly at Henry.

" 'e didn't . . . 'e didn't say that, did 'e?"

"He called me a liar, and said I'd shown criminal indiscretion and he was going to tell Sir Bertram and see to it that I lost my job."

Mr. Easter pushed his glass aside and ran a hand agitatedly through his fuzz of hair.

" 'enry, I . . . if Joyce could've 'eard . . . look, 'enry, I wouldn't 'ave 'ad this 'appen for the world. Please believe me."

Henry was inclined to; Mr. Easter looked close to tears. He waited until Francisco had poured out the drinks, and then spoke slowly.

"What's worrying me," he said, "isn't what the Colonel said. What I'd like to know, what I must know but what I'm afraid to ask is: Did I, when I spoke to you last night, give anything away?"

"Without meaning to, you mean? No. No, you didn't," Mr. Easter answered with conviction, bringing a measure of comfort to Henry.

"Then . . . how did you know?" he asked.

"I didn't know — not then. All you did was set me thinking. Nothing you said would've made any sense to anybody else — per'aps I could say anybody else in the world — but to me, what you said went 'ome."

"Why? The Colonel said you had a special interest in that land. Is that true?"

It was some time before Mr. Easter answered. Then he slid his untouched drink to one side and joined his stubby hands together as though in prayer.

"It's a long story, 'enry," he said.

"We'll have lunch together. You can start now."

"Well . . . it was three, four months ago. Joyce and I came 'ere on 'oliday. We stayed at Albufeira. We'd come out with a view, as you might say, of staying out — if we liked it, and if we found anything in the way of a 'ouse or a bit of land we liked. It was Joyce's idea. I'd been getting restless 'aving nothing to do, and she thought if I got right away from the business, I'd forget about it. So we came out and started looking round. I knew I was a bit late, the cream, as you might say, was nearly gone, but I'm a rich man and I was ready to pay for what was left. See what I mean?"

"Yes. Go on."

"Well, I saw several agents, but nothing really up our street turned up. And then one day, up comes a fisherman we'd always liked to 'ave a chat with on the beach, and he asked us if we'd like to 'ave a little ride, a little jaunt, a little sight-seeing trip. Just a short one, along the coast for a bit towards Faro, and then turn again and come 'ome. Of course, Joyce was all for it, and what she likes, I like. So we got in and shoved off and Joyce sat on a coil of rope on the deck where there wasn't much movement and there we were, just gliding over the nice calm sea. And then suddenly I heard Joyce give a sort of . . . well, an exclamation, sort of. I turned round, and if I live to be a 'undred, I don't forget the look on 'er face. Kind of quiet and . . . wondering. And she was pointing to something ashore. So I took a look, and . . ."

Mr. Easter stopped. He sat gazing absently at the line of bottles above the counter, but Henry knew that he was following the pointing finger of his wife.

"It was a little bay, 'enry," he resumed at last in a slow, dreamy voice. "Just a little, 'alf-moon of a bay, 'idden away, a bay with golden sand and nothing in the world near it but a little white 'ouse. In a pinewood. If you'd drawn a picture of 'eaven, a bit where it ran down to the sea, that's what you'd 'ave seen on the paper.

"We asked the skipper about it, and 'e said where it was an 'ow it was practically impossible to know it was there if you were near it on the land side. 'e said as far as 'e knew, it was for sale, because the chap who lived in the 'ouse 'adn't lived in it for a long time, and anyway 'e was soon going off to do 'is military service. 'e said 'e'd 'ave a word with 'im and arrange for us to see 'im.

And then we turned for 'ome and I promised Joyce — solemnly I promised 'er — that if that beach could be bought, then it was 'ers, for forty-odd years' good behaviour.

"And then we got back to the shore, and I did just what you and me's doing now. I went to the 'otel bar and ordered a soda while Joyce got 'erself tidied up for dinner, sorry, lunch. And I was feeling so full of myself that I stood a drink to a chap sitting near me, just like you're sitting now. 'e was a tall, good-looking, upstanding old chap, and if I'd been in my right mind, I'd 'ave sized 'im up better and I'd 'ave waited till he talked to me first. I'm not 'umble, 'enry, I've explained that, 'aven't I?"

"Yes. Go on."

"I think I'm as good as the next fellow — but sometimes the next fellow takes exception to my way of talking. Well, this fellow wouldn't 'ave a drink, but 'e listened while I talked. 'e looked nice and sympathetic, and 'e smiled when I told 'im the luck I'd 'ad, and the bit of land I'd found, and 'e said he congratulated me because I'd found what 'e said must be the last bit of private beach 'ereabouts. 'e wished me luck. And then, 'enry, do you know what 'e did? 'e went away and rang up 'is lawyer and rushed 'im out from England, and when I went down a couple of days later to ask the fisherman chap if 'e'd got in touch with 'is friend, 'e said I was too late. There was an English gent got in first."

"By the name of Sir Bertram Stonor?"

"That's right. Mark you, 'enry, 'e's your boss and I'm not running 'im down. All I'm saying is —"

"— that he was a low-down swine."

" 'e worked fast. Greased lightning was 'ow 'e must 'ave moved. And that was that." Mr. Easter drained his glass and spoke philosophically. "But if you want to get on in life, 'enry — and you will, I can see that — then you 'ave to remember one thing — what's gone's gone and you mustn't waste time moaning. Joyce didn't. We went round looking at 'ouses for sale, and then we went to England to sort out which ones we liked, and in the end I came back because she'd fixed on this house of the Colstons. And then I got talking to you on the balcony upstairs, and I thought to myself: Why, if everything was settled and sealed, is this young fellow out 'ere straight, as you might say, from the Stonor's mouth, but not able to give a straight yes when you ask 'im if the deal went through? You didn't give anything away but that, 'enry, that the sale 'adn't gone through. You didn't say it 'adn't, but then again, you couldn't say it 'ad, and so I went round asking a few questions. And I found out that Sir B. 'adn't been as slick as 'e'd thought, the dirty old perisher. Mind you, I'm not —"

"— running him down."

"I'm only saying that I found that bit of land first, or Joyce did, and if it's still going, I'm going to 'ave a bash at buying it. So I called off buying the Colonel's 'ouse, and I was glad I did, because I didn't know what a ruddy rude perisher 'e was. If 'e went for you, I'm sorry. But 'enry, I love my wife. Your Sir B. did 'er down, and I've never forgotten it. I want that land. I'm being straight with you, 'enry; I'm after it. You must do what you've been instructed to do, and because I like you, 'enry — in fact, as we've got on to it, I'll say I never came across a young chap I took to more — because I like you, I 'ope you're not going to let this stand in the way of us being friendly. But don't mistake me. I want that land."

"You go ahead and try for it," Henry said. "But don't bank too much on getting it."

Mr. Easter studied him across the table.

"By that, you don't mean nobody's going to get it, do you?"

"I'm only guessing."

"I've found out who owns it. She's called Senhora Silva, isn't she?"

"She is."

"What makes you think nobody'll get the land?"

"She does. If you want my honest, considered opinion as well as that guess I've just given —"

"I do, 'enry. I do."

"She won't sell."

"Of course I won't sell," Senhora Silva said some hours later.

Her voice floated across the quiet, dim room to where Teresa sat curled up on a window seat. This was the time they both liked best, when they sat in the little room that adjoined the large, uncomfortable drawing room and watched the sun turning the walls crimson, and then pink and at last a dusky gray. Each evening they came here to talk, to exchange the news of the day, reluctant to call for the lamps to be lit. This was the time Teresa most liked to listen to her aunt, when she could smile without being seen, when she could watch the fan, forever in the hand waving to and fro, to and fro, swiftly or slowly according to what they were speaking of — the fan that was so much more expressive than her aunt's face or her aunt's voice. This was the time she could learn a little more of the years before she was born, when her mother lived here. She could picture her father in this very room, meeting her mother for the first time and, in her aunt's phrase, losing his head and his heart and his tongue all together.

"Of course I won't sell."

"That girl thinks you will."

"Which . . . oh, Miss Stonor. Well, she will soon know better. Teresa, why aren't you wearing your new dress? Three times already you have appeared in that one when the Vascos have come to dinner. They will think we are paupers."

"They know we're paupers — by their standards, that is. Is Father Vieira really going away?"

"He thinks so. Certainly they want to send him to Oporto, and send someone else here, but if you want to know, I wrote to your cousin Milou and said she must do something, see the bishop, write to the Pope, anything. We have got used to him, and at

Caravela they like him, and to send him away would be to kill Senhor Crespo's mother. Never would she be able to accustom herself to any other confessor."

"Who were they going to send?"

"Father Bastos, from Coimbra. He is younger, and they say not forgetful like Father Vieira. Certainly it would have been a change to have someone who remembered the times of meals."

"Or where he last left his umbrella. Or what time the babies were going to be baptized."

"Nobody else would have been so good with the children. She was beautiful, that Stonor girl. And so fair. If you saw her a mile away, you would say at once — English."

"If your eyesight was all that good."

"Don't say 'all that good.' Say what is more correct: as good as all that. Why do you use these expressions?"

"Because my grammar isn't all that good. I didn't think she was beautiful."

"Yes, you did. Why have you lit the candles in the dining room already?"

"They looked so pretty."

"Pretty, pretty. . . . Look at my accounts, they are not so pretty. Do you know how much those candles cost? And I counted those cartons today, that came back in the cart. How have you used so many kilos of the brown sugar?"

"It's good for the children."

"In one week, all that? And you give them too much fruit. Zeto's skin was patchy, and Nuno's stomach was upset. Do you know how much was paid for fruit, only for fruit alone, last week?"

"Yes."

"And soap. You must speak to Fatima. I saw the suds in the tank running over, all to waste. Yes, you thought Miss Stonor was beautiful, and that is why you sulked."

"I? Sulked?"

"Of course. You did not see yourself."

"And you didn't see her when she arrived. She smiled with her teeth, and put on a princess-and-peasant act."

"Naturally she will think you are a peasant, if you wear dresses so old, and shoes so shabby, and won't let Madalena do your hair. He is handsome, Mr. Eliot. I think I will say I have never seen a man with so good a figure, so tall, so well-built."

"If you saw him a mile away, you would say at once — Greek."

"You are in a bad temper. It is natural.

No girl likes to see a handsome man walk away with another girl. What are you going to do about Agostinho Vasco?"

"Nothing."

"His mother will be upset."

"So will Agostinho."

"He is the third, Teresa. There was Basilio, and after him Raul."

"There were two in London and one in Paris, that makes six. Don't underrate me."

"Is this a joking matter?"

"Only when they're called Agostinho."

"Are you waiting for a man like this one who came to the crèche this morning?"

"Yes. But not this one."

"Why not this one?"

"He loves her, so he must be stupid. He follows her when she calls him, so he must be weak. She can have him."

"She has got him already. But you have been here now for three years, and you continue to refuse young men of good family who wish to marry you. Do you want to be an old maid, like Senhora Vasco's sister?"

"Not like Senhora Vasco's sister, no."

"You spend your time doing all these things, the crèche and other things which are good works, perhaps, but you avoid going out to parties where you would meet the sons, the nephews, the godsons of my old friends. You stay too much at home. Don't you want to get married?"

"In due course."

"You said that exactly like your mother. You know, you are growing like her."

"You said I couldn't do better than grow like her."

"In some ways. But she was extravagant, my God, how she threw money away! When she married your father, she was sure that she was going away forever, and she insisted that I should have all the property, and so I agreed to buy her share, even though I knew it was a mistake to let so much money go. And where did it go? Thrown this way and that, melted, lost. And that is how you are, like her, never keeping proper accounts, wasting flour, sugar, candles. Yes, you are like her. Even about marriage. She joked always, like you."

"Not always. Remember? He was shown into this room and you were alone and he explained that he had come to Portugal for a holiday and wanted permission to photograph the old part of this house because of the legend that his hero, the Infante Dom Henrique, had stayed here. And you were just going to say No, or Yes, when the door opened and she came in, and he turned round and they both stood there, struck dumb, and you said, This is my young sister, who is always joking about marriage, and she said, No more, and you said, But he isn't a Catholic, and she said, Shall I have lace or satin? Did you write to Cousin Milou and ask her to write to the Pope?"

"When you joke about serious things, you are most like her. But I can assure you that it was different then. The house was not so neglected, not so much in disrepair. The servants were young servants, they had not gone away to work for the tourists, leaving only the old ones. And I was not a widow living alone, except for you. I was Ofélia Silva, with your mother heiress to this Quinta and to money which is now lost in Goa. We were the last two of a long and honourable, I might say, noble line. We were sought after, we could have married anybody. I did my duty by looking for a man of my own name, but your mother, no. And now there are no more Silvas, no more in the direct line. There is not enough money to stop the rot which has begun. It only remains to live here, to wait here for the end."

"You could wait more comfortably by selling land. Especially the land near the beach. Those people will pay anything. I saw it in that girl's face."

"No. I have said that I will not be the first to sell our property. I will not slice off this piece and that piece and leave less than I inherited. The foreigners have had enough of our land, they will not get any more from me."

"In that case, will you tell Senhor Crespo so, and tell him to tell them so, and will you fix an early meeting with Mr. Eliot?"

"What is the hurry for this?"

"To get it over and done with."

"I have told them quite clearly —"

"Not clearly enough. Send a message to Senhor Crespo tonight. Tell him you'll see —"

"I do not wish to see that girl. I was asked to see only the young man who came out from England. I will see him, but I will not see them both."

"Then see him, and give him a definite answer and send him back to England."

"Very well. I am sorry for him, that he has to go back and marry that girl. But now, how do you think she got him? Listen, and I will tell you. She did not sit like you, with folded hands, waiting for this or that special man to come. She exerted herself. You can see, anybody can see that she is not the right woman for him, but she did not give him time to find this out. She . . . where are you going?"

"To blow out the candles."

CHAPTER 4

No message came from Senhor Crespo the next morning. Henry took the precaution of staying at the hotel, within reach of any communication that might come by telephone or by hand, but he was only too well aware that Senhor Crespo would require time for assimilation, for contemplation, for final transmission of Senhora Silva's agreement to an interview.

There was an obvious course, one upon which Sir Bertram would have insisted: to drive to Caravela, inform Senhor Crespo that he had met Senhora Silva, add that she had promised to receive him, and then urge him, harry him into instant action. But the thought of urging Senhor Crespo was distasteful, not to say absurd; to image him in instant action was little short of fantasy.

He could at least amuse himself while he was waiting. He decided to swim, and spent some time in the crowded pool, idly paddling or floating, parrying the frequent friendly approaches and studying his fellow guests, almost without exception English, the date of whose arrival could be judged by the degree of tan they had acquired, and who ranged in colour from paleface to Indian.

The majority of them, he found, could be divided into two main groups. The larger of these was made up of elderly couples or not-so-young widows who had come to Portugal to seek relief from cold weather, high taxes, household chores or loneliness. Some of these had vague regrets for what they had left behind, others wondered audibly how they had endured it for so long. The second group, younger and livelier, seemed to be opening boutiques or bars anywhere between Faro and Sagres. There was a scattering of bikini-clad girls, two youths sharing them, and a woman in her late thirties, deeply tanned, over-exposed, with green, greedy eyes and a superb figure, who swam up to Henry, introduced herself simply as Lola, and proceeded to play underwater games that drove him out of the pool in panic.

In the poolside bar, he was unable to

escape the jolly-good-company atmosphere, and took his turn at buying rounds of drinks and listening to opinions on local conditions. The politically conscious denounced the regime, the sociologists deplored the backwardness of the country. The remainder declared frankly that they were here for pleasure and were totally uninterested in peasants or politics.

He paid his bill and wandered back along the path to the hotel, his mind going over the telephone conversation he had had with Sir Bertram the night before. He had picked up the receiver, to be greeted without preamble by a terse sentence from Sir Bertram to the effect that Marly had phoned him.

"She told me you'd run into the Silva woman, and the niece too, without getting anything definite out of either of them. You should have reported to me at once."

"In my opinion —"

"I didn't send you out there to form opinions. You were given specific instructions: find Crespo, fix a meeting with the Silva woman and fix the terms. Marly knows what she's talking about when she says there's been far too much approach work. Get hold of the owner and make an offer. I've given Marly a new set of figures and a higher ceiling — she'll give you the details. Can you hear?"

"Yes."

"Well, speed things up, will you? Everybody knows the pace of these Latins — your job is to ginger them up, get them moving, shake them awake. And one more thing: the Colonel had a word with me. He says you've been talking too much."

"I told him —"

"Well, I'm not going to get into an argument over the phone. He seemed to know a damn sight too much of what's going on, and who could he have got it from but you? Well, that's all for the moment. I'll get through again tomorrow to find out what's happening. Good-bye."

Still holding the receiver, Henry had spoken to the dead line.

"Good-bye, and I wish I could say it for the last time. I'm sorry I ever joined your organization. I don't like you and I don't like working for you. I don't like your cousin Tim. Or his wife. Or his son. I'm engaged to your daughter and I'm going to marry her and I hope to God it works out, but I'm concerned it won't, but whether it does or it doesn't, I'm not going to stand much more bullying from you."

Resentment still burned within him, against Sir Bertram for his Down-Dog manner, against the Colonel for misrepresentation, above all against Marly for going over to the enemy. But through his anger came memories of other occasions on which she had elbowed him aside when her interests seemed threatened, and conducted affairs in her own way. Knowing her as he now did, he should have realized that she would get her revenge for the humiliating role she had played at the crèche.

He came out of his reverie abruptly, brought back to the present by the sound of his name called in Lady Pearling's loud tones. She was coming towards him, too close for him to evade her.

"Ah, there you are," she said, coming to a halt. "I've been looking everywhere. I want you to do something for me."

She led him to the end of the path, sat on a bench, and opened a notebook. Beside her she laid a small pile of Portuguese phrase books.

"They're not the slightest use to me," she said, thumping them angrily with her fist. "Now, sit down, will you, and take this notebook and write down the Portuguese for these sentences. Are you ready?"

"No. I'm rather wet, as a matter of fact."

"My dear young man, your hands are dry. What do you require for writing besides hands? Sit down. Here's a pen. Be careful with it — it's a good one. Now. One: *This service is very slow*. Got that? No, no, *no*. You must write it down *exactly* opposite the sentences I've written. That's it. No, don't bother about pronunciation, I shall simply point to the Portuguese you've written, and they can read it. At least, they will be able to read it if you write more clearly. Larger, if you please. Perhaps you'd better print it. Two: *This coffee is stone cold*. Three: *Kindly direct me to the Ladies' Room*. Four: *Kindly* — what are you stopping for?"

"Do you want me to say Ladies' Room, or something they'd understand better?"

"You may make it clear in whatever way you wish, so long as it isn't indelicate. Four: *Kindly turn off the music at once*. Five: *These people are disturbing me*. Six: *You are too heavy for that poor donkey; get off it at once*. Seven: *This* — are you keeping up with me? — *This cat is starving — feed it*. Eight: is it eight or nine? Eight: *The price you are asking is absurdly high*. That's all for now. Give me back my pen, will you? Speaking of price reminds me that I found out what the Colstons are

asking for their house — it was quite ridic-
ulous, and I shall tell them so. Not that they
can interest me in it now that I've learned
that there's something wrong with it."

"Wrong with it?" Henry could not help
asking.

"I've been talking to Mrs. Restington. She
told me there was a man in this hotel — you
may have seen him — odd-looking little
man, red-faced, with white hair. He went
after the Colstons' house, was on the point
of signing, and then didn't. Mrs. Restington
couldn't find out why, but it's fishy, very
fishy. Easter, that's the name — the name
of this man who backed out. I shall make
him tell me what it was that made him
change his mind at the last moment. I'm
quite certain that you know, but I daresay
you feel you shouldn't tell me, since they're
by way of being friends of yours. And now
about bridge," she proceeded without pause.
"Myself, Mrs. Restington, yourself and a
man who doesn't play at all well, but who is
better than nothing. His wife broke up a
game last night, right in the middle. Threw
her cards down, flounced away and didn't
come back. All because I told her she ought
to have led trumps. When can you play?"

"I can't, I'm afraid. I'm going out now

168

and I shan't be back until well after midnight."

She took it badly. If he had been a nephew or grandson living on her bounty, he thought she could not have displayed more wrath. Unmoved, he heard her out and then went up to his room and changed. Then he looked at his watch. Ten past ten.

He knew that he had no right to nudge Senhor Crespo, who had no interest in the affair beyond a desire to oblige his cousin — and who, even if nudged, was not likely to increase his pace. But perhaps there was no need to nudge him. Perhaps, after all, there was another key that would open the doors of the Quinta do Infante. Teresa Kingsley.

He had very little hope of enlisting her cooperation. The two occasions on which she had seen him had not been of a kind to arouse her friendliness or sympathy. But she was on the inside, and it couldn't hurt to sound her out — the worst she could do was to refuse to help him, which would leave him no worse off than he was at present.

He did not pause to ponder on the matter. He went out and drove swiftly past the western wall of the Quinta do Infante, in the direction of the beach. He parked the car at the edge of the pinewood, got out to begin the walk to the house, and then paused, fighting a sudden sick feeling of panic that welled up in him. Leaning against a tree, he let his mind range with increasing hopelessness over the course of his life since he had been summoned to the Stonor mansion. He recalled his first glimpse of Marly, and smiled grimly as he remembered his tentative advances, and his naïve inability to realize that she was not only responding to them, but also making far less tentative advances of her own.

He knew that at that point, he had ceased to think, he had surrendered to his emotions. He could not decide exactly where or how his head had begun to clear — but it was clear enough now, and he realized that he cut himself adrift from his own life while she had done nothing whatsoever to change hers.

He had been happy enough before he met her. He had friends, books, records; he had two comfortable rooms and a car to take him out of London when he wanted to go. He had little spare money, but there was enough for his amusements, and there would be more if his plans for returning to Brazil were successful. But he had accepted the Stonor offer, he had become engaged and he had promoted himself — prematurely, he now knew — into a penthouse flat, of which he liked nothing but the view. His attempts to like Marly's friends had failed. He could match her pace, but leading her life had left him with a feeling that he was chasing his own tail. He had believed that she would come part of the way to meet him, but she was exactly where she had been. What he would like to assess, if it were not too painful, was where he himself was. As far as he could see, he was in a position in which his pride and his dignity was being stripped from him. He had not put his head into a noose, he had put it into a golden collar. And the collar was attached to a chain.

He shook off his forebodings and walked through the wood in the direction of the little house and the shirts and the washing tank and the trestle table. But when he reached the clearing, he saw that he would not have to go so far. The inmates of the crèche were not at the house. They were on the beach.

It was a pleasant sight, and he paused to look at it. The two women helpers were at the sea's edge, their long skirts trailing in the surf. The children were naked, leaping and shouting and digging, running to the edge of the water and yelling in panic as the waves came near.

He thought at first that Teresa was not with them. As he approached, he saw her sitting apart, curled up on the sand beside a pool. There was a basket of figs beside her, she took one, quartered the skin, drew it back and bent to bite off the dark, dripping center. She tossed the skin over her shoulder and it flew past Henry's leg. His exclamation made her turn.

"Oh . . . I'm sorry," she said. "Did it hit you?"

"You did your best."

She did not move. He dropped onto the sand beside her, and she picked up the basket and held it out.

"If you like them, have one," she offered.

They ate in silence, absorbed in keeping the juice from dropping off their chins onto their clothes. He tried to remember when he had last tasted figs straight from the tree, ripe and purple and sweet. They finished them all and leaned over to dabble their hands in the pool. He scrubbed his chin clean and gave a sigh of repletion.

"Those were good. Thank you." He nodded towards the children. "Sports day?"

"They'll be coming every day from now on. Father Vieira blessed the water yesterday."

"He what?"

"Blessed the sea."

"What for?"

"To pray for the safety of the children, and warmth and sunshine to make them strong."

"*Your* idea?"

"Father Vieira's idea. And a good one, unless you feel that iodine's all they get out of it."

"I wouldn't presume to know. I'd forgotten you must be a Catholic."

"Why 'must' be?"

"Well — they sign you up, don't they, when you marry an outsider? Not that your father —"

"Thank you."

"He might, of course, have been a Catholic himself."

"He wasn't, so you can go back to your signing-on theory, which is now out of date. Didn't your fiancée come with you?"

She was speaking casually, lazily, lying on her back, one arm shading her eyes from the sun — beautiful eyes, he thought, large, dark and at once humorous and serene. The depression that had seized him a short while ago began to evaporate.

Peace filled him. He felt soothed, relaxed. He lay back, shovelled the sand with his shoulders to make a comfortable hollow, and squinted up at the cloudless sky.

"No, Marly didn't come," he said. "I came to ask you a favour."

"What is it?"

He did not answer at once. This was not Senhor Crespo's courtyard, and there was no wine, but he was experiencing the same difficulty in keeping his mind alert. He had come with a sense of urgency, he had walked through the pinewood at a pace that had made him perspire. Now, as he sat up to remove his jacket and turned to look down at the almost-dozing Teresa, his haste seemed ludicrous.

"It was about this interview with your aunt," he said.

"My aunt sent a message to Senhor Crespo — didn't you get it?"

"I daresay *he* got it. When I left the hotel, it hadn't been transmitted."

Teresa yawned, displaying flawless teeth and a very healthy tongue.

"It will be," she said. "Perhaps this afternoon."

"Perhaps tomorrow afternoon. Perhaps next week."

She raised herself on an elbow to study him.

"It's so urgent?"

"Well, at this moment it doesn't seem so. But last night I was rung up by Sir Bertram Stonor and reproached, not kindly, for dila . . . dilatoriousness. Is that right?"

"Nearly."

"Dilatoriation?"

"Getting warmer."

"Dilatoriness?"

"You're home. What were you being dilatory about?"

"Getting through to your aunt. Getting an interview with her. When I left England — whenever that was — I was told that only through Senhor Crespo could this be brought about. And Senhor Crespo, I discover, is more concerned with keeping his mother alive than with making appointments for land-buyers. For which, in a way, he can't be blamed. But it doesn't improve my relations with my employer."

"Is that your job — buying land for him?"

"No. I'm one of his team of architects. The only reason I got this assignment was because I happen to speak Portuguese and because Sir Bertram thought a prospective son-in-law could act in a kind of half-business, half-personal capacity. How can anyone act through Senhor Crespo? I daresay he's a perfect intermediary between people of his own nationality and his own pace, but in this affair you have to admit that he lags behind a bit."

"He's old."

"I'll be old before I get an interview with your aunt. That is, if I wait for him to fix one. So I came to you."

"I told you. My aunt sent him a message last night. It's already fixed, as far as she is concerned."

"Did she give him a date and a time?"

"I . . . I don't know."

"If she didn't, then she was wasting the messenger's time."

She made no reply. She sat watching the children, and after a time he put a question.

"Why are you in charge of those brats?"

"Why call them brats?"

"One of them kicked me. Look. I shall carry the mark until I die. Whose brats are they?"

"They're the children, legitimate or illegitimate, of parents who were born at the Quinta do Infante. Before the tourist boom, the parents would in most cases have been working for us, but we can't pay the new wages, so they go into the towns."

"And you support the children?"

"Only the children whose grandparents are too old, or too busy to take charge of them. My aunt used to look after their mothers — there's been a maternity home in the grounds of the Quinta for years — my mother started it and my aunt took it over when my mother died. But nothing was being done about the babies, so I asked for this house near the beach, and started a crèche."

"Why not inside the Quinta?"

"I wanted the children to be near the sea. I could have used one of the Quinta buildings — there are servants' cottages I could have used, empty ones — but it would have meant a long walk for the children to reach the beach."

He turned to look at her.

"What else do you do?"

"Nothing else, on weekdays. How could I? I come early in the morning and I stay all day and only go back to the Quinta for dinner."

"Not Sundays?"

"Not Sundays. On Sundays, the mothers or fathers or some other relations come and take them out for the day."

"And return them at night?"

"Yes. They live at the beach house, in charge of those two women at night and in my charge during the day."

"When do you fit in your amusements?"

"This is more amusing than anything I've ever done. You should have seen your face when José Antonio, Zeto, kicked you."

"I'm glad you enjoyed it. But you're young and lovely," he pointed out. "Don't your friends — your male friends — protest?"

"Some do."

"What about all that glittering crowd in Albufeira and Praia da Luz and so on?"

She hesitated.

"I don't meet many English people," she said at last. "My father's relations appear in Portugal now and then, but apart from them, hardly any. When I came out here three years ago, I decided to be Portuguese."

"Why can't you be both?"

"Because the two don't mix."

"They *have* mixed. You're the result."

There was a pause, then she gave a slight, helpless shrug.

"It's no use explaining, because it sounds fantastic."

"I like fantasy."

"Well . . . my mother died out here when

I was eight. My aunt sent me to my father's family because she thought I ought to go to school in England. She doesn't care for England or for English education particularly, but she's got strong ideas on doing everything the way my mother probably would have done if she'd lived."

"So that accounts for her speaking English to you?"

"Yes. When I left school, I did all the things my cousins were doing — flat in London, jobs in London. Then my aunt's mother-in-law, Teotonia Silva, died. I came out for the funeral . . . and never went back."

"Because you thought you ought to fill in for your aunt's mother-in-law?"

"I stayed because I liked the life here better than the one in England. But staying meant living in the Portuguese way."

"I don't see why."

"You would if you knew more about Portuguese parents. They don't believe in complete freedom for young girls."

"But you do."

"So does my aunt, secretly. But her friends, her relations all belong, without exception, to deep-rooted, intensely proud, completely conventional Portuguese families.

If I went out alone with Englishmen — or Swedes, or Dutchmen, or South Sea Islanders — if I went alone to night clubs . . . it would make things awkward for my aunt."

"Because?"

"Because she wants me to marry, in due course. And she'd like me to marry a Portuguese. And if I don't follow the conventions of the country, the mothers of young Portuguese men of good family will advise their sons not to marry me."

He stared at her, his eyes narrowed to detect signs of joking.

"You're not serious?"

"If you mean am I stating plain facts — yes."

"You mean . . . it actually works? *Still?* Today?"

"Why shouldn't it work? It worked in England not so long ago. There must be ex-chaperones still living, like ex-memsahibs and ex-governesses. Yes, it works."

"And you accept this?"

She smiled. "So far, I haven't given a single anxious mother of a single young single Portuguese gentleman of good family a single anxious moment."

"And when you go to England — how often do you go?"

"I don't."

"Don't you miss it all?"

"What, for instance?"

He hesitated.

"I'm not really qualified to draw up a list," he confessed. "I was planning to go back to Brazil and then I took the job at Stonor's."

"Were you born in England?"

"Yes. I was taken to Brazil when I was about two. My father died there when I was thirteen, and my uncle, my mother's brother, wrote and insisted on my being sent to England to be educated. My mother was strongly against it, but she couldn't argue because we ran out of money. My father left a reasonable amount, but she invested it in stock which had musical names — she was very musical. So I went to England and she went to live in Madeira. My uncle paid for me — school and the university — and died just as I'd embarked on an architect's career. I always thought he was a rich man, but when he died, I discovered that he'd never had much money, and what he had, he'd spent on me. Plus a sizable sum he hadn't got. I paid his debts, my debts, in due course. I was with a firm of architects in London. Then I decided to go back to Brazil. There's where we came in."

"Are you the only one? I mean, no brothers or sisters?"

"Fortunately for my uncle, no brothers or sisters."

"Were both your parents English?"

"My father was English, my mother was half Irish by blood and wholly Irish by temperament. She was beautiful and generous and warmhearted and she hadn't a grain of horse sense in her entire makeup."

"Like my mother. My aunt had all the horse sense. I suppose . . ." she broke off. "Why are we sitting here exchanging life histories? Why don't you go and see Senhor Crespo?"

"The reason I came here — didn't you listen? — was to try to bypass Senhor Crespo. The reason I'm sitting and talking is because there's warm sun above me, figs inside me and a girl next to me who might in time grasp the fact that all she has to do in order to put me in touch with her aunt is say Open sesame."

"That would hurt Senhor Crespo's feelings."

"I have to consider Senhor Crespo's feelings?"

"You needn't. I shall."

"That sounds like an ultimatum."

"No. Just courtesy. He's my aunt's oldest friend, he's my godfather, and his cousin Urbano made him an intermediary between you and my aunt. He'll get my aunt's message and —"

"He'll mull it over, put it aside while he takes his mother for a walk and while he visits your aunt to further his suit — I've heard he's wooing her. He'll ask her to name a day and an hour, not for receiving me, but for their nuptials. One day, perhaps in autumn, he'll remember me and remember he's an intermediary and he'll inform me that your aunt will see me. He will then return to her to . . . oh look, Teresa, be reasonable! I don't want to hurt anybody's feelings, though I doubt whether Senhor Crespo's got any feelings to spare from his mother and your aunt. But I can't hang about forever, can I?"

"Not forever, no."

"Aren't you going to do anything?"

"I told my aunt you were in a hurry."

"Thank you. What effect will that have?"

"How do I know? Why must you rush things? What difference will a week, two, three weeks make? There's no possibility of my aunt selling the land to anybody else, and not much probability of her selling it to you. This is the loveliest time of the year. Why can't you persuade your fiancée to stay here and enjoy it?"

"For one thing, she's a girl who's got a lot of engagements lined up in London, things she doesn't want to miss. For another, she feels that hanging about will mean that the word will get round and a swarm of other people will start pestering your aunt. She's got a special interest in this land."

"What special interest?"

"Her father is giving it to her as a wedding present."

There was a pause. Teresa said nothing, and Henry, glancing at her, saw that she was sitting with her knees drawn up and her arms clasping them, her eyes on the gradually encroaching sea.

"If that's the case," she said at last, "I must wish you success."

"But you're not optimistic?"

"No. In fact . . ."

"In fact, you're convinced your aunt won't sell. And who would know better than you?"

"It's her land. She can do as she likes with it."

"Senhor Moreira said that when she died, it would be yours. Which puzzled me when

I thought about it later. I know there's no primogeniture law in Portugal. All the —"

"All the children inherit equally, and so do their children and grandchildren and so on. Yes. There are properties in my aunt's family which are owned today by more than two hundred people but from the very beginning, it's been traditional at the Quinta do Infante for the eldest son to keep the property and stay in Portugal, while the younger sons sold their shares and went away."

"Went away where to?"

"Mozambique, Madeira, Macao, Goa. They were all seafarers."

"All?"

"All, at first. The house was built by Pedro Silva, on land granted to him by the Infante Dom Henrique. He was one of his navigators, one of the Discoverers. He left the sea in 1458, which was a pity, because if he'd kept going a few years longer, he might have beaten Bartolomeu Dias de Novaes, Bartholomew Diaz to you, round the Cape of Good Hope, and then we would have been in all the history books and the nation would have made pilgrimages to the Quinta do Infante and put up a statue to Pedro. An authentic log of his last voyage existed at the Quinta until 1690, kept in a special little shrine whose remains I can show you on the west side of the house."

"What happened to it in 1690?"

"Stolen."

"By?"

"A younger brother. He took it with him when he sailed for Mozambique."

"And built another little shrine for it there?"

"He never got there."

"Bottom of the sea, log and all?"

"Yes. Nemesis."

"What happened to all the daughters of the family? Did they sell out too?"

"They claimed their share when they married. If they didn't marry, they left their share to the elder brother."

"Expensive business, wasn't it, buying out the others?"

"So expensive that it explains why there has never been any spare money."

"If your aunt needs money —"

"She could never raise enough to restore the Quinta."

"Is it as ruined as rumour reports?"

"The original part was always looked after — that's in good repair. The later additions aren't, in fact, parts of them are about to fall down. And inside, it's medieval."

"How about amenities?"

"None. I think all the modern improvements came too soon after one another: gas, electricity, plumbing, central heating, telephone. By the time they'd got round to deciding to put in one thing, it was out of date and the next thing had come along. I suppose you can't understand why nobody ever got to grips with modernizing the house, but I can. If you prefer lamplight, and if you have an army of servants to attend to the lamps, why change? Why pipe water to the house when you like to sit in the garden on a warm evening, listening to the creak of the mule carts as they come up from the well, bringing huge scarlet barrels of water for the household? The maids wash the clothes in the stream. The orchard has its own well. Telephone? Put it in the gatekeeper's lodge where it won't disturb anybody. You're an architect. You haven't seen the Quinta, but you'd be able to give it one glance and assess how much money would have to be poured into it to make it even reasonably comfortable by today's standards. To get a sum like that would mean selling extensively, and my aunt wants to keep the property intact, as she received it. As it has been from the beginning. And why restore it? No Silva, no direct line Silva, will ever live in it again."

She fell silent. They could see the children leaping in panic as the waves approached, they could hear their cries, and the loud protests or warnings of the two women looking after them.

"If you owned the land, would you sell?" Henry asked.

"No."

"For the same reasons as your aunt?"

"Not quite. I wouldn't sell this particular piece of land because I know, or I think I know, what kind of house you and your fiancée — your wife — would build on it. You'd build what most other foreigners are building in the Algarve, a holiday house. You'd live in it for two, perhaps three months of the year. You'd pay your servants enormous wages. Then you'd go away and shut up the villa, and the servants would make their money stretch until you came back — if you came back. The cats and the dogs you'd befriended — 'oh, look at that poor, half-starved cat, how cruel these Latins are to animals, let's feed the poor thing' — the cats and dogs are left to the maids, but no money is left to feed them, and so they starve again, only now it's worse, because they've become used to being well fed. No.

188

I wouldn't sell. I'd sell to anybody who'd fallen in love with Portugal, who wanted to live here forever, who tried to speak the language, who didn't condescend to the peasants, who tried to understand the country's problems. But I wouldn't sell to the transients. Not to people like you and Miss Stonor, who are simply looking for a playground."

She had spoken without emphasis, slowly, almost absently, staring over the sea, but there was something in her tone that carried complete conviction to Henry and made him understand that these were the arguments he would hear from Senhora Silva, if and when he was received by her. These were the reasons he would have to relay, if he could, to Sir Bertram.

"The tourists," he pointed out after a time, "bring a lot of money into the country."

"True." She stood up and shook the sand from her dress. "They do. They pay high wages and they bribe the workers off the farms but they don't look after them and their wives and their families for life, as my grandfather did, as my aunt does. The land you want to buy . . . twenty-eight years ago it was given to an old man who couldn't work any longer, to put up a little house and fish, and live out his life peacefully. That seems to me a better purpose than using it for a villa with a jetty for water skiing for two months of the year. But it isn't my land, it's my aunt's, and the only way to see her is to see Senhor Crespo. I'm sorry; I have to go to the children now."

He watched her as she left him and walked along the sand towards the sea, small and slim, her shoes discarded where she had been sitting, her hair blowing in the soft breeze.

Then he turned and went through the pinewood to his car, drove to Caravela and drew up at Senhor Crespo's gate.

CHAPTER 5

There was a large group gathered outside as Henry stopped the car; for a moment he wondered whether Senhora Crespo had been taken ill again. Then he saw Senhor Crespo coming out of the house to greet him, his expression reassuringly cheerful. Smiling, he explained to Henry that he had just returned from a short, a very short walk with his mother. She was refreshed, she was not at all tired. Their anxiety at rest, the waiting villagers dispersed.

"Come in, please, Senhor Eliot." Senhor Crespo took Henry's hands in his own. "Please come in. I did not expect you so soon. When I telephoned to the hotel, they said they could not find you, but I left the message and they promised that it would reach you and so it did, and now you are here almost at once. Perhaps you were surprised to learn that Senhora Silva had offered today, this very morning, for your meeting with her?"

Henry, deciding to dispense with explanations, said that he had indeed been surprised.

"So we shall go together." Senhor Crespo was ushering him into a large, glacial hall. "But I have, first, a favour to beg of you." He indicated one of the hard, high-backed chairs. "Will you sit here, or would you prefer to go on to the terrace?"

"If we're going to see Senhora Silva —"

"You are quite right, it will be better here. Sit down, please, and I will explain this favour which I am going to ask. Will you take a little refreshment?"

"No, thank you."

"Then let me begin. When I received the message from Senhora Silva, I went in to see my mother, and I found that she had awakened feeling better than she has felt for months past. When I told her that I would have to leave her in order to accompany you to the Quinta do Infante, then . . . you will not believe this, but she actually expressed a wish — how can one not believe this is an answer to all our prayers? — she actually

said that she would like to take this opportunity of going to see her goddaughter. Yes,
Ofélia Silva is her goddaughter, just as Teresa is mine. So, Senhor, the favour is this:
Would my mother's presence in your car in
any way incommode you?"

Henry took a moment to realize what was
wanted of him.

"You mean . . . she'd like to come with
us?"

"You may well be astonished, Senhor. I
cannot yet believe it. I wished her to forego
our little *passeo*, but she said she would go a
little way. She did not wish to disappoint
those who were waiting to see her, those
people you saw at the gate."

"I'd be happy to take her," Henry said.

Senhor Crespo rose and came forward to
press his hands once again.

"I cannot thank you enough," he said. "I
will go and tell her, and she will make herself
ready. Excuse me."

Left alone, Henry shifted on his seat,
contemplated the eight holy pictures round
the walls and wondered whether he could
open the door and escape into the warmth
and sunshine outside. He heard Senhor
Crespo returning.

"Senhor Eliot, my mother sends you her

thanks. She is getting ready to come." His expression became grave. "You understand, Senhor, that this will be the very first time since —"

"Since her illness, yes."

"No, no, no, Senhor, since her *accident*. You remember that I told you she had been, with me, in an accident?"

"Yes. I —"

"It was like this."

It was word for word as it had been before. Henry wondered how many times the tale had been told. The chill from the tiled floor crept up his legs, his toes grew numb. While Senhor Crespo was tracing the taxi's path with his stick on the tiles, he glanced at his watch — eleven-twenty. He wondered whether Senhora Silva had fixed any definite time. When the story of the collision had ended and he had made the appropriate comments, he inquired.

"Time? No, no. She did not mention an exact hour. She asked only that I should bring you this morning, because you are anxious to hear her decision."

"You don't think it's rather late to —"

"Late? This is the best time," Senhor Crespo declared.

Henry said no more. Whether it was the

best time for old Senhora Crespo, or for her son, or for Senhora Silva, he did not inquire. His talk with Teresa had left him with very little hope of a successful end to his quest; this hasty summons meant only that Senhora Silva was as anxious as he was to conclude the negotiations. Good morning, Mr. Eliot, no sale, good-bye, Mr. Eliot. By which time it would be too late to get hold of Marly and take her somewhere for lunch.

There was nothing to listen to but Senhor Crespo's mild, courteous voice relating stories of his mother's piety. There was nothing to look at except the holy pictures and a row of Senhor Crespo's hats neatly aligned on a shelf. Soon, the cold penetrated the old man's layers of wool, a servant was summoned, a stove was carried in.

Eleven-forty. Even Senhor Crespo began to wonder if his mother had perhaps felt herself, after all, unable to make the journey. He went to investigate, and to Henry's relief returned with her, a frail, appealing figure in all-enveloping black, jewels winking at her ears, her throat, her bosom, and tiny, shining black shoes taking little faltering footsteps. The front door was flung open to allow her passage, clinging to her son's arm, while Henry supported her on the other side.

Behind came two maids, one with a sunshade which she opened and held over the old lady, the other carrying a spectacle case, long black gloves, a black handbag, a black shawl and a length of delicate black lace.

Henry opened the front door of the car. Senhor Crespo begged that his mother might sit in the back. Henry was about to hand her in when the cracked summons of the Church bell rang out the Angelus. The little claw slipped from his grasp to make the Sign of the Cross, heads were bowed, Hail Marys murmured. Prayers over, Senhora Crespo made her farewell, as solemn as though it were the last, to the servants. They crowded round the windows of the car to wish her a safe journey and a safe return, sent messages of respectful greeting for Senhora Silva, and warned against sitting in the sun, catching cold in the shade and exposing herself to breezes. Above all, she was to close her eyes in the car, to guard against dizziness brought on by seeing the trees fly by so fast.

Senhor Crespo, in the front seat, twisted himself round to ask if the journey might begin. The old lady bowed assent. They were off.

"Slower, Senhor Eliot, please," he lowered his voice to whisper. "My mother is being daring, very daring, but we must not permit too much recklessness."

He was watching the road anxiously, he pointed out every approaching curve, advising caution. He turned at intervals to gaze inquiringly at his mother, and reported that she was smiling, or closing her eyes, or praying. Henry subdued his impatience and irritability, and to each report gave a sign of his admiration for her courage and durability.

"I remember," Senhor Crespo said reminiscently, "how busy this road used to be in the old days. Carriages, oxen carts, riders on horses and donkeys, workers coming and going — ah! it was so full of life. You remember, *Mai?* And if a stranger, an *estrangeiro* passed by, we all looked with great interest: Look, we would say, there is someone from England, or France. Didn't we, *Mai?* There were many families here then, so many visits to pay, so many friends to receive. Now, so few. So many have sold their land, their houses. Now there are many foreigners, so many that sometimes I feel that there are more of them than of us. *Mai,* you are not feeling fatigued?"

A reassuring sound came from the old lady, and Henry saw with relief the entrance to the Quinta do Infante coming into view. He followed the wall, mile after mile; at last he saw a large, wrought-iron gate beyond it, a small gatehouse almost smothered in bougainvillaea. An old man emerged from the flowery doorway, inserted a huge key into the lock of the gate and, with Henry's assistance, pushed it open. The car went on along an avenue of tall eucalyptus trees, with thick woodland on either side. The trees began to thin, and Henry saw the shimmer of water in a large irrigation tank. Pines gave way to fig and almond and olive. Round the next curve was a wilderness which had once been a formal garden; there were marble seats half-hidden by weeds, and paths whose ornamental tiles could only now and then be glimpsed beneath thick undergrowth.

Henry expected that the signs of neglect would lessen as they neared the house but decay and weeds persisted. The road skirted a small ornamental lake, now dry and cracked and stony. And then he negotiated the last bend and saw the house.

His first feeling, as he drove the last few hundred yards and brought the car to a halt, was one of surprise. He had formed no definite picture in his mind, but from the perimeter of the walls and his estimate of the area they enclosed, he had expected an imposing dwelling, something like a miniature castle. What he was looking at was a long, simple, stone, single-storied building, standing at one side of a vast, rectangular enclosure, like innumerable other properties of the same kind in the country. Directly opposite was a long line of stables for mules and donkeys and horses, living quarters, a coach house and what appeared to be a storehouse. Along the third side of the rectangle ran an open pavilion. The fourth side was formed by a very high, thick hedge in the center of which had been cut an opening wide enough to admit several mule carts abreast.

Henry sat in the car, forgetful of his passengers, gazing about him. There was nothing about the house to draw an architect's eye, unless it was the strength and simplicity of its central portion — the original house, he saw, built by Pedro Silva. The additions stretching on either side were elaborate, hideous and entirely out of keeping; they showed clear signs of their approaching ruin, and he thought it could not come too soon. Stripped of them, the middle portion would emerge in its original role; a simple, sturdy house for a simple, sturdy sailor. Its stone had weathered to a beautiful tone of dusky rose. Above the door was a barely decipherable representation of a caravel and, beside it, the historic figure that had given the place its name, the Infante Dom Henrique, Henry the Navigator, son of a Portuguese king and his English wife. The large-brimmed hat was blurred, but its outlines could be traced. On either side of the door ran a row of windows with graceful, curving grilles. The uncompromising, almost somber aspect of the original house was softened by the flowers that climbed lovingly up its walls and spilled from both sides of the worn stone steps: roses, scarlet and yellow and pink, geraniums, scarlet and white and a strawberry-and-cream mixture, flowering creepers, bougainvillaea both purple and crimson, their beauty and brilliance contrasting with the grim, centuries-old walls.

He saw the brass-studded door opening, and came to himself. A servant appeared, and then another; both were in faded, dark green livery. At sight of the old lady seated in the car, a cry went up — surprise, joy and a call for reinforcements. Two more green liveries appeared, and then two aged maids dressed in black; Senhora Crespo greeted them all by name. A chair was carried out and Senhora Crespo was carried in, followed by the shawl, the handbag, the sunshade, the lace and the gloves. Henry thought that only a brass band was missing.

He was ushered in politely, Senhor Crespo bowing and insisting that Henry precede him. Henry found himself in a large hall, dark, gloomy and so icy that Senhor Crespo's seemed by comparison over-heated. They followed the chair-bearers along a wide corridor, turned right and walked down another, and then they were in a room full of light and warmth, with a row of windows on one side leading to a wide, flagged, vine-shaded terrace.

Henry stopped in the doorway to look round. The room was immensely long — about sixty feet, he thought. It conformed to no style; it could not even be said to be a mixture of styles; it contained a collection of furniture, dim pictures, cabinets filled with ornaments: jade, china, silver, amber, ivory, ebony. Down its great length there were no dividing doors, but the furniture was arranged in groups, forming a sitting room, a card room and, at the end, a music room with a grand piano, a harp and three elaborate music stands. The carpets were thin, the covers faded, but floor and furniture shone, flowers filled every vase, no speck of dust appeared anywhere. There was an inanimate, unlived-in look over it all that made Henry feel the room had waited through the centuries, ready to receive guests who never came.

Beyond the terrace he saw a lawn of bright green, Brazilian grass; in its center was a small marble fountain from which rose an armless Niobe. His gaze went to the pine-woods beyond, thick, dark-green, seemingly impenetrable.

On the terrace itself, the visitors were being settled, but there was no sign of Senhora Silva. Senhora Crespo was installed in a cushioned wicker chair; trays with tall glasses were carried out; Henry, stepping out on to the terrace, was offered lemonade which he refused. While Senhor Crespo fussed over his mother, Henry went down to make a leisurely inspection of the garden.

There was not much of it. Lawn, flower beds in the shape of diamonds. Once out of sight of the terrace, the weeds had their way. Henry walked down a sloping, sunny path, stopping now and then to examine a curious line of upturned roof tiles that formed a narrow drain parallel to the path along which he was walking. He was pondering on their possible use when he heard his name called, and looked up to see Senhora Silva gesticulating from the top of the slope. He took a step forward to hear what she was saying, and as he did so, he saw a swift current of water cascading towards him. Before he could leap aside, it had reached him and was swirling around his ankles, drenching the ends of his trouser legs, and then coursing down, to leave him standing in a muddy pool. Stepping out of it, he saw Senhora Silva coming unhurriedly down the slope towards him, stout, elegant, her dress black and close-fitting like the one she had worn the day before, her shoes high-heeled, her hair smooth and shining.

"I called to you, Mr. Eliot; you did not listen when I warned you about the water. I cannot imagine why there is no servant here to attend to this. Please will you stop the water from wasting? If I do it myself, I shall get wet, like you."

He followed her pointing finger and saw that the tiles at this point formed a T-junction; in the absence of the attendant whose duty it was to divert the stream to right or left, it had overrun its banks. Stooping, Henry groped under the stream, found the tiles that would redirect the flow and rammed them into position. The stream checked, bubbled and then began to flow smoothly to the right.

"Thank you. Now that is all right," Senhora Silva said. "It is a pity that you got wet; you should have acted more quickly and seen what it was that was needed. I myself invented this way of watering my garden. It is clever, don't you think? Usually, it works very well."

"When the man's on point duty, I presume."

"I can't think where he has gone to. Always in the alternate mornings, I do this. I stand at the top to let out the water, which is in a big tank. My servants stand in their positions, ready to change the tiles to where I say, depending on what is to be watered. I have never before known someone to be out of his place. You received my message that I sent to Senhor Crespo?"

"Yes, thank you."

"Did he come with you?"

"Yes. So did his mother."

Her large, long-lashed, cowlike eyes rested on him. More blank astonishment, he thought.

"Did you say his mother?"

"Yes."

"Eulália Crespo?"

"I wouldn't know about the Eulália. But she's his mother."

"I cannot belive this — I mean, that she is here. She came with you in the car?"

"Yes."

"She trusted you? He trusted you?"

"They both trusted me," Henry said, and bent to squeeze the water from his trouser legs.

"I cannot believe this — I mean that I cannot believe that after so long, she is in my house. Come, we shall go at once. Now I understand what has happened to my servants; after so long, to see her here — they must be so surprised, so happy. They have lost their heads. Come, we shall hurry."

It was not the word he would have applied to their pace. But they reached the terrace at last, and Senhora Silva abandoned English for her native tongue, and embraced her old friend.

"Eulália! This is a miracle! Wait, only wait until Father Vieira sees you here, in my house, after so long. Go quickly," she ordered, "and ask the Senhor Prior to come. Sit down, sit down," she urged Senhor Crespo. "See, here is your favourite chair. Mr. Eliot, if you go into that corner, out of the breeze, you will find it warm and dry, and you will not catch cold. Just imagine, Mr. Eliot got in the way of the water. Eulália, I am of course not going to allow you to go away now that you are here. You will stay to lunch."

"No, no . . ."

"Yes, you will. I have a good lunch that Enrico will enjoy, but for you I shall order some special light things that you can eat. I still have Maria-José; when she hears that she is actually to prepare something for you, she will be delighted, she will surpass herself. Come, tell me what you would like; yes, yes, I insist. Something light, perhaps a soufflé that you used to enjoy."

Henry, drying out in his corner, estimated that it took them eleven minutes to reach an agreement about fish soufflé and a little, just a little thin soup and perhaps a mouthful, no more, of some rich sweet. These vital matters being settled, Senhora Silva was free to turn to minor ones, one of which was Henry's inclusion in the feast. He thanked her, said that he would be delighted, and mentally marked down the occasion as yet another proof that after you got what you wanted, you didn't want it. He wanted above all things to get into the Quinta do Infante;

here he was, in — and far from feeling elated, he was worrying about whether he would ever get out again.

His spirits rose slightly as servants came out with a new supply of glasses on a tray. Henry once again refused lemonade, and was brought black coffee in a cup no bigger than a thimble. He managed to swallow it without swallowing the cup too, and stood staring moodily at the others. When he was not working, this was the hour at which he liked to linger over a good dry sherry while pondering what he would have for lunch.

Old Senhora Crespo was saying something; they all bent forward to catch her words.

"Teresa? But, of course! I shall send for her," said Senhora Silva. She turned to address Father Vieira. "See, Father, I have a surprise for you. And for you, too, Eulália, I have a surprise; Father Vieira is not, after all, to go away from us. This morning I heard that he is to stay. I had many difficulties in arranging this, but now it is settled. Thank God, he is not going to be taken away."

Henry left them to mutual congratulations, and wandered into the drawing room, strolling from cabinet to cabinet and idly inspecting their contents. He could not assess their value, but he thought it must be considerable.

Glancing out of a window, he saw a movement in the distance. Something, someone was approaching, now visible, now hidden by trees. He identified it at last as a bicycle ridden by Teresa, and forgot his thirst as he watched her unsteady approach along a path that was not meant for wheeled traffic.

She stopped at the end of the garden; a servant took her bicycle and she came up to the terrace.

"Here is Teresa," her aunt announced. "Teresa, come and kiss the Senhora. How long is it since we saw her in this house? An age!"

"A year and a half," Teresa said.

"They are staying to lunch, of course. And Mr. Eliot, too. Where is Mr. Eliot? Oh, he is in there. He got wet, Teresa; he saw the water coming down but he did not move in time. Perhaps he would like to go with Manuel and wait while his clothes are dried?"

"Would you?" Teresa asked, joining him in the drawing room.

"No, thanks. Tell me, does your aunt serve anything stronger than lemonade?"

"No. Wine, wine and more wine. But for

hard drinkers like you, nothing. Except —"

"Except the odd bottle you keep for alcoholics?"

"Correct."

"Where?"

She opened a small cupboard; it contained only one bottle, but several glasses.

"Dry white port," she said. "Yes or no?"

"Yes, please."

She poured out two glasses and handed one to him.

"I suppose you'd prefer it chilled?"

"Not this time I wouldn't. Look at my trousers. I said look, not laugh."

"Did you fall into the trough?"

"No. The man wasn't there to switch the points. Don't go," he begged, as she moved towards the terrace. "They're all quite happy. Stay here. I'll need at least two more drinks."

She came back, and he nodded towards the group seated outside.

"Period piece," he said. "Does Father Vieira live here?"

"Only while his house at Caravela is being repaired. He would have stayed with Senhor Crespo if his mother hadn't been so ill. He's in charge of two villages — normally, he comes over here to say Mass in the Chapel on Sundays, but now he stays here and only goes to Caravela to say Mass there. He's supposed to be going away soon, but my aunt's trying to keep him here."

"She's just announced that she's succeeded."

"He's *not* going?"

"The Papal Bull has given him a dispensation or something of that kind. This white port is rather good. Have you noticed that my glass is empty?"

"Yes. As soon as mine is, I'll refill them both. I told you that my aunt would make an appointment, didn't I?"

"You did. What you didn't tell me was that this house — I'm speaking of the original house and not of the unfortunate accretions — is what the fanciful call an architectural gem."

She flushed with pleasure.

"Want to see?"

"Please."

She led him on a tour of inspection. The plan was as straightforward as the New York streets; they had only to walk down the broad, central corridor and inspect the rooms to right and left of it. On one side, the windows faced north and gave a view of the stables and the coach house; on the other side were the rooms facing south, sun-filled, warm, looking on to the garden. To cross the corridor was to step from an arctic to a sub-tropical temperature.

To east and west of the original building, the rooms, no longer in use, were larger, with ornate ceilings and huge, over-decorated fireplaces; here, Henry saw, had once been kept a great deal of state; some of the gilded furniture was still in place, portraits hung on the walls, heavy silver gleamed on long, narrow tables. The lower part of the walls were covered with ornamental tiles; above them was peeling plaster and the marks of damp and decay. The wooden floors were rotting.

"Smell the damp?" Teresa asked him. "That's one of my earliest memories — this smell. I used to cry because they wouldn't cut down trees and burn them in the fireplaces. Whenever they looked for me, they located me wandering about in these rooms, among the ghosts. Want to see the stables?"

They walked over the rock-hard, beaten-down earth to the stables, and Henry learned that where there had been a dozen mule carts, there were now only three. The stalls were occupied by the three mules, four ponies, a baby donkey and a sheep which, Teresa explained, harboured the delusion that it was a horse and could not be induced to stay with its own species.

In the coach house there were two carriages, one small and plain, the other large and imposing.

"My aunt would still use a carriage if she thought it was safe," Teresa said. "But there are too many cars on the road. When she leaves the Quinta, which is seldom, she goes by car. If you can call it a car. Come and see."

An adjoining building contained two cars, one a high, black, brilliantly polished museum piece on which Henry's gaze rested in wonder.

"How old?" he asked.

"Bought by my grandfather, but it didn't stop short, never to go again when the old man died. My mother drove it when she lived here, and when she came later on visits."

"Don't you?"

"Never." She pointed to the small, green one beside it. "That one's mine. It looks battered because I drive it through the woods on Sundays when I go down to the crèche — I take the weekly stores, or I'd go by bike. Driving round by the road is a bore, and the woods are all right except in wet weather, when you're apt to skid on the pine needles. If my aunt has to go to funerals or weddings, if they don't take place in our Chapel, she's driven in my grandfather's car by one of the gardeners who doubles as a chauffeur. Now come to the house and I'll give you another drink."

When they reached the house, he asked, "What did you do in England? By way of work, I mean. If any."

"Several jobs. All total failures."

"What were they?"

"Teaching in a language school but I couldn't get anything into the pupils' heads. Secretary, but I couldn't spell; in times of stress I used to lapse into spelling by sound, and they sacked me when I wrote sweater as *sueta*. Then receptionist in one of those fancy country hotels, and finally a firm which did business in the three languages I knew: Portuguese, Spanish and French. The work was easy; the difficult part was trying to cram all my leisure pursuits into my leisure hours. After I'd fought my way home from the coal-black office in Fenchurch Street, and cooked and cleared away my supper and tried to get some of the London fog off my underwear, it was time to go to bed."

"What are your leisure pursuits?"

213

"Painting, badly, playing the piano quite well. That piano over there is a good one, but in winter, even when all three fires are going in here, my fingers freeze. Do you like music?"

"I'll tell you when we've worked down my list of questions about you. How about men friends?"

"A silly question. Look at me and be reassured. But I can't say I was popular in London; half my escorts got tired of taking me to concerts and the other half gave up because they decided, after one or two skirmishes, that I was the cold type. It was really rather a relief; I got fewer dinners, but I could digest them in peace. Do you play any instruments?"

"No. But I've got some rather special records."

"Dance? Opera?"

"Orchestral, chiefly."

"Who?"

"Holst — my favourite. Britten. Bartók. And for the lightweights in the audience, some quite good folk music, Russian, chiefly, and Calypsos, and fados."

"You must have a mixed lot of listeners."

"Before I got engaged, I had a crowd of friends who used to drop in three or four times a week and sit around drinking beer and listening to what I'd got. But Marly got bored. I suppose most people would, except the addicts. She tried, but she couldn't take the kind of stuff I liked."

"Can you take the kind of stuff she likes?"

He kept his gaze on her for some moments, but she made her expression as blank as her aunt's.

"She isn't musical," he explained. "She likes dance music because she likes dancing." He picked up a small carved box. "Does this play a tune when you open it?"

"Yes." She took it from him, and they stood listening until the tinkle ended. She took the box to see if it had run down, holding it against her ear, her hair falling forward against her cheek, her expression absorbed, her lips parted. He had a sudden, shaking desire to prolong the moment, to stand and watch her, to forget (as he had forgotten until Marly's name was mentioned) all the things that had crowded in on him in the past few months, pushing out one by one the old, quiet, satisfying pleasures. While he had talked to this girl, in this timeless room, he had forgotten everything but the things he had had — and lost. Not lost, he corrected himself bitterly. Thrown away.

He was so engrossed in his thoughts that Teresa had to recall him by a touch on his arm. He saw that a manservant was standing beside them.

"Hanibal is waiting to take you along to wash before lunch," she said.

Henry followed Hanibal — not over the Alps, though it might well have been, so cold was the bedroom to which he was led. On a marble-topped washstand stood a copper jug; from this the man poured hot water, standing by while Henry washed his hands, ready to hand him a linen towel. Then he conducted him to a tile-floored lavatory; when Henry emerged, he was waiting for him. A single note of a gong reverberated through the house; Hanibal led the way to the dining room and handed Henry over to the care of another servant, who led the way to a long table at which the others were already seated. Senhora Crespo was settled in the chair next to her hostess; Henry was placed next to her and saw, to his annoyance, Teresa going to a place on the other side, between Senhor Crespo and the priest.

One of the servants drew out Henry's high-backed chair while the other unfolded his napkin and placed it across his knees; Henry had half-expected them to tie it round his neck while they fed him. He watched Senhora Crespo eating fish soufflé and a little cream of chicken. Pressed, begged, encouraged, applauded, she later consented to try just a little of the successive dishes of *bacalhau*, mutton stew, meat balls in tomato sauce, caramel custard, cheese and fruit. The service was leisurely, the plates and the food cold after the long journey from the kitchen, but the food was abundant, and well cooked.

He liked timing events. They sat down at two o'clock; they rose and filed out on to the terrace for coffee at exactly four. At four-fifteen, Senhora Crespo began to nod; a shawl was placed over her, cushions were put on either side to steady her. Senhor Crespo and the priest drew their chairs closer together to converse without disturbing her.

"And now, Mr. Eliot" — Senhora Silva turned to him — "if you wish, you and I will go into the garden and we shall have this little talk you wish to have with me. Teresa, you will be going back to the children, I suppose?"

"Yes, if you don't mind."

The bicycle was wheeled round; she mounted, and Henry saw her go with a heavy sense of loss. He wanted to go with her. He wanted to return to the beach, to recapture the mood of the morning. His eyes rested on her until she was out of sight; then he followed Senhora Silva and remembered that at last he was to embark on the business which had brought him out to Portugal.

She led him to a bench beside a magnificent fig tree, its branches sweeping the ground like a great hooped skirt. The sun was hot, but they were out of reach. Senhora Silva sat down, plied her fan slowly and prepared herself to listen but for some moments Henry, seated beside her, had nothing to say. He was staring at the flower beds with their dusty geraniums, their half-wild roses, their undisturbed weeds, and wondering why this whole vast, seedy property, this house and its grounds, which should have filled the visitor with a sense of gloom, if not doom, instead breathed out an infinite peace. This was a dying world. The real world was out there, bustling, thriving, changing, rolling in great waves round the walls of the estate — but within the walls, though there was awareness, there was no fretting and no fuss. This woman seated beside him was living out her life watching the inevitable end to the conditions in which she had been born and reared. She knew, she understood, and she cared deeply — but she could shelter it to the last, Henry realized, under the canopy that had been erected by hundreds of years of safe, unthreatened existence. He could not explain his impressions to those outside; they would sound unrealistic to the point of idiocy — but he knew that this place cast a spell, and that he had fallen under it. Marly, Sir Bertram, the Colonel . . . he could call them to mind, but only dimly; at this moment they seemed to him remote figures in a far-off, half-forgotten, infinitely less desirable existence.

Senhora Silva glanced at him.

"Now we are ready to talk," she pointed out.

"Yes." Henry pulled himself together, struggling to assume a businesslike air. "About the land, Senhora, I —"

"Yes, of course, about the land. That is why you wished to see me, no? But first I should like to know who is this Sir Bertram Stonor?"

"He's the head of the Stonor Development Corporation."

"He wishes to develop this land?"

"No. He wants it for purely private reasons."

"What is so special, that he wishes to build a house in just that place?"

"The beach, of course, and the view and —"

"There are other beaches here."

"This one is exceptionally secluded. I know that the question of access —"

"One moment. About you, yourself. You were in Brazil?"

"Yes."

"Your parents lived there, your father worked there?"

"He was an engineer, with headquarters in Santos."

"And then he died?"

"Yes. My mother would have liked to stay in Brazil because she didn't think she would be able to settle in England after having been away so long."

"And then?"

"My uncle sent for me."

"To England?"

"Yes."

"You were obliged to go?"

"Yes. He paid for my education. My mother went to Madeira, and died there. About this land, Senhora —"

"One moment; you have not finished about yourself. This uncle was rich?"

Like Mr. Easter, Henry thought, anything you want to know, just ask.

"I thought he was rich, but he wasn't. Before he died, he got into debt because of me."

"And you became an architect?"

"I wanted to be a painter, but —"

"— but this uncle did not permit it?"

"He felt it was important for me to have a profession."

"Painting is not a profession?"

"I put that badly. I meant that he —"

"Yes, yes, yes. You must have certificates to show, diplomas to frame on your walls, letters to put after your name so that everybody will be reassured. That is what Teresa's English relations were always saying, that she must have a profession, she must be trained and so on. It was all very silly, and useless too, because she did not learn anything at all."

"About the land. Sir Bertram —"

"You are a good employee; you keep your master's affairs always in mind."

"The matter of price can be —"

"I understand that he is prepared to offer me a great deal. Senhor Crespo's cousin, Urbano Moreira, was authorized to say this to me. But I will tell you now, Mr. Eliot, I would rather keep my land. You are an architect. You know, then, that my house is in bad condition. I could sell this land, I could sell other land within the Quinta. I would get money, quite a lot — and then? I would call for an army: builders, carpenters, stone-masons, *canalisadors* — how do you call them? Yes, plumbers. They would go to work, and soon where would the money be? It would be gone."

"The house would have been saved."

"You think it is worth saving?"

"The central, the original part, yes."

"For what? For whom? There is nobody left, only myself and Teresa. She will get everything, of course. But if she marries an Englishman, which I hope not, she will have to go away to live in England, as her mother did. If she marries a Portuguese, which I hope, it will be a man of good family who will have a property of his own where she will go to live, and her husband, you may be sure, will not care to drain his money out on this Quinta. The house will be left empty. It will become a ruin. This is what must happen. Sir Bertram's money could not do more than make a little delay."

"He is hoping very much that he will be able to persuade you —"

"If Teresa needed the money, I would of course consider. But I have enough for her.

I have not enough to make this house live again, be beautiful again, but I have enough for our needs, even for Teresa's if she does not marry, she will be able to live out her life here. She would like that; there is no place she loves as much, as deeply as she loves this Quinta. She could live here, and she would be the last and then everything would end. When our line ends, who will care what happens to the house? It would have been different if I had had sons; they would not have been the direct line, but they would have been Silvas. Now there are no more."

"Money is money; it can be used for other purposes."

"Such as what purposes, Mr. Eliot? I do not care for travel. I can entertain my friends in sufficient style. My servants will remain until I am dead. I do not wish for any other kind of life; my niece does not, either. Shall I sell my land and give the money to charity? No, because already I have given enough, and done enough. Also, I think it is important to keep the land because so much already has gone into the hands of foreigners. If they were serious people, I would be glad — but mostly, they are not. They are, for the most part, holiday people, restless people, rootless people. Only one in fifty cares for our customs, or our music, or our festivals or our traditions. They eat our food and drink our wine and buy our land, and if there is too much rain, or if the servants are stupid, or there is not as much gaiety as they had hoped, they pack up and go away. Sir Bertram, I think, is not making a plan to live in this house that he will put on the land?"

"No. He's buying the land . . . he's hoping to buy the land as a wedding present for his daughter."

She stopped fanning herself and turned slowly towards him.

"And so for you, too?"

"Yes."

"So that you have a personal interest?"

"I suppose so. To tell you the truth, my interest didn't really stir until I went through the pinewoods the day before yesterday and saw exactly what Sir Bertram was after. Now that I've seen it, I know that he will be prepared to make generous terms."

"He will blame you if you fail to persuade me?"

"Blame? He'll feel I'm less . . . effective than he had hoped."

"And your fiancée, Miss Stonor?"

Henry frowned.

"I think she'll ask to see you. Her father rang me up last night and seemed to feel I wasn't moving fast enough."

"He was angry?"

"Yes. So this morning I decided to go to the crèche and speak to Teresa. She sent me to Senhor Crespo and I found he had already had a message from you which he'd sent to my hotel."

"Your fiancée is staying at the same hotel?"

"No. She's staying with friends. I'll see her tonight and I'll tell her what you've said, but I think —"

"You think she will insist on hearing this for herself? She will not accept my refusal through you?"

"She will ask you to reconsider."

"You must tell her that I will not."

"Won't you at least see her?"

"No, Mr. Eliot, I will not. I do not like her."

Surprise at her frankness, rather than affront at her opinion, kept Henry silent for some time. Then he spoke slowly.

"I don't think you should allow feelings of that kind to influence you in business matters, Senhora."

225

"No? Why not? I am not a shopkeeper, who has to bow politely to each customer."

"How can you make up your mind about Marly in a few moments?"

"Marly — that is her name? In a few moments, I saw that she was bad-tempered. In a few moments, she showed me that she did not care for the children, so small, so sweet, so poor, so defenseless. In a few moments she showed me that she has no good manners, and does not know how to behave in the presence of an older person — I will not mention a priest."

"She had no idea who you were."

"That is an excuse? When she knew, she was worse, because she became arrogant. No, I will not see her."

"Am I to tell Sir Bertram that you refuse to see his daughter because you don't like her?"

"That is for you, not for me. I would not have seen you if I had not been assured first of all by Urbano Moreira, and also by Senhor Crespo, of your good bearing. You must not blame me for appearing to be unobliging; you cannot have an idea of what it has been like for the past year, and more. I have had strangers, absolute strangers, I assure you, pushing past my gatekeeper and demanding to see me and shouting, yes, I promise you, shouting to me to listen to their offers of money. One actually, this you cannot believe but it is true, one of them took out a pen and his book of checks, and offered that I should fill in the amount. After this, I said: No More, and I took steps for my own protection. I was sorry that my servants were too old to throw them out — but as you see, I have only old men and old women; their sons and daughters, who used to work for me, are earning unimaginable sums working for the foreigners. They say they are happy, and I am glad for them, but I am sorry for the old, who are left without strong hands to help them on the land, on the farms, in the fields. I am —"

She broke off abruptly. Getting to her feet, she stood listening intently. Henry at first heard nothing; then he made out a wailing sound coming from the woods. He remembered that Teresa had told him of a maternity home in one of the outbuildings; this might be a mother, or a baby.

He saw Senhora Silva hurrying towards the trees, calling loudly as she went.

"Guilhermo! Nuno! Arturo! Here, at once! Hurry!"

To Henry the three men seemed to fall off

the trees. Senhora Silva addressed them, her manner hurried, her tone as flat as ever.

"Quickly! Go and find Gonsalves."

One of the men hobbled away; the other two followed Senhora Silva through the pinewood, and Henry, left alone, stood pondering. The interview was over. He could go back to the house and shake Senhora Crespo awake, but he could not take her away until she had taken leave of her hostess. Teresa was out of reach. He was not anxious to encounter any expectant mothers, but he might as well follow Senhora Silva and find out the reason for her agitation.

He walked in the direction she had taken. There was no path, and the wood became thicker. He tried to get his bearing, but there was nothing to guide him. He went on, stumbling over stones and roots; through the trees he glimpsed small buildings, and was about to turn towards one of them when he heard Senhora Silva's voice, and a renewal of the wailing he had heard before. The noise became louder, and suddenly he identified it. Not mothers. Not babies. Cats.

And then he saw them.

He stood rooted to the spot, openmouthed. Behind a high, stout wire screen he saw countless cats: gray cats, tabby cats, black and ginger and streaky cats. They were clawing at the wire, scratching, mewing, screeching. The wire enclosed a large area; near him was a wooden door, and through this he saw the two men entering, in their hands nets attached to long bamboo handles.

"There!" Senhora Silva, outside the enclosure, was directing them. "That's the one! Catch it! Quick, Arturo, round this way!"

Henry forgot everything in the excitement of the chase. The nets hovered, descended and always, with a lightning twist, the quarry got away. It was a gray cat, lean and long; it leaped among the other cats, dodged, swerved — and then at last Guilhermo had it and was walking up to wind it securely into the net.

"Good!" Senhora Silva drew a long breath of relief. "Good. We have got him."

"What for?" Henry inquired.

"Did you not see? That cat was a he-cat. Always I said, from the very beginning, that he is a male, but we could not be sure, and Teresa said to wait. And if I hadn't been in the garden with you, if I hadn't heard that noise that only he-cats make when they are after a she-cat, then what would have happened? The men could not have heard; Nuno is old and does not hear well, and the others had work to do where they could not hear. It was fortunate that I was in time. Now we have got him."

"What happens to him now?" Henry asked, and found her turning to stare at him.

"But surely . . . this is childish, to ask this! Did you . . . didn't Teresa tell you about the cats?"

"No."

"Then I will tell you." She turned and began to lead him back to the house. "Until Teresa came to live here, three years ago, there was not one cat. Not one. I do not like cats. Perhaps one, two, I would have liked, but soon they would have been six and then twelve and then more. So I refused to have them. And one day, Teresa found one on the road, a very small cat, dying because it had no food. She brought it home and looked after it and I allowed this because I thought it was only a kitten — and then what? A litter. Three, no bigger than mice. That was the beginning. When people outside the Quinta heard that here was a girl who liked to make herself a guardian angel to cats, what did they do? They put, if you will believe this, cats, kittens, young, old, some sick but all hungry — they put them at my gates. And Teresa took them in, and still takes them in. But from the first, I said: Very well, but if there is a he-cat, he shall not be allowed to make future generations. I watched carefully, and caught them and sent them to the *veterinario*, who is the father of Gonsalves, and he arranges them and then they cannot make more little cats. Only in this way can I be assured that I shall not have to go away from the Quinta and leave it for the cats. Everybody agrees with me that it is madness to allow Teresa to do this but about children and animals, it is not I who can be called crazy, but Teresa. Come, let us hurry. I have left my friends alone for too long."

He made only one more attempt to draw her mind away from her own affairs. As they reached the terrace steps, he said, "May I tell Sir Bertram —"

She did not pause.

"Of course, Mr. Eliot. Please tell him that you have done everything possible."

"And your answer —"

"It is as I told you: No."

There was complete finality in her tone. He walked up the steps in silence, resigned to the knowledge that the business was over — if there had been any business. They had not come to terms, because no terms had been mentioned. How he was to embody the substance of the conversation in a stark report to Sir Bertram, he could not imagine; how describe negotiations when none had taken place? He, who had seen her and heard her, had lost all hope that she would ever sell the land, but he knew that it would prove impossible to ask Marly or her father to accept defeat at what would seem to them merely the approach to hard bargaining.

Senhora Silva was already calling to her friends.

"Eulália, I am sorry to have been so long. Are you feeling rested?"

Senhor Crespo said that his mother looked better than she had looked for many months but it was time, he added, to take her home; she must not exhaust herself.

"Certainly she must go away now to rest," Senhora Silva agreed, "but I have thought of a good idea. Tomorrow all day she will rest. The day after that is Sunday, and you shall bring her to Mass here in our Chapel. Mr. Eliot will bring you both. Mr. Eliot, will you do this? Mass will be said by Father Vieira at ten o'clock, after he has said Mass at Caravela. Please to drive Senhor Crespo and his mother."

Senhor Crespo was making low, embarrassed sounds.

"But Ofélia," he reminded her, "you do not know if Mr. Eliot . . . that is to say, he may not be —"

"You mean not a Catholic? But he could drive you here — isn't it, Mr. Eliot? Senhora Crespo would trust nobody but you to drive her. If you are not of our religion, you can amuse yourself in some way, and then join us for lunch. Yes, yes, yes, Eulália, I insist; you shall not go away without first having lunch. Mr. Eliot, you agree?"

Henry agreed, and fell into line as the ceremonial procession formed to conduct Senhora Crespo to the car. He drove to Caravela, saw his passengers safely into their house and then left them and went to the hotel.

After he had had a shower and changed, he telephoned Marly. A maid informed him that Colonel and Mrs. Colston and their guests had gone to Albufeira, and would not return for dinner.

He put down the receiver and stood staring at it. When next he picked it up, he reflected, it would be to hear Sir Bertram inquiring what progress had been made.

"What did you tell him?" asked Teresa

at dusk.

"I told him exactly what I told you: I will not sell."

"What did he say?"

"Naturally, he tried to persuade me."

"How much did they offer?"

"You mean money? We did not speak of money."

"How could you meet someone to talk about a sale without —"

"I did not meet to speak of a sale. I met only to say clearly that I will not sell. Now it is said and it is finished. It is finished at any rate for him. Now other people will come and ask about it. This is just what I feared. Already one has come."

"Who?"

"Another Englishman. His name was strange — Easter. He came this evening, but I did not receive him. I sent him away. I would never have agreed to receive Mr. Eliot if Urbano Moreira had not given so good an account of him. Now it is finished. The girl and her father will of course wish for more meetings, but I said to Mr. Eliot: No. He is coming on Sunday; I asked him to bring Eulália Crespo to Mass, and he will stay to lunch."

"Didn't you invite his fianceé?"

"Certainly not. To him I said absolutely: I will not receive her."

"You told him that?"

"Why should I not tell him? We did not meet for social matters, where it would not have been possible for me to be so frank. It was business, and I know quite well what she wished to do, come here with an impertinent manner and a mountain of money and make useless arguments."

"What did he say?"

"What could he say? He could not say 'I love this girl, you also must love her.'"

"But if you refuse to see her, she'll blame him."

"This I think, too."

"And if the deal's off, finally, he's going to have to say so to his fiancée's father, and —"

"You mean that they will make him the whipping boy? Well, so much the better for him. She will be angry and she will dismiss him and he will be saved from marrying her."

"Suppose her father dismisses him, too?"

"That is not my business. Do you wish me to follow each one to see how my refusal to sell my land has affected his life?"

"Not each one."

"Then why this one?"

"Because his future's tied up in the deal."

"You care about his future?"

There was silence. The red glow of sunset faded to pink. Senhora Silva's fan slowed and finally stopped.

"Well, Teresa? There is a question to answer. You care for this young man's future?"

"Yes, I do, since we're about to blast it."

"That is a strange word to use. He will simply be blamed for failing to persuade me to sell the land."

"It was to be a —"

"A wedding present from the girl's father. This I already know. What is that to me, or to you?"

"It made the transaction a bit more personal, that's all. If they blame him, he might end by losing more than a wedding present. He might lose his job and his fiancée, too."

"So then he will not need a wedding present. I myself think this is better for him than marrying her."

"He chose her."

"I do not think that men choose a woman like this one. She chose him. When I said this before to you, you agreed with me because you said that he was weak."

"He's not weak."

"Ah, so you changed your mind?"

"Yes. But he's not strong in the way you have to be strong when you're dealing with the kind of people he's up against."

"You seem to be talking in a very mixed-up way. You need not tell me, if that is what you are trying to tell me, that nice people are, in a way, weak. This I know already. But will being abused by them hurt him? Will even dismissal hurt him? If he is employed by a great organization of this kind, he cannot be bad at his work."

"How do you know she didn't get him the job?"

"First, because I do not think he is a man who would need such a way of finding work, and next, because from what I know of this man Stonor, he would not be a man to tolerate in his organization second-rate workers. Of this I am sure. Do you think he will be happy if he marries that girl?"

"No."

"But you object that I should be the reason for losing her?"

"Yes. No."

A maid appeared in the doorway with a lamp; Senhora Silva waved her away. When the door was closed, there was a long, unbroken silence in the room. Then Senhora Silva addressed her niece slowly.

"Teresa, there is a solution for me in this matter. I will tell you what it is. But listen carefully, because it is very important."

"I'm listening."

"I am going to send for Urbano Moreira. I am going to make him prepare some papers. I am going to give this land to you."

"No. I —"

"Please to wait before you speak. I do not care if you have arguments for this or against this; I am going to do it. I have good reasons — many, but two especially. The first, I am sick, sick, sick of being pestered. The second, and perhaps this is more important, sometimes in the night, lately, I have had doubts; I have asked myself: Am I right to refuse to sell?"

"You're quite right to refuse to sell. You know it and I know it, and one of us had better keep a clear head. If you're tired of seeing people, why not let me do your refusing for you?"

"It would be useless. Who will deal with a young girl who does not own the land? But soon it will be yours, and what you do with it, I don't care. If it is sold, it will not change anything for me; if anything is built there, I shall not see it from my windows. I have never used the beach; I do not like to put myself into the sea and I do not like to have picnics with sand in the food, and I do not like exposing myself to heat and I do not wish to go on water-skis or float about on those blown-up rubber beds. When the papers are signed, the land will be yours and you may say to this man you like so much: Look, I shall sell it to you and you can marry this arrogant girl and please your employer. But if I were you, I would keep it, for if nothing else, it is valuable and it will be a good dowry, if you ever make up your mind to have a husband."

"You haven't given up hope?"

"I think, yes, I have, because I say to myself: What sort of man will wish to marry you? He will also have to marry fourteen children and one hundred and eight cats."

"One hundred and twelve."

"You mean . . ."

"This morning. Two black and two black and white. The mother's the cat you thought was so well-fed when it came."

"Can you imagine any husband putting up with this? Teresa, what sort of life is this for you?"

"Absolute heaven. A great big house to

roam around in, an enormous spread of ground with little empty houses and a beautiful Chapel and a tank and your little irrigation drains and dams, and the crèche with the children, and all those cats who used to make you feel sick with misery every time you looked at them, and who now look like real, live happy animals. And a nice climate — lots of sun and torrents of rain, each in due season. And lots and lots and lots . . . and lots . . . and lots of *time*. Time to live slowly. Time to dream. Do you know what they used to do whan I dreamed — daydreamed — in England?"

"Yes, I know. Your mother told me. She dreamed, too."

"They thought I was ill. They thought I had a sort of wasting disease that was sapping my energy. They wanted to give me pep pills. Privately, they put it down to decadence, due to my Portuguese blood. They wanted me to rouse myself and go to parties, but the parties there —"

"— were worse than the parties here. Naturally."

"Naturally. And so when you told me that I could stay here forever if I wanted to . . ."

"Perhaps it was a mistake."

"To let me stay?"

"Yes. I don't know. It is difficult to know these things for certain, but when I thought of you living here, I didn't think — this I can assure you — I didn't think of a girl who would pass her days in an old dress and hair this way and that, going from day to day to a crèche and occupying herself with cats. No, this I could not have imagined. So perhaps it would have been better for you to stay with your father's people, to have more . . . more . . ."

"Discipline?"

"That. Yes. You are too old to run wild, and you are too young to . . . to . . ."

"Go to seed?"

"Yes. I will not say that your life is not happy — I know that it is. I will say only that it is not a life for you. You are very pretty. Sometimes you are almost beautiful, like your mother. You should go out into the world, meet people, meet young men. My friends are old. They have, of course, sons or grandsons, but all are Portuguese and perhaps you should be able to choose more widely, more freely. You have had a good, an expensive education. What use is it to have this and spend your time with cats?"

"A poet named Cowper wrote something about homeborn happiness. That's my kind.

Are you really sorry you let me come here?"

"Yes. I think so. For me, of course, it is a great happiness, but I must think of you."

"Good. If you think of me, you'll never send me away."

"Send you? I could never do that. But I could urge you, persuade you."

"You could never do that either. And if you want to think of me, don't sign those papers. Wait until you're dead."

"No. No, Teresa. In this matter, you must let me decide. You cannot make me change my mind. If that Englishman comes again — and he will — I will send word to say that the land is no longer mine. This I shall say to everybody. Something tells me I am doing what is right. I have this feeling that I had when I married your uncle, and when I saw your mother marrying your father. The land will be yours. If you refuse to sell it, then it will be you who will ruin this young man you are so interested in, and you will not be able to blame me. It will be all in your hands. You understand this?"

"Yes," Teresa said slowly. "Yes, I understand this."

CHAPTER 6

Henry had a bad night. Lying awake hour after slow hour, he came to the conclusion that he had carried out his mission badly.

He had not come out with any great hope of success. Unlike Sir Bertram, he had respected Senhor Moreira's views and had foreseen difficulties that might prove insurmountable. But one thing he had not been prepared for was the poor figure he would make during the negotiations. He had never pretended to be a man of affairs, but he had at least felt himself capable of putting forward a business proposition, ready and able to counter objections with reassurances, to use persuasion against obstinacy.

It hadn't worked out like that, he admitted. From the moment he had set eyes on the land, he realized, he had been filled with foreboding at the thought of what Marly would do to it. It had not needed Senhora Silva's views, or Teresa's; better than either of them, he could visualize the nature and extent of the changes that Marly would make.

He found himself wondering now how much effect Mr. Easter's revelation had had on him. In one sense it had not been a surprise, for he had never harboured illusions about Sir Bertram's business methods, but he realized that after listening to the story he had lost much of his eagerness to obtain the land for Sir Bertram. He did not doubt any part of Mr. Easter's account; had he done so, Colonel Colston's outburst would have convinced him of its truth.

He fell asleep at dawn, woke late and unrefreshed, and decided to go down and have a swim. Crossing the terrace on his way to the pool, he saw Lady Pearling signalling to him and hurried on, ignoring the summons. But as he turned on to the sheltered path leading to the pool, he saw two figures which brought him to an abrupt halt. One was Marly; the other was Mrs. Colston.

A glance was enough to show him that neither was in a mood that could be termed sunny; when they drew near, he saw that Marly was not disposed to receive even a token greeting.

"Time you showed up," she said. "I've been trying to get you all morning."

There was more than ill-temper in her tone; there was contempt. Hearing it, something hardened within Henry.

"I'm sorry." He spoke with no more than politeness. "I had a bad night, and I overslept."

"I would have thought that a phone ringing in your ear would make you at least semi-conscious. What happened to you yesterday?"

"Yes, *what* happened to you?" Mrs. Colston demanded in an angry voice. "Marly rang you several times and they told her you were out."

"I was trying to get hold of you," Marly said, "to tell you I was going into Faro with Edgar to see the Lucases. We stayed to lunch and then we drove with some people to Sagres and ended up by going to the opening of the new restaurant at Albufeira. But I couldn't let you know I'd be away all day, because you didn't answer your phone and — incidentally, did Father get hold of you?"

"Yes."

His tone was abrupt. He saw her eyebrows go up.

"What did he say?"

"He began by saying that you'd rung him up to — as he phrased it — put him in the picture."

"Well, I thought he ought to know what was going on. I told him we'd run into the Silva woman, and he agreed that I ought to go and see her."

"I saw her yesterday."

She had turned to address Mrs. Colston, but the words made her swing round to stare at him.

"You *what?*" she asked him slowly.

"I said I saw Senhora Silva yesterday."

"Where did you see her?" she demanded.

"At the Quinta do Infante."

There was a pause. There was a dangerous glint in her eyes; that was the lightning, he told himself with a feeling of detachment. The thunder would follow.

"I don't understand." Her voice had risen to a pitch that made passers-by slow their footsteps in the hope of hearing more. "I don't know what you're talking about. I told you I wanted to go and see her myself. Why didn't you wait and go with me?"

"Because your father told me, very forcibly, to get going, so I got."

"What difference would one day have

made?" Mrs. Colston put in angrily.

"None, to me," Henry told her politely. "But Sir Bertram pointed out that I was sent here with specific instructions, and that I was to waste no more time in carrying them out."

"You know perfectly well that I was going to see Senhora Silva," said Marly in a high, furious tone.

"Then you shouldn't have wasted time doing the rounds with Edgar," Henry said.

"One day wouldn't have mattered, and you know it!"

"You should have told your father that."

"Now look," Mrs. Colston told him severely, "you can't take that tone. It's not only unreasonable, it's impertinent. Marly rang up her father and had a frank talk with him. Why shouldn't she? He agreed that she ought to go and see Senhora Silva. Marly had told you that she intended to go."

"I went to see Senhor Crespo yesterday morning. He told me he'd already sent a message to the hotel to say that Senhora Silva would see me at noon. We drove to the Quinta together."

That was the truth, he reflected. It wasn't the whole truth, but it was all they were going to get.

"What did she say when you got there?"

Marly demanded.

"What Senhor Moreira and Senhor Crespo said she'd say — that she won't sell."

"But my father told you he'd raised the offer. You mean she turned it down?"

"Money wasn't mentioned. As we were told in London, money hasn't got much to do with her reasons for selling or not selling."

"Money wasn't —" Marly broke off, too astounded to proceed.

"Money wasn't mentioned?" Mrs. Colston sounded dazed. "I don't think you know what you're saying."

"He's crazy," Marly said viciously. "Edgar said so yesterday, and now I believe it. He's crazy; he must be. He goes to see a woman who has land to sell, and now he tells us that no money was mentioned." She swung round on Henry. "Do you think my father is going to be satisfied with that?"

"I'll tell you when he comments on my report."

"You won't be making one," she said. "I'm going back to phone him now, and when I've finished, he won't need any reports from you."

"For your information," Mrs. Colston told him, "Sir Bertram had given Marly a free hand, and promised he'd meet whatever sum it was this Silva woman was holding out for. Marly could have gone to her and —"

"She must think we're a set of fools," Marly said bitterly.

"And the proof," Mrs. Colston told Henry, "is that we used you as a negotiator."

"When you say 'we,' " Henry asked mildly, "do you —"

"I mean we, in the family, as opposed to you, an outsider," she said.

"The land was to be a wedding present to Marly. Wouldn't you say that this concerned me more than it concerned you?" he asked her.

"It was more than a wedding present, once I'd seen it," Marly said. "You know quite well that when I saw it, I realized its possibilities and I made up my mind to get it, whatever it cost. And I will, too. If you think this is going to stop me from going on with —"

She paused. A tall, thin figure had appeared beside them. Lady Pearling, far from pleased, was waving her notebook at Henry.

"Young man, if you didn't see me beckoning to you, you must be blind. If you didn't hear me calling, you must be deaf. I wanted you most particularly to translate something for me. Now it's too late, but you must write some phrases into my book for future use."

"Of course," Henry said. "Lady Pearling, may I introduce Mrs. Colston — and my fiancée, Miss Stonor."

"Howjerdo. Howjerdo. Now, the first sentence, young man —"

Mrs. Colston's expression had undergone a swift transformation.

Oh, *what* a lucky encounter!" she exclaimed. "I've been asked by some friends of yours and mine to look you up — and here you are."

"And here I've been for some time," Lady Pearling informed her.

"Oh, really? Well, they said we might be of some use to you as you were hoping to find a house somewhere in the Algarve. My husband and I —"

"— have a house to offer. I know. But I don't want to see it until I've made some more inquiries. I happen to know that a man in this hotel went after it and was on the point of signing when he withdrew. Peculiar, I thought. I said so to Mr. Eliot. The man who was after it won't say anything; he's afraid, I daresay. But Mr. Eliot seems to know —"

Mrs. Colston was turning away.

"Forgive me; I'm in a hurry," she said abruptly. She called over her shoulder to Marly. "Are you coming?"

"Or are you staying?" Henry inquired.

Their eyes met. In his was merely the question he had asked; what the answer meant to him he could not at this moment assess. But when, without a word, she turned and followed Mrs. Colston, he knew that the tie that bound them was stretched to the utmost, and was unlikely to take the strain for long — and he knew that he would feel nothing but relief when it snapped.

"Bad-tempered gal," Lady Pearling commented, staring after her. She looked round for a bench, found one, and sat down. "I'm not good-tempered myself, but there's a difference, and you'd better learn what it is before tying yourself up. I'm bad-tempered because I won't suffer fools and I won't pander to people who want soft-soaping. I'm bad-tempered because I'm too old to wait for things to be done wrong and then undone and done in the proper way. That's different from being bad-tempered all through, like that gal. You know what they mean by a bad streak? She's got one."

"Perhaps we'd better talk about something

else," Henry suggested.

"Ah. That wasn't the tone you said it in last time I mentioned her. Good. You're coming up for air. A young man like you — you've got a soft streak, since we're speaking of streaks — can't hope to hold your own against that crowd. They're all cheats, and they're not amateur cheats, either. Now sit here, will you, and translate for me. Here's my pen; mind how you write; don't on any account turn the nib sideways. Sit down, sit down; if you had tortured feet, like mine, you wouldn't need to be urged. One: *You are overcharging me.* Two: *I want* — young man, are you paying attention?"

"I wasn't," Henry confessed, "but I will. What were you saying?"

"Never mind." She took away the notebook and the pen. "Your mind's not on it. I suppose you're wondering whether that girl will come back. She won't if Mrs. Colston's got anything to do with it. And what stung *her?* I was in the middle of a sentence when she bolted."

"You gave her the idea that I'd put you against buying her house."

Lady Pearling's small, shrewd eyes narrowed.

"I did what? Nonsense. And even if I did,

it was for your own good."

Henry patted her bony hand.

"You're very kind," he assured her. "But how about letting me manage all by my grown-up self?"

"They'll run rings round you. They'll carve you up. They'll make mincemeat of you."

"Why should you care?"

Before answering the question, she subjected him to a long, frank, unwinking stare.

"I don't know," she said at last. "But the irritating thing is that I do care. Perhaps you've heard of ABC."

"Yes. Allen's Baby Cars."

"Quite so. I'm the A, or I was before I married Pearling. If there's a quicker way of meeting crooks than by being a woman with a million pounds, I don't know it. I've learned to pick them out, and I can still do it. What's more, I can deal with them. But you . . . well, I don't like to see a man like you letting people like those Colstons walk over you."

Henry smiled.

"I'll tell you a secret," he said. "It isn't a soft streak. It's like your bad temper — top layer only."

"Rubbish. Don't you deceive yourself.

You fell in love with that girl, and I know why; she wanted you and she grabbed you and you were in no state to run. But you made the mistake of trying to put it on a permanent basis. That's where men like you go wrong, and prove you're nothing but ninnies. Do you know how long I was married?"

"No."

"Then I'll tell you. Fifty-two years. I was just over twenty-one when I met Pearling, and my temper then was what it is today, only my tongue hadn't had time to grow so sharp. He was like you, ready to legalize every passing fancy. I rescued him practically from the altar's mouth, and I married him and kept him happy till he died. Without me, where would he have been? What you want is someone who'll keep you from the sharks."

"I'll look out for the warning flags," Henry promised. "And as you've been so kind, how about letting me drive you round on a house-hunting expedition?"

"I can well afford taxis, thank you."

He took the notebook and opened it.

"You are overcharging me," he recited. "You see? A taxi driver only has to look at you to see that you've got a soft streak,

and so he —"

"Don't be funny at my expense, young man. Are you free this morning?"

"*And* this afternoon *and* this evening. I have no engagement until tomorrow."

"I'll be ready at the entrance in fifteen minutes. Don't keep me waiting. I hope you're a competent driver."

"I can drive without hands. You'll see."

It was a prolonged, pleasant excursion, and Henry covered a good deal of ground, but it was clear at the outset that Lady Pearling's requirements would prove difficult to fulfill, since she stipulated that she must have a secluded site, an open view, unlimited water, main drainage, acceptable neighbours, and be out of earshot of all cats, dogs, donkeys and church bells. Henry conducted the negotiations, translated her terse demands into more polite form and restrained her from telling English owners exactly what she thought of their property and the price they were asking for it.

When on their way back to the hotel, she ordered him to drive to the Colstons' villa. He hesitated.

"What's the matter?" she demanded. "Scared of them?"

"Do you want to see the house, or do you merely want to engage Mrs. Colston in battle?"

"If she doesn't insult me, I won't insult her. We're only a mile or two away from the place."

"We haven't an appointment to view."

"All the better. Take 'em unawares; always the best way."

He turned in the direction of the villa and wondered what she would think of Edgar's painting; his pictures, like the furniture, were included in the sale. Disparaging remarks about them would be ill-received by the Colonel, whose pride in his own taste exceeded, if possible, his price in his son's work.

But when they reached the house, it was to find that only Mrs. Colston was at home. She received them with an impersonal, business-like air, offered drinks, and when Lady Pearling refused, suggested an immediate tour of the property.

"I've got very little time," Lady Pearling told her. "Not that I need much; a glance here and there, and I know whether I'm going to like a place or not. This is the only drawing room?"

"There's a smaller room, a very pleasant

one which my husband uses as a study. It opens, as this room does, on to the terrace."

"If I'd been in your place," Lady Pearling said, "I wouldn't have chopped off the terrace just there; spoils the sweep. Never does, in my opinion, to spoil the ship for a ha'porth of tar. That pool, now; what's it cost to fill and filter and keep in order?"

"Frankly, a *lot*." Mrs. Colston spoke with the air of one keeping nothing back. "But it's a splendid pool; we didn't spare the ha'porth of tar there, I can assure you."

"Where's the study you mentioned?"

"This way." Mrs. Colston led them to it.

"Smaller is right," Lady Pearling commented. "Why didn't you put in a west window? I like to have the sun in the evening."

"Really?"

"Yes. The furniture's for sale too, isn't it?"

"It is. As you see, there are some fine pieces, and —"

"You're not hoping to sell those pictures, by any chance?"

The tone was not that of a possible buyer. Lady Pearling had stopped in front of one of Edgar's canvases and Henry held his breath. But beyond twisting her head this way and that in an apparent effort to discover whether the work had been framed upside down, she made no comment.

"Shall we go upstairs?" Mrs. Colston suggested frigidly.

"Six bedrooms, you said?" Lady Pearling asked on the way up.

"All with bathrooms." Mrs. Colston threw open a door. "And three with balconies."

"This isn't a bathroom, it's only got a shower," Lady Pearling pointed out.

"We prefer showers."

"I prefer baths. What are those doors along there?"

"They lead to the maids' rooms."

"Rooms, plural?"

"I'm afraid you won't be able to run a house like this on fewer than three maids. It isn't like England, where —"

"If it were like England, I wouldn't be here."

"Oh, really? If it weren't for my husband's health, we should never live anywhere else. Sometimes" — Mrs. Colston smiled bravely — "we feel like exiles."

"The cure for that," Lady Pearling said briskly, "is to dismiss all your maids, do all your own housework and cooking, chop wood and stagger to the gate with your dustbin every Friday. You'll get over feeling an exile, and decide to be an expatriate."

"My husband and I regard England as —"

"— a country to live in if you're under fifty. Quite. But try to put your feet up, and there's nothing to put them on. I was there two months ago, so I'm in touch. Could we look at the garden?"

It was not a long look. Lady Pearling gave it a glance, looked at her watch and said that she must be going.

"How about price?" she asked. "I'd better know."

The price was named. There was a long silence — so long, that Mrs. Colston lost her nerve.

"You've got to remember that land round here is extremely expensive," she said aggressively. "We had to pay an enormous price for this site alone."

"Ah. Well, I hope you get it back," Lady Pearling said kindly. "But not, I'm afraid, from me. Thank you for showing me round. Good-bye."

Mrs. Colston bowed and rang for a maid. The visitors were shown out.

"Ill-planned and ill-constructed," Lady Pearling said, when barely out of earshot.

"But somebody will buy it; there are just as many fools here as there are anywhere else."

Henry settled her in the car for the return journey.

"Are you really thinking of staying in Portugal permanently?" he asked.

"I'm going to have a good try. I spent fifteen years in Switzerland — I suppose you know how much my husband did for the winter sports industry? No, you don't; it was well before your time. He did more than anyone else, I think, to popularize skiing in Britain; he began this yearly swarm to the ski slopes. When he died last year, I went to England, to settle down again there but I like to live in the country and I like a spacious house; add those two factors together and the answer is no domestic help. So I came here, and as far as I can see, I shall stay here. I like the people and I like the climate — even the winter climate, because I like rain."

"Has Mrs. Restington found a house yet?"

"She's not here; she's gone to London on business. Went off early this morning, so there won't be a fourth for bridge. You'll have to play. The other two I've got hold of are a naval ex-captain and his wife. Six o'clock to eight. We —" She turned to stare at him. "What did you say?"

"No."

"Then you're extremely ungrateful. I gave you lunch and I offered to pay for your petrol."

"And in return," Henry promised, "I shall provide you with a fourth for bridge, to be carved up and made mincemeat of."

It was easier than he had anticipated. The green-eyed Lola, from whom he had escaped in the hotel pool, had on several subsequent occasions attempted — unsuccessfully — to entrap him; when she waylaid him as he was on his way to his room, he did not try to evade her, but asked, instead, if she would make a fourth at bridge. A certain amount of circumlocution was necessary, but he left her with the impression that it would be his knees she would lock with her own beneath the bridge table; the rest could safely be left to Lady Pearling.

He was walking over to the lift when a page stopped him.

"A lady is outside, Senhor," he said. "She wishes to see you."

Henry raised his eyebrows.

"Won't she come inside the hotel?"

"No, Senhor. She says it is only for a moment. Please come this way."

261

Henry followed him, sensing in his manner something out of the ordinary. When the hall porter, removing his hat with a flourish, hurried to open the rarely-used central glass door and ushered him through with ceremony, the impression deepened. And then, occupying a space usually kept clear for residents' cars, he saw a large black one and without hesitation identified it; he had last seen it at the Quinta do Infante, standing beside Teresa's small green one. In it, upright, grave and dignified, sat Senhora Silva.

She was bare-headed, her hair impeccably dressed. She made a sign to the chauffeur standing stiffly to attention beside the door; he opened it, Senhora Silva held out a hand and Henry bent over it.

"Let me assist you," he said. "You must —"

"No, please." She lifted both hands in a gesture of protest. "No. You must forgive me. I came to say only one thing, and it will take less than a moment. But I wanted to say it to you personally, because I felt this was due to you. It is only this: I have sent for my lawyer, Urbano Moreira, whom you already know. I am going to give this land, about which there has been so much trouble for me, to my niece, Teresa Kingsley. Once it is hers, she will be free to do as she wishes; she may sell or not, just as she decides. From now, please to understand that I have nothing to do with this part of my property. Do you wish to ask me anything before I go?"

"Yes. *Why?*" Henry asked unhesitatingly.

She looked at him for some moments, and he saw a faint smile on her lips.

"Why? To relieve myself of a responsibility, Mr. Eliot. Simply, that is why."

There was no more. She held out her hand, Henry bowed, the chauffeur closed the door and drove away. Henry watched the car out of sight and then turned away, but he did not go into the hotel; he walked absently towards the pool, stared unseeingly at the few swimmers in the water, and then wandered slowly along the paths bordering the gardens. His mind grasped well enough what the announcement meant to him; all hope of getting the land was over. He had failed with Senhora Silva; he would not fail with Teresa because he knew beyond any shadow of doubt that he would never ask her to sell. And though he could not, as yet, understand exactly why the transfer had been made, he acknowledged that the move was a clever one.

He had no idea how long he stayed brooding outside the building. He went inside at last, and let himself into his room.

Five minutes later, the telephone rang. Lifting the receiver, he learned that Colonel Colston was below, and wished to see him.

He hesitated for a barely perceptible second.

"Ask him to come up," he directed.

There was not much time to wonder what had brought him. He did not think the Colonel had come to add his own comments to those his wife had made that morning. Perhaps he had learned of Lady Pearling's visit to the villa. He might even be bringing Marly's engagement ring back — but if Marly had finished with him, Henry knew that she would inform him of the fact herself — and she would not return his ring for the simple reason that she would consider he had had his money's worth.

The door opened, and one glance at the visitor's face told him that his guesses were wide of the mark; the Colonel had not come to bully, but to beg, and in the same illuminating second, Henry realized — and was amazed that he had not realized before — that he himself was the only person with whom Senhora Silva would deal. Without his aid, Marly and Sir Bertram and the Colonel would batter on her doors in vain.

There was no hesitation in the Colonel's advance or in his firm, fatherly, man-to-man opening. He had been angry yesterday, he acknowledged freely. He had lost his temper, let off steam, which at his age was a safe and sensible thing to do; never had been much good at bottling things up, and couldn't begin now, but absurd to suppose any real rancour behind his remarks. Damn silly to let a small incident like that build up into a disagreement. Besides, a young fellow had to learn to take people as he found them, the good with the bad.

"Wanda came back this morning — caught me just as I was going out — and said she and Marly had had a chat with you. She said she thought you'd taken things too much to heart. 'Nonsense,' I said to her, 'he's got too much sense.' But I was passing just now, and I thought I'd drop in and prove she was wrong."

"Whisky?" he asked.

"Thanks. Don't mind if I do. I've had a full day and I'm not finished yet."

Only when he was settled in the big chair, drink in hand, did a change of tone indicate that he was coming to the point.

"Marly was telling me you hadn't got much change out of the Silva woman. Pity about that, but you can't gather much from a first try. Time means nothing to these people. You might be in a damned big hurry, but they're built by nature to let things drift along at a nice, easy pace for years. She'll probably say No again — and again. All one has to do is plug on, feeling one's way. Out here, you can't negotiate a brisk, American-type deal; it's a case of tomorrow and tomorrow and tomorrow, as someone said — Hamlet, I daresay." He sipped his whisky-and-water. "You're young, and you haven't learned to talk brass-tack business; you'll find out that 'No' usually means 'Perhaps.' This woman expects to be bargained with. She expects to be approached by someone who knows values and it was here, I think, that Marly's father fell down. He relied too much on the personal and forgot to be practical. I'm not going to pretend to you that I wasn't a bit peeved, hurt, if you like, to find that I hadn't been asked to go along with you. You understand, don't you?"

"Yes."

"Now, when Marly suggested changing her father's original plan, she wasn't pushing you aside. You didn't think she was, did you?"

"Yes."

"Nonsense! Nonsense, my dear Henry. I can't believe that you don't know her better than that. All she was doing was lining up a few big guns, that's all. It's a pity Bertram got you on the line and let himself go but you mustn't take any notice of that. I daresay every time he loses his temper, he loses his tact too and points out how lucky you were to have got Marly and got the job and so on. Between you and me, he's a chap who likes to remind people what they owe him. Just you forget what he said, and let's keep our eyes on the ball. You saw Senhora Silva, and got nowhere. Now we've got to consider the next step, which is —" He broke off. "What the hell's that?"

It was a cough — discreet, informative; Mr. Easter was on his balcony and could hear everything that was being said. With detached interest, Henry watched the Colonel fighting an impulse to get up and bang the balcony door so hard that the glass would shatter and shower over Mr. Easter and teach him not to eavesdrop. But he composed his face, walked on to the balcony and addressed Mr. Easter in a manner almost genial.

"Hello, there. I just dropped in for a chat with Henry. Henry, why don't you ask Mr. Easter to come round and join us?"

"Eh? Oh, no, no, no," Mr. Easter protested. "No, certainly not. I just walked out on to the balcony for a bit of air, heard voices and thought I'd better disclose my presence, as you might say, before you got to talking secrets."

The Colonel, laughing heartily, said that the only secret he was likely to have touched on was one well known to Mr. Easter.

"Come along, come along," he urged. "Perhaps you can give us another angle on the business we're discussing."

Mr. Easter, meeting Henry's eyes and finding reassurance, walked along the corridor, entered the room and accepted a soda water. He sat on a straight-backed chair opposite the Colonel, and Henry sat on his bed and prepared to listen.

"To be frank," the Colonel said, "we were talking about Senhora Silva. I know quite well there's a bit of friendly rivalry between us over this business; when you dropped the idea of buying my house, I knew you'd decided to go after the land again. I hope you're doing better than we are. You went to see Senhora Silva this afternoon, didn't you?"

"Yes. Who told you?" Mr. Easter asked bluntly.

"My dear fellow, I saw you. I'd just called there myself and been turned away; you passed me in a taxi and I saw it stop at the Quinta gates."

"Yes, I went," Mr. Easter admitted. "I'd been there the day before, but she wouldn't see me. So I went along today, and this time, I wrote a letter and took it along with me — a letter telling 'er what I wanted and asking 'er to let me in."

"But she didn't," the Colonel said.

"That's right; she didn't. She sent back a note, though — and that's what I was going to show 'enry, only I 'eard he 'ad a visitor and I was going to wait till you'd gone. But now that we're all out in the open, as you might say, I'll read you what she says."

He plunged a hand into a pocket, brought out a folded sheet of paper, opened it and read aloud:

Senhora Silva wishes to inform Mr. Easter that she is no longer the owner of the land about which 'e 'as called to see 'er.

For a long time, nobody spoke. Mr. Easter was looking puzzled; the Colonel was looking dazed. Only Henry was unmoved.

"My God!" the Colonel brought out slowly at last. "So that was it! She had another buyer up her sleeve all the time!" His face darkened with rage and suspicion and he twisted in his chair to confront Henry. "She didn't tell you it was sold, did she?"

"No, she didn't," Henry said calmly.

The Colonel, without finishing his drink, banged the glass on the table with a force that almost shattered it, got to his feet and stood glaring down at Henry, still seated comfortably on the bed.

"You know why we lost it?" he shouted. "We lost it because you didn't name a figure, that's why. Because you didn't make her understand that we would have matched any bid, *any* bid, any bloody bid, however high. You went to see her, you sat there oozing boyish charm at her and letting her run rings round you, and you made not one sin-gle —"

" 'ere, there's no need to turn nasty," Mr. Easter said resentfully.

"Keep out of this, you interfering old twister, you!" the Colonel roared. "If there's one bright speck in this whole bloody busi-ness, it's the fact that you didn't succeed in buying it. If you'd —"

The door was opened, and Marly was on the threshold. She looked only at the Colonel.

"What's wrong?" she asked.

"Wrong? Ask him what's wrong." The Colonel, purple-faced, pointed a shaking finger in Henry's direction. "Ask him, go on! What's wrong is that the land's been sold, that's what's wrong."

"I don't belive it," Marly said flatly, and swung round to face Mr. Easter. "You got it!"

"That I didn't," Mr. Easter told her. "I wanted it just as much as you did, but I didn't throw myself on the floor and kick and scream with rage like the Colonel's doing, when I 'eard it 'ad gone. I saw it first and your father played a dirty trick and if you're waiting for me to say I'm sorry you've 'ad this disappointment, you'll wait a long time, Miss."

The Colonel addressed Marly bitterly.

"I told you your ex-boyfriend would make a hash of it, didn't I?"

"Yes, you did."

"But you believed it too late. If you'd been more communicative when you rang up from England, instead of waiting until you came out here to tell me what was going on,

271

I would have warned your father that the matter needed experienced handling. Now you can ring him up and tell him that next time, he won't send a boy to do man's work. Well, what are we waiting for? Are you coming, or are you staying?"

She looked at Henry. This was it, he thought. In the silence, he saw Mr. Easter making an embarrassed exit. The Colonel marched out, leaving the door open.

"Would you like me to take you back to the villa?" Henry asked her.

"No. I've got Wanda's car. Edgar's in it, waiting."

"You could tell Edgar to go home."

"When Edgar goes home, I'll go with him. You may as well know that I'll probably marry him. And before I go, you may as well know something else, too — that my father is going to have something to say about the way you've bungled this job."

"He's said a good deal of it already."

"Wait till he hears the land's gone. Perhaps in a way it was worth it — at least it showed me what you were like. If I'd married you, this is how it would have been: everybody getting ahead and pushing you out of the way. You'll always let other people push you out of the way. But I'm like my father: if I want things, I want them and I know how to get them, and when I marry, my husband's got to be able to keep up. Edgar says —"

"Let's keep Edgar out of it, shall we?"

"Not any more. Edgar's in. You're out. From now on, as far as I'm concerned, you can go to hell."

She stormed out and he closed the door quietly after her. Things had ended as they had begun, in a burst of passion. He was free to find his way back to his old life, his neglected friends. He was free to take up the threads . . . if he wanted to.

His mind felt blank — not from shock, for there had been none, but because he had lost his way and was not too sure that he could find it again.

And she had been wearing his ring still, the buying of which had caused him the first prick of uneasiness. She had insisted on choosing it herself. She had known that all he possessed in the world was a six-year-old car and some gramophone records; she had chosen one of the most expensive rings on the tray and it had taken him three months to pay for it.

He looked outside and saw that it had grown dark. There was a tap on the door, and Mr. Easter's head appeared round it.

"Everything all right?" he asked hesitantly.

"Everything's fine. Come in. Switch on a light."

"You was so quiet, I . . . well, I came in to see. 'ow about a bite of something? If you'll take me to dinner at one of those posh places I'm always afraid to go into, I'll pay the bill."

"You'll regret it. I'm fond of lobster."

"Then let's go. By the way, 'enry, I went down to look at the dinner menu, and I ran into your friend, Lady Pearling. She was looking for you. Upset, she was. I told 'er you was out."

"Thanks. In case she's still around, let's go down by the staff elevator."

They made a stealthy getaway. Over a table in a corner of a justly-famed restaurant, Mr. Easter grew philosophical.

"Can't always get what we want in life, can we? But I know what Joyce'll say when I tell 'er what's 'appened. She'll say I'd 'ave got in to see Senhora Silva quick enough if I'd sent in my business card. She says that ninety-nine women out of every 'undred suffer with their feet, and if Senhora Silva 'ad seen who I was, she'd 'ave 'ad me in a jiffy, to ask about shoes. If she 'ad a niece in England all those years, she must 'ave 'eard about Ayr shoes."

Henry stared at him in astonishment.

"Are you Ayr shoes?"

"I certainly am. Didn't I tell you?"

"No."

"Then I'm telling you now."

"But . . . I walk on Ayr."

"I know you do, son. You walked into that airplane on Ayr, and so did nine out of ten of the other passengers. I only did men before I met Joyce — it was 'er who said why couldn't women walk on Ayr, too. It's not a trade name, you know. It was Joyce's name before she married, and she said we'd call the shoes after 'er. After that, we couldn't miss. I never 'ad to pay a penny to any of those advertising firms, not a cent. *Walk on Ayr* — simply that. Walk On Ayr — and everybody did. Everybody still does, and not only in England, either. No, not everybody. The Colonel doesn't. If 'e 'adn't shown 'imself up like 'e did, I might have given him a hint. I only make it a hint, in case people think I'm pushing my goods at 'em. I would 'ave told 'im 'e'd look better and feel better if 'e got out of those shoes 'e was wearing, and walked on Ayr." He paused apologetically. "Sorry, 'enry. I'm off again. Shoes and my wife; my wife and shoes. When're you getting married?"

Henry looked at him. Mr. Easter got very red, choked on a piece of fish and recovered himself.

"All right, all right," he admitted. "She's got a loud voice and I'm not deaf. All the same, if I was asked to point out a miserable man at this minute, I wouldn't exactly pick on you. Which brings me to something I've been thinking."

"Well?"

"Just this, 'enry. If you ever thought of getting out of Stonor's, I . . . well, I'd like you to 'ave a chat with me, that's all."

Henry decided not to tell him that getting out of Stonor's would soon be an involuntary act. Instead, he smiled.

"What do I know about shoes?" he asked.

"Who mentioned shoes? I'm out of shoes. I'm out, and my sons are in. I'm just trying to tell you that if ever you decide to leave Stonor's, I'd like to talk to you. See what I mean?"

"You're very kind. Thank you. But there's always a job for me out in Brazil."

"Why do you 'ave to go that far? There's things nearer 'ome."

"I'll remember that. Look, your food's getting cold."

Mr. Easter picked up his fork, and Henry brooded on the future. It was only a question of time — hours — before Sir Bertram would follow his daughter's lead, and dismiss him.

"I suppose," he heard Mr. Easter say, "this affair's over."

The words echoed Henry's thoughts so clearly that he laughed.

"You mean buying the land?"

"Yes. You won't be seeing Senhora Silva again?"

"I'm seeing her tomorrow. She's asked me to drive a friend of hers to Mass."

"Mass? You a Catholic?"

"No. I'm taking an old lady to the chapel at the Quinta do Infante."

"Oh, I see. You're waiting to take 'er back again?"

"No. I'm having lunch there."

"At Senhora Silva's?"

"Yes."

"You're . . . you mean you're going on seeing 'er, sort of friendly?"

"Why not?"

"Well, no reason, I suppose. I just thought that with the land gone, it'd all be over and done with. Is this a sort of private chapel?"

"It's in the Quinta grounds, but it's open to anybody who wants to attend services. Not that many people live near enough to go there instead of to their own churches."

They finished their coffee; Mr. Easter paid the bill and Henry thanked him and drove him back to the hotel. As they entered, they saw Lady Pearling seated, stiff and vigilant, on a chair that commanded a view of the revolving doors.

"Ha!" she snorted, on seeing Henry.

"May I present Mr. Easter? He —"

"I am not in a social mood," she declared. "I have been waiting for you for some time. I want to know if you were aware of what you were doing when you sent that . . . that creature to —"

"Most certainly not," said Henry. "She wanted to play bridge and she claimed to be a good player —"

"She wanted to play with you. And bridge was not what she had in mind, and well you know it. Never before have I had to sit and watch a woman shamelessly making up to a man in the presence of —"

"Didn't you say he had been a captain in the navy?"

"He was. He —"

"Being made up to was one of the hazards of his profession. Now will you forget him and look well at Mr. Easter? You and he are made for one another. You complained of sore feet; he has a cure for them."

"My dear young man, I have been from chiropodist to —"

"*Shoes*. He's a creator of Ayr shoes, and he knows you don't wear them, because he goes about with his eyes on the ground, studying people's footwear."

"Didn't your ladyship ever try Ayr shoes?" Mr. Easter inquired.

"Never. I have, always have had, always will have my shoes especially made for me. And specially fitted."

"If they fit," Mr. Easter declared, "they don't ruin your feet. If they ruin your feet, they don't fit. It'll be a privilege, if you'll allow me, to measure you up and get a pair for you. They stock them in Albufeira. I know, because I've seen them — well-displayed, right in the middle of the window, as they should be. If you once put 'em on, I guarantee your ladyship'll forget all about foot troubles. Walk on Ayr."

"I understand they're extremely expensive," Lady Pearling said suspiciously.

"Naturally. Nat-cher-ally," Mr. Easter said

stoutly. "They might even cost you more than you pay that chap who's ruining your feet but once you've got 'em on, if you've got the right fit, which with me supervising you can't do otherwise, then we'll see you in this very lounge tomorrow, doing a two-step. No, not tomorrow; tomorrow's Sunday. Monday, then."

Lady Pearling looked at him; her sharp, shrewd eyes took him in from top to toe.

"Very well," she said at last. "You may come to my room on Monday to take my measurements."

"Why not now?" Henry asked. "Postponement is the thief of . . . I've forgotten. Why not now?"

They went up to her room; she displayed a long, thin foot and Mr. Easter, kneeling on the carpet, took thorough and complicated measurements. When the figures were safely in his pocket, she offered the two men drinks.

"As a rule, I say No," Mr. Easter told her, "but as a matter of fact, I'd like to break the rule tonight. If we 'adn't met you downstairs, I was going to ask 'enry to join me in a little special celebration."

"Of what?" demanded Lady Pearling.

"Well, 'e was engaged, and she gave 'im

the boot this evening, and —"

"Champagne," Lady Pearling broke in imperiously. "Mr. Eliot, kindly order it on my account. We shall drink to your release together."

"Sure you're all right?" Henry asked outside Mr. Easter's door, an hour later.

"Look," Mr. Easter held up a hand as steady as a rock.

"Good. I thought your addiction to soda —"

"A glass of champagne — specially that champagne — can't 'arm anybody, 'enry. You know that as well as I do. But you 'ave to do it in moderation if you've got a 'ead like mine."

"I'm glad I haven't. Good night."

"Oh, 'enry. Just a sec. About this Mass in the morning. If I went along and just sat quietly, they wouldn't object, would they?"

"Hardly."

"I'd like to 'ave just one look at the Senhora, and it's the only chance I'll ever get."

"Want a lift?"

"No. I want to go on my own. It'll sort of round off the episode, as you might say. I'd like to see 'er, even though the land's gone.

Who bought it; any idea?"

"Nobody."

Mr. Easter had opened the door of his room. He turned slowly and stared at Henry.

"Eh?"

"Nobody."

Mr. Easter's mouth opened and closed.

"But I . . . I saw it! I saw it written down. I saw the message that —"

"The message merely stated that Senhora Silva was no longer the owner of the land. Nobody bought it. She gave it away."

"She . . . gave it away?"

"She gave it, handed it, had it made over to her niece."

" 'er . . . 'er niece?"

"Yes. But she won't sell it. If you don't believe me, go to Mass tomorrow and look at her, look at her aunt, look at the place — and then you'll understand. Or you won't; but go anyway."

"You knew she was 'anding it to her niece?"

"Yes. She told me yesterday."

"But you said nothing to the Colonel, to Miss Stonor . . ."

"The matter is being dealt with by Senhor Moreira, who is Senhora Silva's lawyer and who is also representing Sir Bertram. When

282

the transfer of the land is completed, Senhor Moreira will naturally inform Sir Bertram. Any more questions?"

"Yes. One. Do you . . . no. I'll put it another way. Shall I see the niece tomorrow morning if I go to this chapel?"

"Most probably."

"Then I'll be able to answer my own question," Mr. Easter said. "Good night."

Henry's telephone was ringing. He picked up the receiver and heard what he had expected to hear. Brief, brutal. But when the voice ceased, and he cradled the receiver once more, he took a deep breath and drew blessed freedom into his lungs.

First the collar . . . and then the chain.

He went to bed and slept soundly.

CHAPTER 7

As the timid little bell rang out on the following morning, Henry drove past the main entrance to the Quinta do Infante and through a smaller, less ornamental gateway a kilometer or two beyond it, to see before him an unpretentious little four-square, stone-built building which he would have mistaken for the village school, if it had not been for the large cross surmounting it, and the bell swinging from a crumbling tower on one side.

It was of a later date than any of the additions that had been made to the Quinta; he would have liked to study it and guess at its probable period, but his assistance was required to disembark Senhora Crespo and her lace head-covering, her purse, her pills, her missal and her reading glasses. She took her son's arm, signalled to Henry that he was to walk at her other side, and slowly ascended the steps leading up to the door. Henry saw that a wall on either side of the chapel curved to join the one which surrounded the Quinta, so that there was no way into the grounds except through the narrow doorway, he saw almost opposite it another entrance through which members of the household were coming in.

The interior of the building could accommodate about eighty people; it was already half full. Senhora Crespo walked slowly to one of the plush-covered seats in the front row; as she rose from her genuflexion, Senhora Silva entered from the private door and took her place between the old lady and her son. Henry retired to the rear and sat at the end of a bench which soon became so crowded that he had to grip the side to prevent himself from being pushed off.

The cold building became warmer; the whispering rose and fell. At the altar, little boys in long robes reached up with tapers to light the tall candles. In niches round the walls were foot-high statues, wooden, unidentifiable, some of them not unlike gnomes. To right and left of the altar were large, gleaming figures of the Virgin and the Sacred Heart.

Father Vieira entered, and over the intervening heads, Henry studied the colourful vestments, the scarlet-and-white of the small boys, the almost unrelieved black of the two front rows and the gay patterns of the women's dresses alternating with their menfolks' sober attire on the benches. He had looked for Teresa and failed to find her; now he saw her coming in by the Quinta entrance, late, slipping quietly into a seat beside her aunt, her blue dress and white lace headdress a pretty touch beside the black.

There was a slight commotion at the back. Glancing round, Henry saw in the doorway a group of people who had been unable to get seats; they were moving to allow passage to a latecomer. The figure emerged; Mr. Easter, flushed and perspiring, was urged forward; a small boy, prodded by his parents, unwillingly gave up his seat to the *estrangeiro* and Mr. Easter sat down whispering husky thanks.

There was no organ. A stout woman enveloped in a heavy woollen shawl, seated near — too near — Henry, opened her mouth and without warning, emitted a strident, nasal note; the congregation echoed it, give or take a semitone, and began to chant the responses. The sound bore no relation to the sweet singing of cathedral choirs, but it was in keeping with the family atmosphere, with the ceaseless shuffle of feet, the restless whispering of children and the occasional wail of an infant. At the altar, the priest dipped and rose in the ritual movements; when the time came for the sermon, he spoke for no more than ten minutes, his manner nicely balanced between the priestly and the paternal.

The service ended. Father Vieira and his acolytes filed out, but there was no movement from the congregation until Senhora Silva had left the chapel. She did not, as Henry expected, go by the private door but by the main one, and the reason for this became apparent as soon as she had stepped into the sunlight; every member of the congregation hurried out and stood waiting their turn to exchange a word with her. Babies received a pat on the head, little children were lifted up to be kissed; among these, Henry recognized many of the underclad inmates of the crèche, now in beautifully-laundered, immaculate cotton suits.

Mr. Easter did his best to get to Henry's side, but was trapped between two mothers holding babies in their arms; unable to escape, he was borne nearer and nearer to Senhora Silva. Confronting her at last, he removed his soft, white straw hat, revolved it rapidly by the brim, squeezed it between his fingers and gave a stiff little bow.

"Good morning, Madam."

Senhora Silva scrutinized him.

"I do not know you," she concluded at last.

"That's right; you don't," Mr. Easter agreed nervously. "I just came —"

Henry had reached them.

"This is a friend of mine, Senhora," he said. "Mr. Easter. He wanted very much to meet you. And to come to Mass here," he added belatedly.

"Easter? The gentleman who came twice to the Quinta?"

"That's the one, Madam, But this isn't . . . I mean to say I'm not . . ."

"He means," Henry put in, "that he received your note and understands that the negotiations have broken down and has no thought of reviving them. But before going back to his wife, he wanted very much to see you so that he could tell her about you."

Senhora Silva turned her glance on Mr. Easter.

"Perhaps you would care to stay to

lunch," she said.

"Eh? Oh, no! Well, as you're so kind, Madam . . . well, thank you, I'd like to."

The crowd was pressing close; he was carried past. He spoke gratefully to Henry.

"That was a nice thing you did," he said, mopping his brow. "I felt a proper fool till you rescued me." He paused and went on thoughtfully. "I didn't expect 'er to look like that."

"Look like what?"

"'andsome. Well set up. She's a fine-looking woman."

Henry had caught sight of Teresa and was stretching a hand between intervening forms to draw her beside him. She acknowledged the introduction to Mr. Easter with a smile.

"I can't stop, I'm afraid. I've got a few jobs to see to. I'll see you later."

But Henry was still beside her when she re-entered the chapel and went down the steps on the other side.

"I'm really busy," she warned him. "Sunday chores."

"Such as?"

"Feeding cats, for a start."

"All four dozen assistants off duty?"

"No. It's my Sunday amusement. If you come, you'll find yourself helping and you won't be amused. Still want to come?"

"Yes."

She was removing her lacy headdress; her skin looked glowing, her eyes were soft and dark. He saw for the first time that she was not unlike her aunt, an infinitely softer version, but with the same small, rather high-bridged nose, the same level brows, the same direct gaze.

As they left the chapel behind them, Henry glanced back. Senhora Silva was coming out of the door.

"Look" — he stopped and turned back — "shouldn't I drive Senhora Crespo round to the house? She can't manage the walk. I'd better —"

There was no need to finish the sentence. Coming down the steps in the wake of Senhora Silva were two servants carrying a chair in which, smiling and placid, sat Senhora Crespo. Beside her walked her son; behind came Mr. Easter, Father Vieira and a long and seemingly unending line of friends. Henry walked on with Teresa.

"Are all those people staying to lunch?" he asked.

"Twenty-four to lunch every Sunday in the garden, all through the summer. Mostly Silva cousins."

"The same cousins every Sunday?"

"More or less. It was these Sunday gatherings I missed more than anything else when I lived in England."

"You had cousins there," Henry pointed out.

"Not the rallying kind. I don't know one — of my age — who would have been seen dead attending regular Sunday sessions with grandfathers and grandmothers and ancient cronies."

He looked down at her curiously.

"Do you feel much two-way pull?" he asked.

"You mean between England and Portugal? No. I always meant to live here if I could."

They were walking slowly through the woods, in which direction Henry neither knew nor cared. He halted, and she leaned against a tree, idly picking off twigs.

"Does your aunt regret not having been born a male?" he asked.

She laughed.

"She'd have hated it; she hasn't much use for men as a whole. But she's sorry to be the last Silva, and she's sorry she didn't have a son. It was a disappointing end to all her travels."

"Do you have to travel before you can have sons?"

"She wanted sons named Silva. When my mother married an Englishman and went away, my aunt got out the family annals and picked out two or three likely kinsmen, announced she was in need of a holiday, and set off on a round of visits. She took in a lot of territory. Finally she chose Henrique Armando Xavier Silva, who up to then had been living a quiet, peaceful life at his mother's Quinta in Amarante. He wouldn't leave his mother, so she lived here after the wedding. Armando Xavier only lived for four years, but she went on and on. She died just over three years ago. It's a shame poor Armando Xavier didn't inherit some of her toughness; there might have been some little Silvas running around. Why are we wasting time?"

They walked on for some distance without coming within sight or sound of cats, and for the first time Henry began to have some realization of the extent of the property. He thought of the present-day price of land in the Algarve and the resultant cheek-by-jowl siting of villas, with a mere surrounding deck by way of garden. He began to do some mental arithmetic to arrive at a rough estimate of the value of the estate, and gave it up when the row of figures grew too long. But the answer to another problem had come to him, and he confided it to Teresa.

"I think I know," he said, "why this place has such a relaxing effect on me."

She glanced at him.

"I didn't know it was this place. I thought it was your normal state of mind. Nobody could call you an unrelaxed person."

"Then let's say the place has a somnolent effect. It has. Because —"

" — it's been asleep for hundreds of years?"

"Perhaps. But my job is designing houses, or converting houses. For one client who'll leave well enough alone, there are two hundred who won't. If any one of the two hundred came here, they'd work a transformation."

"Wake the place up?"

"Yes. No more dim, cool, quiet woods. No more odd, empty, unexpected little houses appearing suddenly in clearings. No more half-hidden paths, forgotten little retreats; no more sagging shutters or crumbling chimneys. When I was young, I used to like to look over our veranda and watch the men settling down for their afternoon siestas — huddled against a wall in the cool shade, a blanket round them, head down. The young ones got up after a time to do some work but the old ones sat and dozed, and dreamed, and nobody took any notice of them. Old, content to sit, happy to dream the rest of their lives away. Just looking at them gave you a feeling of restfulness. Like this Quinta. I didn't know, until I came to it, how sick to death I am of new, brash, repetitive, rich-man's, imitation-Spanish set-ups: white paint, blue pool, green lawn, striped umbrella and parboiled human bodies laid out in rows and turned over at intervals to parboil on the other side. I didn't know . . . look, I think I'm talking too much."

They had stopped again; unwillingly, they went slowly on, this time in silence.

They passed some low buildings. Henry followed her into one and watched as she filled pails with strong-smelling fish and scraps. From somewhere nearby a cats' chorus rose and swelled. By the time they had walked to the enclosure, the noise was ear-splitting.

They made three journeys to fill the food-troughs; not hard work, Teresa said, but unrewarding.

"Why don't they show some gratitude?" she complained. "All they do is spit."

"Don't they ever get tame?"

"Never. If you could get the kittens young, it would be different but you can't. When a new cat arrives that's going to have a litter, I try to find out where she has it — but she's too clever. By the time you see the family walking round, it's too late — they're as wild as the mother. Now the next job."

"Which is?"

"Visiting the expectant mothers."

The *Maternidade* was a long, low whitewashed house with a raised wooden balcony; on this, or on the wooden steps leading to it, sat about a dozen women, some pregnant, some nursing infants. A stout, smiling woman in a white overall came out of the house to greet the visitors.

"How's everything?" Teresa asked, adding — prudently, Henry thought — "This gentleman speaks Portuguese."

There was a stir of interest; several pairs of dark eyes rested on Henry for a second glance. Making a rapid and discreet survey, he was left with the pleasant impression that at another time and in another place many of those seated on the cool, shady balcony would be happy to get to know him better.

Then he saw Teresa's raised eyebrows and realized he was being addressed.

"Sorry. You said something?" he apologized.

"Twice. You were preoccupied. The midwife wants to know if you'd like to see the two new babies that were born last night."

"I can't wait."

The babies were exhibited and admired; the mothers were congratulated. After this, the kitchen was inspected; coffee was offered and refused. After a word or two with the mothers on the balcony, Henry and Teresa left.

"Next job?" he asked.

"Turning on the water for my aunt's garden. And that's all."

"She doesn't run this place single-handed, does she?" Henry asked.

"No. She's got a steward, a bailiff, who's supposed to deal with the estate, but she manages the house and the grounds, she runs the *Maternidade* and the feast-day charities, she provisions the crèche and she looks after every man, woman and child connected with the Quinta. She knows all the annual yields of almonds, figs, olives and lemons. And oranges. And honey. She counts every grain of rice and sugar. But on Sundays, as you see, she doesn't water her garden."

She stood at the top of the slope and gave him instructions, and he arranged the tiles to direct the flow of water. Above its gentle bubbling, he could hear the hum of voices floating across from the terrace of the house.

"Thank you," Teresa said, coming down the slope to join him. "That's the lot. Now we can join the others."

"Do we have to?"

She glanced at her watch.

"Not yet. What else do you want to do?"

"Talk. Can we sit on that wall?"

"Don't you want to go in and have a drink?"

"No."

The wall was low and crumbling; he settled her on a relatively safe part of it and sat on the rough ground at her feet. The sun filtered through the mimosa trees above them; the water trickled musically; children's laughter sounded from time to time.

"You're not talking," he heard Teresa say after a time.

"I'm thinking. Do you realize you're living the kind of life that most people have left behind them?"

"Of course I do. If I didn't know, my English cousins would remind me."

"How long will it be before the rat race begins here?"

"Not for a long, long time. The tourists have arrived, industry's growing, wages are soaring, but the changes won't go down deep yet. You won't change the national character, which is slow and mild and amiable and in my opinion, rather beautiful. If you don't agree, read Portuguese history and compare it with the bloodbaths of some other nations. Yes, I'm lucky. What else did you want to talk about?"

"Nothing. Just you."

"We've covered most of the ground, haven't we? What else is there?"

"Were you ever in love?"

"Yes — for a week, when I was fifteen. Since then, I've had leanings now and then, only to find out that he was married, or — like you — engaged."

"Did that cure the leaning?"

She smiled tranquilly.

"Up to now," she said.

He stared up at her. She looked calmly back, the smile still on her lips. He saw a faint colour rise in her cheeks.

"Teresa —" he began.

"Teresa Margarida."

"I'd like to tell you something, if you'd

298

listen. It's —"

"It's my turn. How often were you in love before you got engaged?"

He twisted round and leaned his back against a tree trunk and stared absently at the little stream trickling past them.

"It sounds a little suspect," he said slowly, "but I don't think I ever was. Between the ages of eighteen and twenty-six, I worked pretty hard; there wasn't much time to look for girls and there was certainly no money to amuse them. You have to take girls somewhere besides a bench in the park — and it costs. Then I was out of debt and earning, and free to go around but I found that the kind of life I'd got used to, even though quiet, was satisfying — and fun it its way. I had friends who, like me, enjoyed listening to music. I could afford to hire a horse now and again. I had a car, rather like yours, but with fewer dents. I'd discovered that I was a good architect, and I enjoyed doing a bit of homework. That was the program when I met Marly."

"Where did you live?"

"Putney. Two nice big rooms, one above the other, both looking on to the river. There was room for my friends; we could make as much noise as we liked, because there were shops on both sides of the house which closed down for the night, so that we couldn't keep the neighbours awake."

"And then?"

"Then Marly's father offered me a job. I went to his house. She . . . well, you've seen her, but not in the setting I first saw her in — or against. Her father promised me a golden future, and Marly . . ."

"You can skip that part. Go on to the next bit."

"We got engaged. It worked, at first. It was amusing for her to go out in a battered old car. She could make her friends hysterical by imitating the landlady who looked after me. She even gave a couple of parties in my rooms — caterers and white-coated waiters against the Victorian wallpaper, and my friends trying to find one another in odd corners. And then the novelty wore off and she took me in hand — her expression — and I moved to a penthouse and the parties were in night clubs, and because I thought she'd tried to accommodate herself in the beginning to my circle, I thought it was fair to try to fit into hers. And couldn't. The thing began to limp badly, but it kept on its legs. Until now. And then it fell down. Here."

She looked down at him, frowning.

"I don't understand."

"It's quite simple. In England, Marly regarded your aunt's land as just another wedding present. Once she saw it, it turned into a status symbol, something to flaunt at her envious friends. Yesterday, Mr. Easter came here and got a note from your aunt telling him she no longer owned the land. He showed it to Marly's cousin, who happened to have called to see me. He took it badly. When Marly dropped in a few minutes later, he told her. She took it badly, too. She went home and rang up her father. Her father rang me up last night — to say good-bye. Marly had said good-bye before leaving the hotel. Now do you understand?"

"I . . . I don't believe it." She was very pale. "I don't believe anybody could . . . could . . ."

"— dismiss such a promising young man? Well, they both did — father and daughter, though not in that order."

"But it wasn't *your* fault!" she cried angrily. "How could you make my aunt sell if she didn't want to? And do they think that if they come to me, after having done this to you, I —"

"They won't come to you for the simple

reason that they don't know you own the land. Your aunt merely said she was no longer the owner."

"You would have had to tell them."

"No, I wouldn't. If I hadn't been sacked before I could make a report, I would have stated simply that your aunt had parted with the land."

"But don't you realize . . ."

She stopped. Someone had called Henry's name. A figure came out of the shadow of the pines, and they saw that it was Mr. Easter, red and breathless and perspiring, his straw hat limp in his hand.

"Glad to see you," he said with deep thankfulness. "Got myself lost and thought I'd never see 'ome again." He dried his face on his handkerchief. "Never dreamed this place was the size it is."

Teresa moved to make room for him beside her; he sank down thankfully.

"You're looking pale," he told her. " 'eat does that to some people, but with me it's just the opposite. I feel like a roasted turkey. Serves me right for trotting about in the sun at my age."

"Where did you go?" Henry asked him.

"Just for a stroll — I thought. You and Teresa went off and I did my best with

Father Veera and 'is 'arf-dozen words of English, but then the Senhora introduced me to some of 'er friends and my 'ead began to go round. So I went to look round a bit. Miles, I must've gone. Don't tell me I've missed the grub."

"Lunch on Sundays is always late," Teresa said. "But you must come and have a cool drink first."

"Let me cool down 'ere first," he begged. " 'enry been telling you about the row those people kicked up in 'is room yesterday?"

"Yes."

"What that Stonor chap needs to work for 'im is a bulldozer. 'enry's not built for that kind of job. What a bulldozer 'asn't got is feelings."

"And so it gets the job done," Henry smiled.

"I'm not denying that," Mr. Easter said. "All I'm trying to say is that if you use a bulldozer when you ought to use something lighter, you do more 'arm than good. See what I mean?"

"No," said Henry.

"Yes, you do; you're only pretending not to. Teresa wasn't there listening when they chewed you up yesterday, but I was. What they were really saying was that when they want something, to 'ell with anything that's in the way. To 'ear them, you'd never 'ave thought that I saw that land first, and got gypped."

"You what?" Teresa asked.

"I saw it first. Ask 'enry. Well, my wife saw it first, and I promised she should 'ave it if it was to be 'ad. Then I opened my mouth too wide, and to Sir Bertram, of all people. And before you could say Dirty Doublecrosser, 'e'd got 'is lawyer out from England. And now 'enry says it's yours, and I 'ope you'll keep it. If my wife was 'ere, she'd say the same. You keep it, Teresa my dear, and keep the sharks outside the gates, same as your aunt did."

He stopped and mopped his face again. Nobody spoke. What broke the silence at last was the sound of a gong, booming, penetrating the pinewoods, calling stragglers to table.

They walked slowly towards the house. On the terrace, a long table was set for the grown-ups; in the garden below, children were already seated round a large trestle table, their attendants standing behind their chairs.

Senhora Silva placed Father Vieira on her right and Senhor Crespo on her left. Mr.

Easter was put between a middle-aged couple who spoke a little English. Then she smiled at Henry.

"For you, Mr. Eliot, I have a friend. Look."

Henry turned. Coming out of the house was Senhor Moreira, dark, smiling, as impeccably groomed as ever.

"So, Mr. Eliot" — he held out a hand — "we meet again, and on the same business." He took his seat beside Henry, bowed to his acquaintances round the table and unfolded his napkin. "What have you been doing since we last met?"

"Not what I was sent out to do. You were right: No Sale. I came to Mass this morning to pray for my future prospects. Sir Bertram sacked me."

Senhor Moreira's glance, grave and a little shocked, rested on him.

"You mean, surely, that he threatened to do so?"

"He didn't threaten. He sacked me."

"Because you told him of the change of ownership?"

"Because his daughter told him Senhora Silva no longer owned the land. They don't know Teresa is to have it."

"You did not tell them that?"

"No. Need you?"

"You are not going to send a report of any kind?"

"No. I told you — I'm out. You'll have to do the reporting, and if you can do it without letting them know what Senhora Silva did with the land, I'll be grateful."

"There will be no need to go into details. But Miss Stonor will surely —"

"She sacked me, too. About four hours before her father did."

"I am sorry. No," Senhor Moreira amended resolutely, "I must be truthful. I am not sorry, Senhor Eliot."

"Henry."

"Thank you. In fact, Henry, I shall go as far as to congratulate you."

"That's the end of that. When did you come down?"

"Last night. My wife drove down with me; she is staying with a cousin at Loule."

Henry glanced round the table. Far removed, Teresa sat among a group of young men and girls; he felt old and envious. Senhora Crespo was holding up a trembling little hand to halt the servant who was refilling her wine glass. Father Vieira was trying to assess how much longer the repairs to his house would drag on. Mr. Easter had discovered that the claim of his neighbours had been to speak English, not to understand it, and was attempting to explain that Darby and Joan had no connection with the famous horse race, which in any case he didn't think should be pronounced Darby because that was the sort of thing that confused foreigners, if they would excuse him for calling them foreigners, seeing that he was in fact the foreigner here. Henry turned to his own neighbour, a portly, middle-aged gentleman who was the brother of the portly, middle-aged gentleman seated on Senhor Moreira's left; both, he learned, were engaged in writing and illustrating a book on the birds of Sagres.

"Bit windswept for birds, isn't it?" Henry asked.

"So. You are another one," the gentleman mourned, "who knows nothing of Sagres except the ships. It has always astonished my brother and myself, the way tourists come year after year, and not one of them seems to be interested in the birds. But they are worth study, I assure you. Blue rock thrushes — you can see them, sometimes in the rock crevices, sometimes sitting on the compass dial, sometimes even on the car of a tourist. Hoopoes. Crested larks. Linnets.

And then the south-flying birds. If you have not seen a thousand small birds resting before crossing the ocean, you have missed a memorable sight. My brother and I have photographs that would astonish you. Puffins. Quail. And razorbills at the foot of those magnificent cliffs. And —"

He paused. The fish had arrived. He helped himself liberally, picked up his fork, leaned forward and forgot Henry. His brother was equally absorbed. Henry and Senhor Moreira could resume their conversation.

"How did Miss Stonor learn about the change of ownership?"

"Mr. Easter, the pink and white gentleman sitting opposite you, called here to see Senhora Silva. He had seen the land before Sir Bertram saw it, and Sir Bertram heard him talking about it, and got in first. Senhora Silva sent him a note and Miss Marly was in my room at the hotel, with her cousin Colonel Colston, and Mr. Easter dropped his little bomb. The end. Now can I ask you some questions?"

"Anything you wish."

"This house. Hasn't the possibility of restoration ever been raised seriously?"

"Certainly. But two things were against it — expense, and the fact that there was nobody to inherit it."

"It's surely one of the country's historic houses? Couldn't the state —"

"No. There is no real historic interest. That is to say, it has nothing that would interest the general public, here in Portugal, or foreigners who visit the Algarve. What do you think of the building?"

"The original part, the central bit, is beautiful. The later embellishments or excrescences are unfortunate, to say the least, but they can be removed. And when you're left with the house built by Pedro Silva, isn't that historic?"

"Apart from its connection with the Infante Dom Henrique, no. It has no history. The family, since Pedro, has done nothing of note. And he was simply one of a number of intrepid sailors sent out by the Navigator."

"Isn't that enough?"

"No. All the history of those times is to be seen at Sagres. The *forteleza* is there; there is the restored chapel where the Infante prayed; there is his compass dial still as it was when he was planning the voyages. This house is interesting, certainly — but historic? No. And it has no museum value. In your opinion, how much would it cost to restore?"

"More than it's worth. Only the central part is worth keeping. But I think it's . . ."

"Well?" prompted Senhor Moreira.

"Waste!" Henry said explosively, causing his neighbour to start. "The estate, I mean. The whole enormous area of the place — what's to happen to it? When Senhora Silva dies, it'll be carved up, won't it?"

"If Teresa has married and left it, yes."

"She'll marry, Senhora Silva will die and the place will be sold and the speculators will come in and another forest of white tourist villas will spring up and the house will be pulled down, central portion and all, to make more room, and the Silvas and their sailor ancestor will be forgotten."

"That is probably what will happen. It is sad, but" — Senhor Moreira raised his shoulders in the age-old gesture of What-would-you? — "we have really thought with great regret about this, Mr. Eliot. We —"

"Henry."

"Henry. We have discussed it here, and in Lisbon. We have approached other branches of the family; none is sufficiently interested to take over the property on the death of Senhora Silva. You are the first person, apart from Teresa, who has ever pondered on its future, and even you cannot offer an alternative. Unless you are thinking of a Development Company — Stonor's?"

"God forbid!" Henry spoke with such force that his neighbour choked over his wine and gazed at him protestingly.

He had forgotten the food on his plate. He saw it removed and realized that the meal was almost at an end. The children had finished eating and were streaming noisily up the steps to make their farewells; little girls curtsied, small boys bowed gravely to kiss Senhora Silva's hand. Well-fed-looking chauffeurs waited below to conduct their charges to cars. The last small figure disappeared, the servants cleared the garden table and soon the adults rose and went down to take coffee. Teresa joined Henry and Senhor Moreira; together they rescued Mr. Easter, scarlet from overeating and the effort of making himself understood.

"Come into the shade," Teresa said compassionately. "You look so hot."

He followed her gratefully and sank on to the shady bench to which she led him. Senhor Moreira sat by his side; Teresa sat on the warm, sandy ground.

"If we're not all talking the same language in another 'undred years," Mr. Easter said feelingly, "then we deserve to be called fat fools, if not worse. What's the use of jet travel if you can't say anything when you get anywhere?" He put away his damp handkerchief and took a cup of coffee from the tray offered by a maid, and looked at the guests some distance away.

"When I tell Joyce about this, she'll be pleased; she's always been one for family life, and this is family life if ever I saw it. From babies right up to oct . . . octa . . ."

"Wait till you're cooler," Teresa suggested. "Sugar in your coffee?"

"Yes, please. Plenty. That's right." He glanced at Senhor Moreira. "I don't know this gentleman."

"I'm so sorry," Teresa apologized. "I forgot you hadn't met. This is Senhor Moreira, who's my aunt's lawyer, who has come here to —"

"Ah, yes. Well, you know my views," Mr. Easter told her."You 'ang on to your little bit of property."

"Speaking of property," Senhor Moreira said, "Henry was interrupted in the middle of his plan for the future of the Quinta do Infante."

"Plan?" Teresa turned inquiringly to Henry. "What plan?"

"Not Sir Bertram, please God," prayed Mr. Easter.

"No, certainly not that," Senhor Moreira assured him. "A project to build . . . I am not sure what."

"Nothing. I was merely talking," Henry said. "All I was about to tell you was that the job I was going out to do in Brazil — the job I gave up in order to take Sir Bertram's — was a project which could quite well be carried out here. All you'd need would be Senhora Silva's consent, which she wouldn't give; money, which we haven't got; and State permission, which we wouldn't get."

"And what is this doomed project?" Senhor Moreira asked.

"A village."

The others looked blank.

"A what?" Teresa asked.

"A village," Henry repeated.

"You mean a whole *village?*" Mr. Easter said in astonishment.

"That's right; a village. The idea's not new," Henry told them. "It's been done in various places — south of Spain, which I've seen. Sardinia, which I took a professional look at. The Bahamas, the Canaries, which I didn't see but which a colleague of mine did. But all those projects were aimed at the tourist and prettied up accordingly. The one in Brazil was different. It was to be exactly what it sounds; a village in Brazil, built by Brazilians for Brazilians. A real village. Not — as elsewhere — an imitation village whose houses would be lived in by tourists, but a village laid out as a village — a copy, certainly, but a copy based on a sound knowledge of local conditions, local weather, local facilities, local amenities. Houses for the rich man and the poor man: a post office, a tavern, cottages with a patch of land for peasants, a small school, a church, and a cemetary. It's all going up now, eighty miles from Santos; the prices are geared to the type of dwelling, and when it's finished, you won't have a string of tourists occupying the houses for a few months of the year, you'll have a permanent, purposeful . . ."He broke off. "I'm sorry; when I get onto this subject, I talk too much."

"Please go on," Senhor Moreira said.

"It's being done there, and it could be done here — here in this Quinta. With, as I said, permission from the owner and from the State. And a mint of money. I don't know anybody who's got that kind of money. All I know is, that the thing, once created, would work. It would pay for itself. The houses would fill up as fast as they were built, and if you opened the wall on the south side and broke through to the land bordering the beach, you could build a miniature harbour for your fisherman. It's not a dream, it's a practical proposition. And if it isn't done on a more general scale, you'll soon have the kind of thing you're getting all over the States — whole estates built to pattern, every house on them within a fixed price limit, secluded, segregated, separated, and as featureless as a sandscape in the Sahara. Even the shops are lined up in one big enclosure, and the people who serve the customers aren't grocers or greengrocers or butchers or iron-mongers — they're nameless, anonymous; they're merely faces fixed onto the machine that goes click click and hands you your change. What's needed are the sights and sounds and smells of real, lovely, lusty life. Village life — real life. Peasant and patron, rich man, poor man, fisherman and cobbler, stonemason, prior and pastry cook. If people live among a picked crowd in their own income group, they're living artificially. Village life has existed since the world began — the community, a natural way of life, the houses graded according to a man's means and abilities and manner of work. I think that . . ." He pulled himself up abruptly. "Well, that's all I think," he ended.

Senhora Silva was coming towards them. She stumbled over a piece of rough grass, and Mr. Easter was first at her side to assist her. He stood looking down at her feet, his head shaking sadly from side to side.

"I am not hurt, thank you," she told him.

"You were lucky, Madam," he said gravely. "You'll 'ave to excuse me, but this I've got to say; those shoes weren't built to walk about in."

"Mr. Easter," explained Henry, "makes, he claims, the best shoes in the world. People mistake him for a shy man, because he always goes about with his eyes cast down modestly but he's merely looking to see if people are comfortable in his shoes, or ruining their feet in someone else's."

"You sell shoes?" Senhora Silva asked Mr. Easter.

"Not now, Madam. My sons do that for me. I've retired, and as there's nobody 'ere to say it for me, I'd like to say it for myself; a man never deserved success more than I did, because I thought first, last and all the time of my customers' comfort. You've got beautiful feet, if I may say so, and it 'urts me to see you 'urting them. I'm not in business, I'm only advising you because you've been kind enough to 'ave me as your guest. All I say is: get into a pair of my shoes and be 'appy. I'd be glad to measure you any day you name and tell you your requirements."

She bowed.

"Thank you. We shall arrange this," she said. "Perhaps when you come next Sunday to Mass, you —"

Mr. Easter blushed.

"I'll be honest with you, Madam. I'm not a Catholic. But Mr. Eliot said 'e was coming, and . . . I came to see you. And . . . the 'ouse."

"Then come with me. I shall send someone to show you the house — and in return," Senhora Silva said, "you will perhaps tell some of my friends about your shoes, because they will be interested. And Father Vieira," she added, leading him away, "will be the most interested, because the poor man is sometimes on only one foot at the altar, to rest the other."

They went slowly away, Mr. Easter steering her carefully round the offending tuft of grass. Senhor Moreira looked inquiringly at Henry.

"Which shoes?" he asked.

"Walk on Ayr."

"I shall tell my wife. She walks on pins, five inches high." He rose and followed the others.

Henry and Teresa were left alone. Most of the guests had finished their coffee and wandered away; servants were spreading a white cloth on the garden table, moving quietly round Senhora Crespo, who was slumbering in a wide wicker chair, cushions propping her up on either side. At the foot of the steps, Senhor Crespo snored loudly. Senhor Moreira paused to speak to Father Vieira, and Henry watched them walking slowing to and fro, to and fro . . . to . . . and . . .

He woke with a start and struggled to an upright position.

"Sorry, I fell asleep," he said to Teresa.

"Twenty-five minutes," she confirmed. "Snoring, like Senhor Crespo."

"It was all that food. Where's everybody?"

"My aunt is listening to Mr. Easter, chapter forty-two, the years of success. The Crespos are in the drawing room, listening but not understanding. Father Vieira has gone to christen some children at Caravela, but he will be back soon. Senhor Moreira went with him, as his wife's godson is being christened. If you've recovered, I'll give you some tea and then you can drive the Crespos home. Mr. Easter, too, if there's room. He didn't keep his taxi."

"What do you do for the rest of the day?"

"I go to the crèche to see the children coming back. I like to be there; their parents bring them in donkey carts or on donkeys, or on the backs of bicycles or motor-bikes. I watch them having their supper, and then I come back here."

"Can I come with you?"

"If you want to."

"What time?"

"About six."

"Will you come out to dinner with me afterwards?"

"Didn't you listen when I told you about the local conventions?"

"Yes, but —"

"The thing you have to remember about rules is when to break them. I'll bring a picnic and we'll have it on the beach."

"Shall I come here, or meet you at the crèche?"

She hesitated.

"Come here," she said. "We'll drive

down in my car."

Senhor Crespo sat with his mother at the back of the car when Henry drove them back to Caravela. In front was Mr. Easter. Between Caravela and the hotel, there was silence. Mr. Easter seemed to be thinking deeply, and Henry did not disturb him.

"I liked that lawyer chap," he told Henry at last.

Henry parked the car and they walked into the hotel.

"I like him too," he said. "I don't envy him having to send in a report to Sir Bertram."

Mr. Easter pressed the button for the elevator. "It's your job, isn't it, sending in a report?"

"No longer. I'm out. Would your son — wasn't his name Leslie? — consider me as a shoe salesman? I'd be — look, this is our floor."

As Mr. Easter seemed to be in a daze, he opened the elevator door and ushered him out.

"*Sacked?*" Mr. Easter breathed incredulously, in the corridor.

"Yes. I'd make a good shoe salesman."

"Sacked! You, by that . . . that . . .

why, he's a . . ."

"Steady!"

"A fellow like you, who anybody'd be proud to 'ave as an employee. A fellow like you . . ."

"How about a drink?" Henry suggested.

"No." Mr. Easter made an effort to recover himself. "No, I won't 'ave a drink. But if you'll let me take you out to dinner again, I'd be right glad to —"

"I'm sorry, I'd like to, but I'm going out. As a matter of fact, I'm going back to the Quinta."

There was a pause.

"Back to the Quinta? This evening?" Mr. Easter asked at length.

"Yes. I'm going to the crèche with Teresa."

"To the crèche?"

"Yes."

"With Teresa?"

"Yes." Henry took Mr. Easter's key and opened his door for him. "Sure you don't want that drink?"

"No." Mr. Easter stood on the threshold. "No, I . . . sacked! What'll you do?"

"Haven't you just said that I'm a fellow anybody would be proud to have as an employee?"

"Yes. And I meant it. But . . . but 'enry, what are you going to *do?*"

"When I know," Henry said, "I'll tell you."

CHAPTER 8

Drying himself after a shower, getting into fresh clothes, Henry pondered on Mr. Easter's question. What was he going to do with his future?

One or two alternatives sent up his spirits to a pitch which was reflected in the speed at which he drove to the Quinta do Infante; he put it down to natural reaction after having acted as chauffeur to Senhora Crespo.

He reached the Quinta gates and was admitted. He drove on wondering whether there was not something seriously wrong with a man who, having lost both beauty and success, felt nothing but a vast sense of relief. He ought at least to be feeling shame at having come so near to wrecking his life but all he could remember was that he was free. He was free. He was driving to see

Teresa, through a wood which he was prepared to believe enchanted. He was free, he was happy, and success could mean many things, he mused, besides a berth in the Stonor setup.

Teresa was beside her small green car on the drive, superintending the loading of stores. When the last package was checked, she looked at Henry.

"Want to drive?" she asked.

"Through the woods? No, I think not."

"Then get in and shut your eyes. I don't even have to steer; the car's so used to this road, it goes practically by itself."

Henry, his legs folded as best he could in the confined space at his disposal, kept his eyes open and then regretted not having followed her advice to close them. He had anticipated a cautious zigzagging between trees; instead, he found himself bumping over the roots of the trees at dizzying speed, the car slithering and skidding and twisting and bringing him near to nausea.

"Hey!" he protested.

It was a mistake to disturb her concentration; the car grazed four trees, almost overturned on a stump and came to a dead stop, its engine stalled, with two wheels on either side of a fallen pine.

"Now she won't start again," Teresa complained. "What did you shout for?"

"Help, of course. You're not driving me any further."

"You're not frightened, are you?"

"What colour am I?"

"Sort of green. Then you *are* frightened!"

"It's your car, but it'll be my corpse," he pointed out, and took the wheel.

The engine remained deaf to urging and coaxing; after a time, he got out and pushed, Teresa keeping a hand on the steering wheel. When he heard the engine revive, he bounded in and had begun to weave his way in and out of the trees, when he made the interesting discovery that the brakes did not work.

"Hey!" he yelled again.

"*Now* what?"

"The blasted brakes! What's the matter with them? They —"

He saw a tree advancing rapidly, and spun the wheel. The car skidded; there was a thud. The engine stopped.

"What is one more dent among so many?" Teresa asked to no one in particular.

He was gazing at her, speechless.

"You mean to tell me," he managed at last, "you drive this thing without brakes?"

"The brakes are there, of course. I keep having them fixed, but they always go wrong again."

"So how do you stop?"

"Easy. Go into top gear, and stall."

Without a word, he got out and changed places with her, and sat clinging to his seat until the crèche came into view. She judged to a nicety the time and place to let the engine give its dying cough.

She left Henry, and he stood watching the children's return. Carts lurched and lumbered through the trees; peasants dressed in Sunday suits lifted out small boys and girls who showed no distress whatever as they were handed over to Teresa and her helpers. The last one having arrived and been checked off on the list, each child was given milk and bread and then taken to have his Sunday clothing removed and folded away, to be replaced by the institutional shirt. The rows of small beds filled up. The shutters of the little house were closed; the two helpers sat down to their own meal. Teresa was free.

"I'm hungry," she announced.

"After that enormous lunch?"

"You couldn't see what I was eating. Will you get the basket out of the car?"

He found it unexpectedly heavy.

"Sandwiches?" he asked in surprise.

"Et cetera."

They walked onto the beach. The sand was smooth, the sea silver; the moon was round and full and looked so low that Teresa, staring up at it, said that she could count the astronauts. There was no sound but their voices and the lapping of the sea and the creak of the basket lid. They laid the food out on a car seat placed on the sand.

"About your village," Teresa said musingly after a time. "Why can't it be built?"

"Because for every bag of sand and cement, you need a bag of gold, that's why." He bit into a chicken leg. "If your aunt had had children," he asked, "do you think she would have been a domineering mother?"

"Do you?"

"In her nice quiet way, yes."

"Then you're wrong. She's got, deep down, a fatal defect. When it comes to making big decisions, she can never believe —"

"— she's made the right one?"

"Yes. The proof is —"

She pulled herself up abruptly, and busied herself with seeing that he had enough to eat. Later, she poured out the coffee. They finished the meal in silence, leaning against the ends of the basket, cupping the little brown mugs between their palms. He helped her to clear away the remains, then lay back with his head resting on his arms and gave a long sigh of repletion.

"Thank you," he said. "That just about tops it all. The moon, the beach, the girl and a full stomach. You were saying —?"

"I wasn't saying anything."

"Yes, you were. You said that the proof of your aunt's not being domineering could be seen in the fact that she hadn't — blank. Kindly fill in the blank. If you don't, then I will."

"Then do."

"She handed that land — this land — over to you because she wanted you to make the decision. As things turned out, you didn't have to decide — but that was your aunt's idea."

"Yes, but —"

"One moment. She realized that failure, for me, was going to be a serious matter and she realized that you liked me enough to care about my future."

"I didn't —"

He took her by the shoulders and turned her so that they were face to face. Still holding her, he spoke slowly.

"Teresa, listen. We were interrupted this afternoon when I was going to talk about ourselves. Now we're alone again, and we've got to talk — and we've got to tell the truth. We've got to know the truth." He released her and went on speaking in the same serious tone. "We haven't much time. I've got to go away, and whether I come back or not depends on you. Only you. I'm not worried about my prospects; I can get a good job and earn enough to keep a wife and children. All I'm worried about is the fact that we've come together just after I'd made a monumental fool of myself with another girl, and almost wrecked my life. You've seen me as weak and ineffectual but that isn't the true picture. I'm not weak and I'm capable of using my strength if I have to. But not pushing — I can't push — in the Stonor sense. If I wanted something badly — as now — I'd try and get it in my own way."

"What's your own way?"

"It looks like trial and error, doesn't it?" he asked bitterly. "I'm free, and glad to be but what right have I to ask you to take me seriously? I love you but how can I make you believe it? And if you believed it, how could you have any confidence in my ability to stay in love? The other was nothing — oh, Teresa, I swear it — nothing like this. It was . . . I'm not trying to make excuses. I don't want to lie to you — all I'd like to do is make you understand what happened to me, but I can't because I don't really know. I know the facts, but I don't know the reasons. If you believe I'm a man who couldn't refuse an offer of a place in a girl's bed, you're wrong; the offer has been made before, and by women almost as attractive as Marly, and turned down. So why did I lose my head so completely over her? I don't know. How can I, how can you guard against my losing my head like that again? I don't know. Teresa, look at me. Are you listening to what I'm saying?"

"Yes."

"Do you believe I love you?"

"Yes."

"Thank God for that. Do you believe I can stay in love with you — always and forever?"

"Yes. But . . ."

"But what?"

"Did you ever really love her?"

"I thought I did."

"Did you think of a home, and children?"

"Good God, no! I thought of her long,

white, lovely body. How do I know I won't again — hers or somebody else's?"

He saw a slight smile on her lips.

"It's a risk," she agreed. "But knowing about your past is a kind of insurance — isn't it? — against the future?"

"Teresa . . ."

"Well?"

"Some day, when we've forgotten all this and you've had a chance to see me with my head on, could you marry me?"

"You've skipped a line."

"Yes, I have. Do you, could you, would you love me?"

"Yes. But when will I have a chance to see you?"

"If I took this job in Brazil, which I think they'd still give me, would you go with me?"

"Yes. But why go to Brazil to build houses? There's lots of land here. What about your village?"

"Just a dream."

"If it was more substantial than a dream, would you stay in Portugal?"

"Yes. But as it isn't, I'll go back to England at once to clear things up, and then start thinking straight again. And if you promise to go with me wherever and whenever I go, then —"

"Of course I will."

"Will you mind leaving your aunt?"

"When the time comes, I'll tell you. But —"

"But —"

"Maybe we won't have to go very far."

He drove her back — by the road. He had decided to say goodbye to Senhora Silva. The maid who admitted them said she was still up, and Teresa led him to a small, rather dim, book-lined room, near the window of which was a large winged chair. Seated on it was Senhora Silva.

It was a brief meeting. Henry thanked her, regretted any inconvenience she had suffered and told her that he was leaving for England.

"Senhor Moreira came here to look for you," she said. "He waited, but you did not come, and so he has gone to your hotel. I hope, Mr. Eliot, that we shall meet again. I am sorry this visit has been unhappy for you."

When he had gone, Teresa came back to the little room.

"You are late," her aunt observed.

"Not very. It's only ten something."

"Ten fifty-five. Fifty-five is something. I

hope the children were well?"

"What did Urbano want?" Teresa asked.

"He wished to see Mr. Eliot."

There was silence. Teresa waited; nothing more was vouch-safed.

"What's so secret?" she asked at last.

"Nothing is secret. Urbano came simply to see me and ask about Mr. Eliot."

"What about Mr. Eliot?"

"Simply, he wished to know what Mr. Eliot was going to do now that he has no fiancée and no employment. Now he will learn that he is going back to England. That is where he came from — naturally he would go back."

"But as I'm here, naturally he won't go back for long," Teresa said.

The fan faltered.

"He has told you this?"

"Most convincingly."

"You wish me to welcome this man, who yesterday was to marry some other woman. Are you satisfied with his stability, his judgment, his taste?"

"Yes. He loves me."

"He told you this?"

"Yes."

"He said to you: I have been freed from one, now it is your turn?"

"I suppose you could put it that way."

"How would you put it?"

"From the morning we met, it was settled. Settled between us . . . inside us. You don't dislike him, do you?"

"Dislike? No."

Teresa settled herself on the carpet beside her aunt's chair.

"Would you mind?"

"If you married him? How could I prevent it?"

"He's not just an architect — he's a brilliant architect. He'll do well — once he gets started."

"Since I have no special knowledge, I will not contradict you."

"Would Urbano give him a job?"

"He is a lawyer, not an architect."

"*Get* him a job. Is that what he came for?"

"He spoke of a fantastic scheme, a village which is to be built on my property with only permission from the Government and — this seemed less important — permission from the owner. There was also, Urbano said, a little difficulty about money."

"Aunt Ofélia —"

"Well?"

"Need it be just a dream?"

"Of course not. Just the permission from

334

the Gover —"

"If it could be done, wouldn't you like to see it coming into being, instead of knowing that . . . that . . ."

"That when I am dead, everything is finished? Urbano was kind enough to say that this house would be preserved. Not all the house — only part. They will not pull it all down about me. Yes, Urbano has this dream as well as Mr. Eliot. They have not got State permission, but in a dream, practical things do not matter."

"If Urbano's thinking about it, he must know there's some hope of building it. Can't you . . . can't you *imagine* it?"

"No. What is there to imagine? My estate, now so peaceful, so spacious, so private, to be streets and houses, people and dogs, noise and shops and the cries of fishwomen and the piping of knifegrinders. Is that what you wish me to imagine?"

"Yes. Exactly that. The creation of a village which will save the Silvas from complete and final obliteration."

"You are not a Silva."

"In our veins, yours and mine, we've got the blood of a man who was one of the Discoverers. No seaman who ever sails the seas will ever forget Henry the Navigator.

335

But no tourist roaming round the *fortaleza* at Sagres ever hears that Pedro Silva existed. If we build a village and name it after Pedro Silva's ship, the *Esperanza*, and if we save the house he built, then everybody who looks at the stone caravel above the doorway will know that he was one of the Discoverers. Is that just a dream?"

The fan waved swiftly to and fro.

"Teresa, I do not know. You cannot go so fast. You cannot say: Look, today this man is free, yesterday I fell in love with him, tomorrow we will marry and the next day we will somehow build a village. This is not reasonable. Your mother was reckless, but this is worse. What do you know of this man? What is his behaviour in the six months that have just gone by? To engage himself to a woman clearly undesirable. To accept a position he could not keep. To speak of love to a girl like you, without any seemly interval, without prospects, even without my permission; after all, I am your aunt and your guardian. It is all impracticable, all impossible. Besides building this village, what does he plan to do?"

"Go back to Brazil."

The fan stopped again.

"To . . . Brazil?"

"Yes."

"And he . . . you would . . ."

"Go with him? Yes. And Brazil is a long way away — on the other side of the Atlantic. We should, of course, ask you to come too, but I know you're too fond of this house and this place ever to leave it. That's why it's such a pity you rejected that village idea without really studying it. You in this house, Henry and myself and our children in the very first house to be built in the village, with a private road from you to us. I would have liked that. When I'm in Brazil, I shall often think how wonderful it would have been."

There was silence.

"Blackmail!" Senhora Silva said at last.

"Yes," Teresa admitted. "Blackmail."

CHAPTER 9

When Henry entered the hotel, Senhor Moreira was sitting in the deserted foyer, waiting with the calmness and patience of his race. As Henry came in, he rose and walked forward.

"Good evening, Henry."

"I'm sorry to have kept you. Senhora Silva told me you were here. Come on up to my room."

"If you don't mind, no; we are almost alone here, and what I have to say will not take long."

"You can at least sit and have a drink?"

"Thank you."

"Are you going back to Lisbon tomorrow?" Henry asked, when the waiter had taken the order.

"Yes. But by air; my wife needs the car

338

down here."

"You wouldn't care to drive up with me tomorrow morning?"

"You're surely not leaving so soon?"

"Yes. I've got to give the car back; it was hired in my name. Then the afternoon plane next day to England. I've got things to settle."

"And after that?"

"At the moment, nothing definite."

"It's about the 'after that' that I came to see you."

"I thought perhaps you'd come to get the Silva documents Sir Bertram gave me when I came out to Portugal. He said I was to hand them over to you. I was going to leave them at your office in Lisbon."

"You were under contract?"

"He'll fix that."

"I was certain that he would vent his disappointment on someone. You first, and then probably myself. It will be a relief for me; he is not a pleasant man to deal with. We shall survive without his patronage — but it is about you that I came to speak. I wanted to see you before going back to Lisbon, because I was afraid that you might accept some other offer before you could hear mine."

Henry smiled.

"Let's build the village," he said flippantly.

"One day, who knows? That is for the future. My offer is for now. It is an offer to join my brother's firm —"

He stopped; Henry had made an impulsive movement of negation.

"No?" Senhor Moreira inquired after studying him.

"You're very kind. You're more than kind. Nothing could have been kinder, anyway, than the timing. But I want to think. And I want, if it's at all possible, to get into something of my own."

"Will a partnership in a Portuguese firm of architects not allow you sufficient independence? That was the offer. My brother needs an English architect. He has looked for some time; in fact, when I was in England on Sir Bertram's business, I met, on my brother's behalf, two men who were interested in coming out here. But my report was not favourable. When I returned to Portugal, I told my brother that I had met you and that I felt most strongly that you were in every respect the man he wanted. You were not, I told him, available . . . at present. Please don't think I am claiming any special powers of divination; I knew, almost as surely as I know anything, that Senhora Silva would not sell her land. I knew, from Sir Bertram's attitude, that if you failed to obtain it for him, he would blame you — even dismiss you for having failed. I was correct in both these surmises. You are no longer working for him, or for anyone. At least, I beg you, meet my brother before going back to England. We can drive to Lisbon and you can, if you will, stay at my house, and he will come there to meet you. You need do no more than hear what he has to propose."

"Does he know that I haven't any capital whatsoever? Partnerships don't come gratis."

Senhor Moreira smiled.

"Will you agree to meet him?" he asked again.

"Yes. And as I said — thanks." He rose. "I'll go up and get those papers and you can pack them."

"I'll go up with you, to save you coming down again."

They took the elevator and went up to Henry's floor and walked down the corridor. Before Henry could open his door, the one next to it opened and Mr. Easter came out.

" 'enry —" he began, and then, seeing Senhor Moreira, stopped.

"Coming in for a nightcap?" Henry asked.

Mr. Easter shook his head. His normally cheerful face was grave.

"No. I was . . . well, there was an incident, as you might say, and I wanted to tell you about it."

"Then come in."

Senhor Moreira drew back.

"I'll just wait for the papers," he said, "and then be off."

"I'd rather you stayed," Mr. Easter said. "It might concern you too, in the end."

Senhor Moreira, surprised, entered the room and took the chair Henry indicated. Mr. Easter chose to remain standing; Henry sat on the bed.

"What sort of incident?" he asked.

"Not very pleasant."

"Here, in the hotel?"

"Yes. Just after dinner."

"And you were involved?"

"I was bang in the middle. I'll tell you. I'd gone down to 'ave my dinner. While I was eating it, Lady Pearling came into the dining room. She was alone, and so was I, and if she 'adn't been who she was, I'd have suggested making it a twosome. But I didn't.

And then she came over and said she'd join me if I 'ad no objection. Well, I was pleased. We talked — shoes; and when we'd talked about shoes, we talked about prams — baby cars was 'er line. It was nice and friendly, and interesting, too. Then she said we'd 'ave coffee in the sort of foyer, and we'd just got there when who should walk into the hotel but Miss Stonor. And with 'er was a long, weedy chap —"

"Edgar."

"That's right. The chip off the Colonel's block. I 'eard them asking for you; you wasn't there. Miss Stonor 'esitates a bit and then she sees me, says something under 'er breath to Edgar, and then they come across and say do I know where you are. I was opening my mouth to say yes or no, I can't remember which, but Lady Pearling gets a word in first. I ought to say, which I forgot to say, that as well as talking about shoes and prams, 'enry, we talked a lot about you. Maybe I said too much, but Lady P. 'ad been interested and wanted to know. Well, she opened her mouth and says to Miss Stonor that you're at the Quinta do Infante, and if you're not there, then you're at the crèche with Teresa. After that . . . well, I don't know 'ow the landslide got started, but

343

the two ladies, or I ought to say one lady and Miss Stonor, told each other a few things, and not nice things. As for instance when Miss Stonor said she'd broken 'er engagement to you, and Lady P. said in that case, what was that ring doing on 'er finger? And with that, Miss Stonor pulls it off and tosses it on to the table, and I'm glad to tell you that I got my 'and on it just half a sec before Edgar did." Mr. Easter paused, fished in his pocket and produced a ring. "There," he said, holding it out to Henry.

"Thanks." Henry took it thankfully. Not a partnership, he thought — but not peanuts, either.

"And then," Mr. Easter concluded, "they went away and — oh, she said she wanted the car. That's what they'd come for — to get the car."

"It was hired in my name and I'm driving it back to Lisbon tomorrow morning," Henry said. "The bill will go to Senhor Moreira, to be sent in due course to Sir Bertram. Was that the end of the incident?"

"Yes. It wasn't nice behaviour right in front of the 'otel staff," Mr. Easter commented. "When they'd gone, I made Lady P. sit down and I bought 'er some brandy to put into 'er coffee. And she said what she'd said at dinner: that she was sorry to 'ear you'd been sacked, but glad to know you was out of that set. And" — he put out a hand to detain Senhor Moreira, who had risen. "Just a minute or two more, if you don't mind, Senhor. There's a bit of business I'd like you to 'ear."

Senhor Moreira sat down again and fixed his grave, dark eyes expectantly on the agitated countenance of Mr. Easter.

"Please go on," he invited.

"It's just this. 'enry's out on his ear, and in a way it's my fault. I —"

"Rot," Henry put in without emphasis.

"It's true, 'enry. It began" — Mr. Easter turned and pointed — "it began out there on that balcony, the first night. If I 'adn't smelled a faint 'ope of getting back into the market for that land, if I 'adn't called off buying the Colonel's 'ouse — *that* was what got you into the mess first off. Not that it matters; that's gone and done with, and all I'm thinking of is what's to come." He turned to Senhor Moreira. "You'd better 'ear this, Senhor, because you're a lawyer and you were there today when 'enry talked about 'is village. If that scheme, or any other building scheme in which 'enry is involved, is under discussion, I'd like to state, and I'm willing to put it into writing 'ere and now, my willingness to come up with one-third of the capital needed. Lady Pearling is prepared, also in writing, tied up legally, to put up a further third."

"Look —" Henry began, and was brought up by Mr. Easter's upraised palm.

"No, *you* look, 'enry. I'm not a fool. And I'm not an impulsive man, either. My 'ead's as 'ard as anyone's. And I don't 'ave to tell you that Lady Pearling is a bone-hard business woman. We didn't make our fortunes, or keep our fortunes by offering to support crackpot schemes. I've retired and so 'as she; we're both planning to come out 'ere to settle, and if we can get behind a business venture that we're convinced 'as got a 'undred-and-fifty percent chance of succeeding, then we're in." He looked at Senhor Moreira. "Do you want me to come to Lisbon and get it signed and sealed?"

Senhor Moreira smiled.

"No. All I would like at this stage, Mr. Easter, is a rough, very rough idea of what figure you are prepared to invest."

Mr. Easter told him. The room circled slowly round Henry and came to rest at an unfamiliar angle.

"Thank you," he heard Senhor Moreira

346

say. "I would like to add only that my confidence in Mr. Eliot is as great as yours and Lady Pearling's. It only remains to convince him that if he will lend his cooperation, the scheme —"

"No!" Henry burst out. "The whole thing's crazy!"

"Don't you believe in your village?" Mr. Easter demanded.

"Of course I do! But my God, that's —"

"— only the beginning. That is true," said Senhor Moreira. "There is State permission to obtain — but now, I am sure that we shall get it."

"And when you lay the first stone, there's always a celebration," Mr. Easter said. " 'enry, if you order the champagne, I'll pay for it."

Henry, in a daze, ordered it, saw it opened and handed Mr. Easter his glass. Then he filled Senhor Moreira's and his own.

Some time later, Senhor Moreira drained his glass, stowed Sir Bertram's papers safely into his pocket, made his farewells, went to the door and then returned to do his share in finishing the second bottle. Henry saw him to the elevator, pressed the button and stood looking at him.

"Perhaps I should have told you that Teresa and I —"

"This is something that I have already seen, Henry." Senhor Moreira patted his sleeve in a fatherly manner and stepped into the elevator. "My congratulations. I shall see you tomorrow. By then, who knows?" — he gave a brief, deep-throated bark of amusement — "by then, we may have been offered the third third."

Henry watched him out of sight. He stood for some time, his mind in a whirl, trying to think of something he could say to Mr. Easter. But however hard he stared at the smooth, blank elevator door with its circular red eye, no inspiration came. There were only two words — thank you — and they were totally inadequate. But adequate or not, he would say them from his heart.

When he went back to his room, he found that there would be no need to say them at all. Mr. Easter, stretched out on his bed, was fast asleep and snoring loudly.

The drive to Lisbon was made in perfect weather, and Henry found Senhor Moreira a perfect companion. The conversation was one-sided; Senhor Moreira had much to say, Henry little or nothing. He had not slept well, but lying awake had been a pleasure;

each awakening after each brief snatch of sleep had been a renewed sensation of happiness. He had the feeling, as he drove north, of having been peering at a distant future, only to find his binoculars suddenly reversed. It was now not a case of peering at tomorrow, but of deciding what to do today. And though he had promised himself to take no step without due caution, he knew that Mr. Easter was pushing from behind, Lady Pearling applying spurs on one side and Senhor Moreira making practical propositions on the other. And whatever he did, he remembered with a feeling of gratitude that came from his very depths, whatever he did, wherever he went, Teresa would be with him.

He drove to Senhor Moreira's house, where he was to stay the night. It was large, cool and comfortable; from his host's undisguised enjoyment of his brief bachelor status, he judged that Senhora Moreira did not often leave home.

He did everything that Senhor Moreira asked: he met his brother, visited his office, looking unseeingly at draft agreements which were to be submitted to Mr. Easter and Lady Pearling. He listened to more practical propositions. But nothing seemed real. He had mentioned a village and fallen asleep and dreamed the rest. He listened, answered as clearly as his confused brain would let him, and longed to be away from everything and everybody, alone with Teresa, who would help him to believe what was happening.

That night, at least, he slept soundly and dreamlessly. He was up early; the flight to London was timed for early afternoon, and Senhor Moreira had been too busy the day before to attend to the matter of a ticket.

"First or tourist?" he asked Henry in his office when they arrived.

"I think," Henry said, "I'll get the ticket myself."

Senhor Moreira looked up in surprise from his desk, ten feet by five and deep in papers.

"My dear Henry, I have only to send a boy out —"

"No, thanks. I'll go myself."

"But if it is only to buy a seat on a plane to London —"

"Not to London. To Faro."

There was silence. Then Senhor Moreira smiled.

"You are going back?"

"Yes. I was only going to England to clear up my flat and get rid of my car. Mr. Pugh will fix all that for me."

"You will go back to the hotel?"

"No. I've decided to ask for one of those empty buildings on the grounds of the Quinta do Infante. There's enough spare furniture in the house to furnish it, and twenty like it. I shall make it a sort of headquarters."

"You will live alone? I mean, without servants?"

"If I'm offered a couple of dailies, I won't say no. I don't want to be too near the house. There's a cottage midway between the expectant mothers and the cats; I'll put in a bid for that and see what Senhora Silva says."

Senhor Moreira was no longer smiling.

"She will perhaps refuse."

"Why should she? I'll soon be married to Teresa."

"But before that, you must understand that you will be expected to be . . . discreet. I will be more frank: the fact that you are to marry Teresa will make the Senhora not less conventional, but very much more so. She will . . . I do not think I am exaggerating when I say that she will have her eyes constantly upon you."

"It's not her eyes I'm worried about; it's her ears."

"I am serious, Henry."

"So am I. Deadly serious. Use your head, Urbano. If Senhora Silva heard me uttering one single mating yowl, you know quite well what she'd do. She'd yell for Gonsalves and then what do you suppose would happen to me?"

For some moments Senhor Moreira stared — and then he threw back his head and gave way to long and unrestrained laughter. Then he came up to Henry and took his arm.

"Come," he said. "We will go out and buy your ticket together."

LP/PA